MISSING BY MOONLIGHT

THE SECOND BOOK OF THE DARK GODDESS

MELISSA MCSHANE

G innevra lay on her back and watched the moon as it
hung overhead, mostly obscured by pine branches.
One day past full wasn't enough to alter its perfect
shape, like a white pearl in the sky. Its malevolent eye watched
her through the trees in return, but Ginnevra wasn't superstitious
about being outside during the full moon. Not much, anyway.

She resisted the urge to make the warding sign against the evil
eye and instead brushed her fingers across the grace nestled into
the curve of her throat. The pearl, big as the tip of her thumb and
black as night with the faintest glowing gray aura, was warm
from her body heat and smoother than silk. Ginnevra touched it
again, contemplating the symbolism. The black pearl to counter
the Bright One's white one. Ginnevra had never seen a white
pearl, but she'd been taught about them in her instruction to
become a paladin. They sounded bland by comparison.

Distantly, a wolf howled, a mournful sound that threaded
through the light wind. Ginnevra smiled. There was nothing to be
afraid of, out here in the wilds between the cities, except possibly

herself. She'd seen all manner of wildlife in the past three days, nothing big enough to threaten. And she definitely wasn't afraid of what had made that howl.

She sat up and poked the fire's embers. The summer evening was too warm for her to need a fire for heat, and she'd let this one die as the sun set. Now she checked to see that it was fully extinguished. Summer had been hot and unusually dry, and she had no desire to be the cause of a wildfire that would sweep unchecked across the forest to the great plains southward. She was leaving in the morning, and she could endure without a hot meal until her return to civilization.

Still, the smell of the hot coals roused her, though she couldn't sleep anyway, not tonight. She stood and paced around her small camp nestled between the firs that grew close together, never harvested. Yes, fire was a real threat here. And yet she didn't think the place would be all that improved by humans moving in to chop down trees and build a settlement. True, she was a child of the city, and civilization was far superior to scratching a living in the back end of nowhere, but sometimes one needed time alone in the natural world.

The howl came again, closer now. Ginnevra couldn't see the stars to guess what time it was, but the moon's position said she had another five or so hours until moonset, which meant about four hours to sunrise. She returned to the shelter she'd built between two of the bigger trees and sat. Sleep would at least be something to pass the time, but she'd slept most of the day and now she wasn't tired.

She sat, hugging her knees with her head atop her arms, listening for the night noises closer to hand. Her extraordinary hearing found an owl swooping high above, barely at the extent of her range, and then the squeak of a mouse or vole as the owl snatched up its prey. Hunter in darkness...she wasn't the only person that title fit. Owls, and wolves, and all the other creatures for whom the full moon's brilliant light meant trouble.

As if on cue, the howl sounded again—and cut off mid-note with a barely audible yelp.

Ginnevra sat up straight, listening hard. In the next moment, the howl was back, long and loud, followed immediately by two short barks.

Ginnevra shot to her feet and snatched up her sword. Those sounds meant trouble. She hurried off in the direction she'd heard them, muttering quickly the words *"By Your grace I come home."* The invocation set a tiny fire burning in the center of her chest that tugged northward and oriented her to the camp. She didn't need to be lost in the forest at past midnight.

Another howl sounded, not as long as the first. She corrected her path slightly southwestward. To her enhanced vision, the world looked clear as day, if less bright, and she discovered the trees were thinning out. She hadn't explored in this direction before, and she'd assumed the forest looked the same for a hundred miles in every direction. Now she wondered if she'd made a mistake.

She was sure she'd made a mistake in not strapping on her sword; the great blade, nearly four feet of silvered steel, made running through the forest difficult when it was in her hand rather than over her shoulder. She slowed, thinking about taking a moment to put it on properly, and another howl, very close now, split the peaceful night. She cursed under her breath and ran on.

The ground sloped downhill now, and the trees were spread very thin, thin enough that between that and the moonlight, Ginnevra could have seen her path clearly even if she hadn't been a paladin of the Goddess. From somewhere nearby came the smell of fresh water. She listened, and over the sound of her footsteps heard the chattering flow of a stream, nothing big enough to be called a river, but more than a trickle. She also heard something big ahead, breathing heavily. Again, she swore, pushing herself faster, dreading hearing that terrible pained howl again.

In moments, she saw it: a stream no more than a couple of feet across, cutting a path into the soft ground between the trees and flowing merrily downhill. Beside it, a low, dark-furred shape crouched, still enough to turn Ginnevra's worry into fear.

She hurried toward the shape, and the enormous wolf sat up and growled at her, a sound that despite herself she couldn't help but respond to by freezing in her tracks. She looked around, but saw nothing else moving. "Eodan," she whispered, "what's wrong?"

Eodan settled back on his haunches and let out another howl. This one sounded agonized. Ginnevra knew well he would never vocalize his pain in any self-indulgent way. It was a warning. But a warning against what?

Ginnevra scanned the ground between them. There was a lot more undergrowth here than elsewhere in the forest, where little more than dead needles covered the ground. Here, she saw plants and ferns and little brambles, blanketing and concealing the earth.

She took a step forward, and Eodan growled again. "I know," she told him, "but I can't see anything under—"

Her foot prodded something that shifted, and she heard a metallic noise somewhere between a thump and a clang. The undergrowth beside her boot scattered explosively. Eodan let out a warning yelp and surged upright before wavering and falling back onto his haunches.

Ginnevra bent and examined the thing. "Bear trap," she said. "A new one. This hasn't sat out here for more than a few months." She kicked it aside and jumped as it struck something else with that metallic clonk. Again, the undergrowth scattered.

Ginnevra felt sick. "Did one get you?" she asked.

Eodan nodded.

Ginnevra crouched and examined the ground. There could be dozens of the damn things scattered between where she stood and the stream bank. Maybe later she'd be able to tease Eodan about letting a hunter get the better of him, but first she needed to get him free and get them both out of there.

She sheathed her sword, then looked around and up instead of at the forest floor. A branch not too far above her head that bore only a few tufts of needles was perfect. She snapped it off easily and used the bristles to clear her path. Twice more, she set off traps, and by the time she reached Eodan's side, she was breathing heavily from tension and a desire to find the hunter who'd thought more traps were better and force-feed one of them to him.

Eodan's breath came in quick, sharp pants, and his eyes were unfocused, never a good sign. His left foreleg bled heavily from skin torn by the jaws of the bear trap. Ginnevra examined the trap, looking for something that would release its grip, but in the end she was forced to wrench the thing apart. She flung it away behind her, only barely aware of it setting off yet another of the vile devices. Gently, she felt along his leg. "It's not broken," she said with relief. "Just very bloody, and you're going to have bruises for a few days."

Eodan pressed his head against her chest, and she put her arms around his broad neck. No, she was never going to tease him about this incident.

Eodan's body suddenly tensed, and he let out a low growl. Ginnevra, surprised, said, "What's wrong—"

"Step away from the creature, miss," a harsh male voice said behind her.

Slowly, Ginnevra turned, putting herself between the speaker and Eodan. The man was short and burly, with a thick dark beard and hair barely confined by his flat cap. He looked so much the image of the stereotypical woodsman Ginnevra wanted to laugh. But the arrow he pointed at her heart wasn't the least bit funny.

"Put down your bow," she said, keeping her voice calm. "You're making a mistake."

The arrow didn't waver. "I don't know what you think you're doing, miss, but that is a dangerous animal and I intend to kill it." The man's voice was as steady as Ginnevra's.

"He's not a dangerous animal. Put the bow down," Ginnevra said. Behind her, Eodan moved slightly. The arrow's point immediately shifted to aim at Eodan's head.

"Miss, there are bounties for killing werewolves," the man said. "You're lucky it didn't tear into you."

Ginnevra stood, still putting herself between Eodan and the arrow. Slowly, she drew her sword. "I am a paladin of the Goddess, and I am sworn to protect humans," she said, "but by the Dark Lady I will make an exception if you so much as scratch his hide."

The man's eyes widened. "Damn me," he said. "What is a paladin doing defending the likes of him? He's a monster!"

"He's not a monster, and I don't need to defend my actions to you." Ginnevra took a step forward. "Lower your weapon, and we can have a talk about what you were so afraid of that you salted the earth here with traps."

"Maybe you don't know this, not being a hunter, but the badlands are dangerous," the man said. "This spot is where the big ones come to drink. Bears, wolves. Looks like werewolves, too. I lay my traps thick so they can't escape no matter how wily they are. That's how we do it out here. So don't come over high and mighty on me. I'm not the one protecting a dangerous monster."

Ginnevra ground her back teeth in frustration. Of course this would have to happen during the one time in the month Eodan couldn't change shape voluntarily. It was a lot easier to convince people he wasn't going to hurt them when he wasn't a growling, dark-furred menace. "Master hunter," she said, holding on to politeness with both hands, "do you see this?" She pointed to the grace she wore.

The hunter's aim didn't waver, but his eyes flicked from Eodan to the grace. "I do."

"You have a grace as well, don't you?" Only paladins wore theirs openly; most people, even the anointed servants of the Goddess, wore theirs beneath their clothes.

Now the hunter looked confused. "So?"

"So you know that a grace only remains unblemished so long as its wearer does not betray the oaths they made upon receiving it. Which mine is. Don't you think then, master hunter, that as a paladin in good standing with the Goddess, my behavior should not be questioned even if it seems...unorthodox?"

The hunter's confusion deepened as he tried to follow the twists of Ginnevra's logic. "But," he said, "werewolves are the creation of the Bright One, made to mock and corrupt humans!"

"That's only part of the story. If you'll put your weapon down, I'd be happy to tell you the rest," Ginnevra said.

The arrow wavered. Then the hunter lowered the bow. "What story?" he said, taking a step forward.

There was a snap. The hunter screamed, a long, high-pitched wail of agony, and collapsed on the ground, clutching his leg. Ginnevra started forward and came up short when Eodan's teeth fastened on her leg, just enough to keep her from moving. "All right," Ginnevra said. She used her improvised broom to sweep the ground between herself and the screaming man, then knelt beside him, peeling his hands away from his bloody leg. "Damn it," she muttered. "Things were going so well."

The hunter keened through gritted teeth, his eyes closed and tears leaking from their corners. Ginnevra forced open the trap and tossed it aside. "And I don't believe for one minute this is the accepted way to hunt," she told the man, though he was past hearing her, curled up around himself and sobbing with pain. "Just calm down, I'll take care of you." To Eodan, she said, "Can you walk?"

Eodan got unsteadily to his feet and took a few hobbling steps toward her through the cleared area. Ginnevra took out her belt knife and cut a couple of wide strips from the hem of her long shirt. She used one to bandage the man's leg, though by the way he screamed louder when she touched him, his leg was broken. With the other, she wrapped Eodan's foreleg and tied the bandage off neatly. Eodan nodded in thanks.

Now they just had to get back to camp, and then to civilization. Groaning, she lifted the man over one shoulder and picked up her sword with her other hand. "I'm not sure which of us will be slower," she told Eodan, "but it's not like this is a race."

9

Eodan gave her a look she interpreted easily to mean *it might not be a race, but you'd better try to keep up.* She refrained from sighing heavily. She loved him dearly, but one of the things she'd learned about him in the months they'd been together was that he was fiercely independent when it came to him being wounded and seriously overprotective when she was the one hurt. For a physician like him, it was a strange quirk—or maybe it was *because* he was a physician he had Views on the care of the body.

She let Eodan take the lead, reasoning that he would find the way back to their camp more easily than she and that he'd take the lead anyway regardless of her opinion on the matter. With the hunter balanced on her shoulder, she was slowed enough to match Eodan's limping gait. The hunter still let out a sob now and then, but was otherwise quiet, a gift for which Ginnevra thanked the Goddess. She didn't need to calm a hysterical wounded man on top of everything else.

They didn't bother going silently, but since they were likely the top predators in their part of the forest, it didn't matter. Regardless, Ginnevra saw no other wildlife on their journey and heard nothing. The hunter's odor, the sour smell of someone who hadn't bathed in weeks, filled her immediate world and made her feel sick.

To give herself something else to think about, she said, "Where's your camp?"

The hunter let out another sobbing breath. "No camp," he said. "Travel light. Just some food and a blanket. Horse."

"I guess that's not much of a loss, then. I'll see about finding your horse after we reach our camp." Ginnevra shifted her burden to a slightly more comfortable position. "What are you doing roaming the forest at this time of night, anyway?"

"Heard the wolf cry. Thought it might be a werewolf. Wanted to get the trophy." The hunter sounded as out of breath as if he were the one doing the lugging. "No bounty if they're not in wolf shape."

"That's sick," Ginnevra said.

"I'm not the one who's friends with a monster," the hunter said.

Ginnevra managed not to throw the little man on the ground and kick him. The thought of what might have happened to Eodan at his hands infuriated her. She reminded herself of her oaths to protect humanity, even repulsive representatives of humanity as this man was, and didn't say anything more.

She welcomed the sight of the little camp with joy she didn't think it actually deserved—it wasn't as if it was more than a place to sleep while Eodan roamed the forest under the light of the full moon. But at the moment, it represented something Ginnevra wanted more than anything else: a place to lay down her smelly burden.

"I need water," the man croaked when she set him down beneath the shelter.

"Just a moment." Ginnevra searched through their belongings for a waterskin and found a half-full one. She drank from it herself before handing it to the hunter, not wanting to put her mouth where his had been.

The hunter drank greedily and dropped the empty waterskin beside him. "You'll take me back to Guinio," he said. "Right now."

Guinio was north of Uparde, which was the nearest town to where Ginnevra and Eodan had set up their full moon camp. Guinio wasn't very far away, but the man's assumptions that she would drop everything to cater to him annoyed her. "We're not going to Guinio, we're going to Uparde. We'll take you there," she said, "but your leg is broken, and we'll need to wait for moonset so Eodan can splint it properly."

The hunter glanced past Ginnevra to where Eodan lay with his bandaged leg out in front of him. "That...thing...has a name?"

"All intelligent creatures have names," Ginnevra said irritably. "What's yours?"

"Pellarius Schiatte," the man said, after a hesitation that had Ginnevra wishing she could slap him, he so clearly continued to be suspicious of her and Eodan.

"Well, Pellarius, Eodan is a physician and he's better at treating injury than I am, not to mention I'm not going to drop everything to transport you anywhere in the middle of the night. You can wait."

Now Pellarius stared openly at Eodan, who ignored him. "Werewolves can't be physicians."

"I assure you they can. Now, I'm going to rest, and I suggest you do the same." Ginnevra got up and walked over to where Eodan lay. Now that the crisis was over, she could indulge in sore muscles and the fatigue that comes after great excitement. She settled down next to him and leaned against his broad back, which reared above her head when she was sitting. He was warm and smelled deliciously of werewolf musk, and she smiled to think there had been a time when that smell wasn't dear to her.

Eodan made a sort of snuffling noise and shifted his head closer to her. "I'm glad you're not badly hurt," Ginnevra whispered. "When I think of what might have happened if you'd been alone..."

She stroked Eodan's fur until he nodded off, then stood carefully so she wouldn't disturb him and headed back into the forest. When she reached the little clearing by the stream, she used the branch to sweep the area until she was sure she'd sprung all the traps. She couldn't bear the thought of some animal caught in one and left to die slowly because Pellarius wasn't around to hunt it.

From the clearing, she followed Pellarius's trail, not very

easily; he might not be much of a hunter, but he was an excellent woodsman, not leaving much more trace than Ginnevra herself would. It took much longer than she wanted to locate Pellarius's little camp, where she had an unpleasant surprise: the horse was gone, the ground under one of the trees disturbed. Ginnevra guessed the horse's reins had been wrapped around a low branch, and the creature had managed to pull free. It might be anywhere by now. Cursing under her breath, she gathered up Pellarius's scant supplies. No point leaving them so long as she was already there.

By the time she returned to camp, she was exhausted and in need of sleep. She curled up by Eodan's side and fell instantly unconscious, waking when the sunlight found its way through the branches to shine directly in her eyes. She stood and stretched. Eodan was still asleep, and so was Pellarius.

With a yawn, she rooted around in their provisions for food. They never carried much on these monthly trips into the wilderness, as Eodan was an experienced hunter in either shape, but there was cheese, and some smoked meat, and a handful of berries left from a blackberry bramble Ginnevra had harvested. She ate and thought of nothing much until she heard Eodan say, "I ought to punch that damn hunter right in the face. Bear traps. Is there any water left?"

Ginnevra brought him the second waterskin and sat beside him as he first drank, then washed the deep puncture wounds on his left forearm and rewrapped it. Then he put both arms around Ginnevra and said, "Thank you for coming to my rescue. I didn't think we'd actually need that signal."

"Yes, and wasn't it good that we considered that eventuality?" She kissed him, then disentangled herself and stood. "Let me get your clothes, and then you can see about Pellarius."

"He has a name? Like a person?" Eodan's sarcasm cut through

the morning air like a flensing knife. Ginnevra tossed his shirt and breeches at him, and he caught them out of the air and began dressing. Ginnevra watched, admiring his well-muscled body and the strong, high cheekbones his short beard failed to hide. Blue eyes like nothing Ginnevra had ever seen on any other person narrowed as he contemplated the sleeping Pellarius. "I'm not sure we owe him anything. My arm is going to hurt for a week."

"You don't mean that," Ginnevra said. "You're just cranky because you had a bad night and there's no chance of our usual morning routine with him here." Another thing she hadn't known was how very amorous werewolves got after a night of chasing the full moon. It was probably just as well they traveled into the wilderness rather than risk Eodan being caught in a city in wolf shape.

Eodan sighed. "No, I don't mean that." He tied the laces of his breeches and knelt beside Pellarius, gently unwrapping the bandage. "Love, would you fetch some straight sticks for a splint? It's not a bad break, but it should be immobilized."

Pellarius came awake with a start. "Who are—" Realization dawned, and he tried to scoot away. Eodan held him fast by the other leg. "Don't touch me, monster."

"You have no idea how much I would like to leave you for the wolves," Eodan said without a trace of a smile. "But Ginnevra reminded me I'm not actually a savage beast. Now, hold still and let me look at your leg."

Pellarius stared at Eodan. "Werewolves can't speak," he murmured.

"I assure you we do. Very eloquently, at times." He felt along the leg, prompting a hiss from Pellarius Eodan ignored. "Those are fine, thank you," he said, accepting the sticks Ginnevra extended to him. With a minimum of fuss and no words, he set, splinted, and rewrapped the injured leg, accompanied by Pellarius's cries of pain and occasional struggles. Then he sat back on his heels and said, "So, how are we going to get him out of here?"

"I've been thinking about that," Ginnevra said. "I have a feeling you're not going to like it."

Eodan scowled. "I have a feeling I'm going to hate it."

"Not that much. You're too wounded to handle it by yourself."

"Which only means I'll hate it on both our behalf."

Ginnevra kissed him again. His scowl disappeared, and he grabbed her hand and squeezed it. "All right," he said. "But don't get any ideas about me acting as a pack animal later. These are exigent circumstances."

"Of course," Ginnevra said.

It took her and Eodan a few hours to find the wood they needed for a travois. Then Eodan put it together out of the heavy canvas of their shelter and Ginnevra packed everything else up. Pellarius watched their activities with sullen interest, but he didn't complain about the delay. When Ginnevra picked him up to carry him out of the trees to where the travois waited, though, he said, "This is the best you could do?"

Ginnevra paused a moment before setting him down on the travois, controlling an angry retort. The little man was obnoxious and rude and he was responsible for Eodan being hurt. She would never consider leaving him out here to die, but she didn't have to be nice. "It's your own fault you're in this position," she said. "I'm not sure why you think rudeness to the people who are saving your life is a good plan, but if you're not going to be polite, I don't want to hear anything else out of you."

"You're deviant," Pellarius said, but without any heat behind his words. "Intimate with a monster...how can you call yourself a paladin?"

"She told you to shut up," Eodan said, his voice lower and

more menacing than before. "Call her names again, and this ride will be a lot more unpleasant for you."

Pellarius eyed Eodan. He opened his mouth to speak, and Eodan's lips curled back in a snarl. That shut him up.

Ginnevra loaded the rest of their gear onto the travois and settled the makeshift strap across her upper chest. Beside her, Eodan shifted the strap across his chest to lie even with hers. They gripped the long poles, which were slightly gnarled branches with the bark stripped off at the upper ends, and with a heave got the travois moving. Pellarius yelped, but didn't make any other sound.

After the first hundred or so steps, they fell into a rhythm, matching each other's pace and pulling smoothly despite Eodan being five inches taller. "Just like a couple of oxen," Ginnevra murmured. Eodan let out a short, slightly breathless laugh. The exertion was too great to make conversation comfortable, so they walked in silence, listening to the sounds of birds in the nearby trees and the voice of the wind rustling the branches.

It was nearly noon, and the sun beat down on them out of a clear sky the color of Eodan's eyes. Ginnevra didn't wish for rain, knowing how impossible it would be to lug the travois through sodden ground, but a few clouds might be nice. Sweat ran down her back and pooled beneath her breasts and dampened her hair at the scalp. This was going to take all day, what with having to follow the forest until it opened up into the fields outside Uparde. If they'd been on their own, they could have cut through the woods and saved themselves a few hours.

And yet as irritating and personally repugnant as Ginnevra found Pellarius, leaving him behind was unthinkable. It was counter to everything paladins stood for. It didn't matter if he thought she was deviant for loving a werewolf. The thought depressed her anyway. *She* knew the truth—that werewolves were, for the most part, peaceful people whose Goddess had abused and dominated them for centuries. That they weren't the same as the true monsters who plagued humanity, the malignae and the krokotta and the lamias and all the hundreds of others of the Bright One's creations.

But convincing people of the truth was difficult. Humans were so afraid of werewolves they weren't interested in listening to a story about why they shouldn't be afraid. Ginnevra had looked for opportunities to teach humans the truth for the past few months, but nothing had presented itself. Pellarius was the first person she'd told even part of the story to, and he was like everyone else —so wrapped up in fear and superstition there wasn't room for anything else.

The Blessed, chief of the anointed of the Faith, knew the truth and wasn't horrified by it, and she hadn't stripped Ginnevra of her paladin's rank and grace. But even she hadn't had an answer to the problem, other than to assure Ginnevra she would support her in whatever she chose to do. Though Ginnevra's initial reaction had been to wish the Blessed would make an announcement, over the past months she'd realized what a terrible idea that was. Even the Blessed couldn't change centuries of hidebound tradition, and she couldn't stop people being afraid. And if the holiest woman in the world couldn't make werewolves socially acceptable, what chance did a lone paladin have?

Abruptly, Pellarius said, "What's your game?"

"Excuse me?" Ginnevra panted.

"Not you. Him. The monster. You trying to trick me?"

"I don't care enough about you to work that hard," Eodan said, as breathlessly as Ginnevra.

"Then why not tear me apart?"

Ginnevra inwardly groaned. She didn't have the strength to

spare for this conversation. But Pellarius for once hadn't sounded hostile, just curious.

"He's not a monster," she said, just as Eodan said, "What you think you know about werewolves is wrong."

"I didn't think you were intelligent," Pellarius said. "Thought you attacked humans. Tore them apart and turned them into your kind."

"A werewolf's bite or claws don't turn a human into a werewolf," Eodan said. "And some of us do attack humans. Just not all of us."

"Why not?"

Eodan drew in a deeper breath. "For the same reason you don't attack humans. Because we're not animals. We turned our backs on the Bright Goddess and try to live peacefully."

Pellarius was silent for a moment. Then he said, "But paladins kill your kind."

"Paladins kill monsters," Ginnevra corrected him. Her chest ached from the pressure of the strap and her feet were reminding her that strong as she was, there were limits to her endurance. "The werewolves who don't serve the Bright One aren't monsters." No point in saying she was the only paladin who felt this way. That was even more discouraging than Pellarius's ignorance.

"Don't see how you can tell the difference by looking," Pellarius muttered. "You looked plenty monstrous by the stream."

Ginnevra rolled her eyes, but said nothing. Eodan looked annoyed. He also remained silent. So much for that conversation changing a mind.

THREE

They walked until the sun wasn't directly overhead and then stopped for a rest and something to eat. Ginnevra had put the food at the top of the pile, and she handed out dried meat and cheese gone slightly runny in the heat. They passed around the refilled waterskins, and Pellarius drank as deeply as Eodan and she despite not having done any work. Ginnevra tried not to let it annoy her, though that was a lost cause as everything about Pellarius annoyed her. They were probably going to need a new canvas after this, too.

She and Eodan were settling the strap around their chests again when Pellarius said, "You could have left me back there."

"Not really," Ginnevra said curtly. "You don't know any more about paladins than you do about werewolves, do you?"

"Never met one before now," Pellarius said. "I don't understand you."

"Fortunately for you, that doesn't matter." Ginnevra braced herself against the lurch as they set the travois in motion. Inside, she was miserable. This encounter only proved that nobody would ever believe Eodan wasn't a monster. He might save an entire city and it wouldn't change anyone's mind.

They walked on, step after plodding step, until the sun was in their eyes and Ginnevra couldn't remember a time when life had been more than one foot following the other, over and over again into infinity. Beside her, Eodan's heavy breathing told her he was working as hard as she was. Blood spotted the bandage wrapped around his forearm. Her resentment of Pellarius deepened. This should have been a pleasant walk. Instead, it was grueling torture.

She swiped sweat away from her brow. She was getting a bath when this was over. Her Aunt Caterrina, whom they were staying with, had her own bath house with an enormous cistern and plenty of firewood. Ginnevra didn't care if it was midnight when they reached Uparde. She needed a good, long soak.

She didn't notice they'd reached the road until Eodan pointed it out. The raised highway, paved as all roads to and from the holy city of Abraciabene were, was a welcome sign of civilization. She'd never felt so cheerful in her life, Pellarius's presence notwithstanding. With renewed vigor, she walked a little faster. They might actually make it before sunset.

Only a few steps south along the highway revealed just how hard the cross-country trek had been. The travois slid more smoothly along the stone pavers, which were flat and even with no sign of wear, not like the many side roads paved only with earth and deeply rutted from centuries of travel. "I think it's another hour from here," Ginnevra said. "Aunt Caterrina will be wondering where we are."

"We aren't that late," Eodan said. Ginnevra gave Eodan a cynical look, and he smiled. "All right, we're late. I hope your aunt isn't waiting on us. I hate to inconvenience her."

"She won't mind. It means more time with our horses. I think she was more excited at the prospect of caring for Ginger and Dauntless for three days than in seeing her only niece after two years' absence." Caterrina Cassaline was Ginnevra's favorite relative, a retired paladin who now taught sword fighting in Uparde. She hadn't asked any questions about why Ginnevra wanted to take off into the wilderness for three days when there was a perfectly good town available, she'd listened to Ginnevra's explanation about werewolves without trying to take Eodan's head off, and she'd welcomed Eodan like he was a blood relation. "Besides," Ginnevra added, "if there are no messages waiting for us at the Uparde chapel, we can stay with her for a few days. Then Devoyenne is another day south of Uparde, on the coast. I say we go there next."

"I've never seen the sea," Eodan said. "I like that plan."

"Then—damn. Riders. We'd better get off the road." Ginnevra jerked her head at the oncoming horses, four of them. They didn't look inclined to slow for other traffic.

With some effort, she and Eodan got the travois off the road and down the short slope to the grass that grew on the verge, short and spiky and dry from summer's heat. Rather than continue, Ginnevra removed the strap and stretched. She was going to be sore in the morning. That bath was looking better all the time.

The riders drew nearer. Then, to her astonishment, they slowed and came to a stop. The lead rider brought his horse to the edge of the road. "You in need of assistance?" he asked. "You look like you had an accident."

"Nothing we can't handle," Eodan said. "But you have our thanks for your concern."

Two of the riders at the back of the group exchanged glances. Ginnevra happened to be looking at them rather than their leader, and their sneering, amused expressions unsettled her. She didn't think there was anything funny about their situation.

"Oh, no, friend, we can't just leave you here!" The leader was smiling now, but his eyes were hard and cold and his smile wasn't pleasant. "At least let us lighten your load. Say...any coin you have stashed away in there?"

Ginnevra groaned inwardly. These fools stood between her and a hot bath and a nice bed that wasn't a pallet on the ground. "You're robbing us?" she asked wearily.

"I wouldn't put it that way," the leader said. He withdrew a pistol from beneath his jerkin and aimed it at her. "You'll give us your money, and we won't shoot you all and take it anyway. I think that's fair. Now, friend, I suggest you find your purse so I don't have to shoot your lady."

Ginnevra and Eodan exchanged glances. He nodded slightly in the robbers' direction, a question in his eyes. Ginnevra said, "I guess you'd better do as he says. Get our *other* valuables, too."

Eodan turned and pretended to rummage in the pile of things. Ginnevra took a step back and halted when the pistol's long muzzle followed her. "I didn't say you could move, did I?" the robber said.

"I thought I could help," Ginnevra said, pretending to be scared. She put a hand on the pile, right above where her sword was strapped on, out of sight of the robbers. A sword against a pistol was a bad match, but he'd only get one shot, and Ginnevra was willing to bet her Goddess-enhanced reflexes against that shot.

"Stop!" Pellarius shouted. He twisted around in the bottom of the travois. "She's a paladin! He's a werewolf! You think you can fight them?"

"A what?" the robber said. His pistol wavered. Quick as thought, Ginnevra snatched up her sword and swung at the robber's pistol hand with the flat of the blade. The sword connected, hitting flesh and metal with a resounding crack. The robber cried out and dropped the pistol. Ginnevra pressed the attack immediately, changing her grip and thrusting past his guard until the point of the blade dimpled his thin leather jerkin over his heart.

Beside her, Eodan had her mace in hand and was advancing on the second robber, but rather than swinging the deadly weapon, he grabbed for the horse's reins. The horse, smelling a werewolf, wrenched away, and Eodan had to step backward as the horse reared up and dumped its rider on the paving stones.

The two men at the rear reached for pistols. "Don't," Ginnevra warned, and pressed harder with the sword. "I'll spit him like a suckling pig if you put your hands anywhere near your weapons."

"Listen to her," the robber said hoarsely. "Look, miss—my lady. This was all just a misunderstanding."

"The kind of misunderstanding you have often?" Ginnevra said, raising an eyebrow.

The robber had the good sense to say nothing.

Ginnevra continued, "I am authorized to exercise justice throughout the Lordagne, and it's within my mandate that I can try and execute criminals. You, don't move or Eodan will test his strength on your skull," she said to the fallen robber, over whom Eodan now stood. The man froze like a terrified rabbit facing a fox. Or, rather, a wolf. Eodan smiled pleasantly at him, but held the mace at the ready.

"However," Ginnevra continued, "I'm tired and hungry and holding a criminal trial is more work than I'm interested in doing this afternoon. So—throw down your weapons. All of you."

The robber scowled fiercely at her, but withdrew the long knife he wore shoved into his belt and tossed it aside. The others threw guns and knives well to the side. Ginnevra ignored them.

"Now, on the ground. Face down with your hands above your heads. Not on the road, on the grass." She withdrew her sword slightly so the robber could dismount, but stayed poised for treachery.

Sure enough, the robber kicked at her face before grabbing another, smaller pistol from atop the saddlebag and aiming it at Ginnevra. Ginnevra thrust with her sword, catching the man in the stomach and making him grunt in pain. The pistol discharged, the ball whizzed past Ginnevra's head, and then the weapon fell from the robber's hand to crack against the paving stones. The robber grabbed the blade where it emerged from his body, bloodying his hands, and sagged in death. Ginnevra withdrew her sword, making him fall.

"Do any of the rest of you want to try what that fool did?" she said, her voice wintry cold. The three robbers sank slowly to lie prone on the ground in silence. Ginnevra wiped her blade on the back of the dead man's jerkin, cursing him mentally. Just because she was sworn to protect humans didn't mean she couldn't defend herself or others from evil, even in human shape. But she'd never gotten used to how it felt to take a human life.

Ginnevra rooted through the pile on the travois, ignoring Pellarius's wide, horrified eyes, and came up with a coil of rope she'd used to turn the canvas into a shelter. She bound each robber's hands behind him while Eodan picked up the abandoned weaponry. "Now what?" Eodan asked in a low voice.

"We take them into Uparde," Ginnevra replied. "There's a justiciary there equipped to hold them until trial. Can you ride?" This was directed at Pellarius, who flinched.

"My leg," he said.

"You just have to hold on to the damn horse for a few miles. Can you do that?" She knew her anger should be directed at the robbers and their greed and stupidity rather than at Pellarius, whose only crime was being annoying—well, that was untrue, he'd gotten Eodan injured, but that was the sort of sideways, unintentional evil that paled beside highway robbery—but she'd been forced to kill a man, and that made her both angry and irrational about it.

Pellarius cringed. "I suppose so."

"Fine. Four horses, four of us if you count the body. We can't just leave it here," she said to Eodan's astonished face. "The others can walk. Let's get the load distributed."

It took very little time to load up their gear on the robbers' horses, get Pellarius into a secure position atop one mount, and tie ropes from the captives to Ginnevra's saddle. It still felt like an eternity. When they finally rode out, the sun touched the western mountains and Ginnevra felt like screaming at the world.

They'd gone a few hundred paces before Eodan said, "Ginnevra. You did the right thing."

"I know," Ginnevra shot back. "I know that. I don't need reassuring."

"Not reassuring. But you need to let go of that anger. Stop telling yourself things should have worked out differently. That's blasphemous."

Ginnevra glared at him. "I don't need lessons in my religion from you."

Eodan lost all expression. Ginnevra immediately knew she'd gone too far. "Eodan, I'm sorry. I can't believe I took my anger out on you. You're right, I shouldn't behave as if there was only one right outcome to that situation. I'm sorry."

Eodan shrugged, a casual gesture, but he still looked angry, and it made Ginnevra's heart ache. She cast about for something else to say, anything that might make things right between them. "I hate taking a human life," she said in a low voice she was sure Pellarius couldn't hear. "It always feels wrong no matter the circumstances. And since I know that's the wrong way to feel about it, I want to turn that anger outward. I should have yelled at Pellarius instead. At least he deserves it."

"Does he?" Eodan asked.

"You're injured thanks to him. I don't know why I didn't tear him a new one earlier instead of being forbearing."

That made him smile. "I forgive you," he said. "But I think you owe me."

"I do? Owe you what?"

Eodan smiled wickedly. "I'll let you know tonight," he said.

CHAPTER

FOUR

They reached Uparde as the sun sank fully beyond the western mountains, turning the sky peach and gold. The highway stopped being stone pavers and became cobbles the horses' hooves rang out clearly on despite the noise and crowds filling the streets. To Ginnevra, whose vision sharpened as dusk approached, the lanterns lighting the streets gave an odd doubled look to the houses and the passersby, as if she saw them twice, separated by the space of two breaths. She blinked, and the illusion vanished.

She'd only been to Uparde a few times, once with her paladin company, three times visiting her aunt, who'd settled in the town ten years ago. Uparde was a thriving young town in the republic of Devoyenne, too young to have acquired the grimy patina of the big city, but old enough to have had its rough edges knocked off by life. Tall, narrow buildings of wood or stone loomed over the street, most of them with glass-paned windows that opened into the street, and men and women leaned out of the windows and called out to their neighbors or to people on the street. Couples walked arm in arm and saluted their friends with noisy good cheer. Uparde by evening was loud and boisterous and looked to be gearing up to become even more so as the hour latened.

"I need to report in to the justiciary, see these louts handed over for trial," Ginnevra told Eodan. "Will you do something about Pellarius?"

"Something?" Eodan asked, his eyebrows arching.

"Just an inn, love. I'm not going to impose on Aunt Caterrina by bringing him back with us." Ginnevra looked over at Pellarius, who clung to his horse as if it might take a prybar to get him off it. Despite herself, Ginnevra felt sorry for the man. "I don't know. Maybe he's learned something from all of this."

"You are the most optimistic person I know." Eodan gripped her hand briefly, then wrenched at his reins to keep the horse from nervously mincing away. Convincing it to carry Eodan had taken a lot of patience and skill, and even then it had come close to bolting once or twice. "All right. I'll find him someplace. We'll meet back at Caterrina's house."

"I'll see you soon." Ginnevra took the reins of the horse bearing the dead robber and led it and her string of captives down the street.

The crowd made way for her even though without her plate mail, she wasn't obviously a paladin. Possibly some of them recognized the sword bound to her saddle, its long hilt extending past the horse's shoulder. But it was more likely they made way for the body and the bound men following her. The noise even dropped a little as people stopped their conversations in favor of hushed words speculating about Ginnevra and her captives. Ginnevra ignored them. It was hard enough keeping everyone pointed in the same direction without acknowledging questions from the crowd.

She found her attention wandering to the posters and handbills plastered against the walls. Anyone with property along the main roads ended up serving as impromptu advertising for every entertainer and merchant in town, and when you added the WANTED posters and other public announcements, it meant the foundations of Uparde had an unexpectedly colorful appearance. She drew her gaze away from a rather plain broadsheet with MISSING printed crookedly across the top and gave the ropes tying the bandits a good yank to keep them moving.

She found the justiciary with little trouble despite having only seen it in passing. It occupied the entire space between two narrow side streets and was shorter than the surrounding buildings, two stories of fitted granite blocks that no one would ever mistake for anything but a prison. Two guards flanked the front door, which was of iron that showed traces of rust along the hinges where it hadn't been properly cleaned and treated.

Ginnevra came to a stop there and dismounted. "I have some prisoners to be bound over for trial," she said.

The guards' attention was on those prisoners rather than on Ginnevra, but they clearly recognized her rank. "What's the crime, my lady?" one man asked.

"They tried to rob me and my companion on the road north of here," Ginnevra said.

The two men smirked. "Attempted suicide, then," the other man said. "What about the deader?"

"He succeeded at his attempt," Ginnevra said without cracking a smile. "I didn't want to leave his body to frighten other travelers."

"Fair enough. Wait here, my lady, while I fetch someone to take them into custody." The first guard nodded at her politely and shoved the iron door open with some effort, disappearing within.

"You're not with your company, then?" the other guard said.

Ginnevra recognized an attempt at casual conversation and not a challenge. It was rare to see a paladin separated from her company, as she now knew well. "I serve the Blessed," she said.

The guard's eyes widened in surprise. "Never seen one of the primes before," he said. "What's that like?"

She hadn't expected awe. Everyone knew the Blessed, the highest ranking of the anointed of the Goddess, used some lone paladins to solve problems too subtle for a company, but Ginnevra had only rarely been in a position to identify herself as a prime in the two months since her new calling. "I...it's interesting," she said, startled into candor. "I see all sorts of challenges." She hadn't actually seen many challenges, had witnessed judgment a few times and hunted a couple of monsters, but it was true those were things she wouldn't have faced as part of a company.

"Bet these fools were surprised as hell to find out who they'd attacked," the guard said, jabbing a thumb at the prisoners. Ginnevra glanced over the men. They looked exhausted and thoroughly subdued, which satisfied her.

The door creaked open again, revealing the first guard and four other men wearing leather armor and carrying clubs. "This squad will take them around to the cells, and dispose of the body," the man said, "if you wouldn't mind coming with me? You can make your statement and be on your way."

It took another hour, Ginnevra judged, to tell her story to the clerk who wrote it all down with some excitement. The girl couldn't have been more than seventeen and clearly thought Ginnevra the most wonderful thing ever. As exhaustion set in, Ginnevra found herself stumbling over words and repeating herself, but the clerk didn't seem to notice. Finally, Ginnevra spoke to the justicer on duty, who assured her the statement was enough and she could go. "But it would help to know where you're staying, in case there are any questions," the man added.

Ginnevra directed him to inquire at Caterrina's house, to which she gave directions as complete as she could manage; she wasn't all that familiar with the town. The justicer looked impressed, and Ginnevra wasn't sure if that was because Caterrina lived in a high-class part of town or because he recognized Caterrina Cassaline's name. Either way might deter him from sending for her on frivolous grounds.

Then she had to endure more friendly small talk while she waited for the robbers' two horses to be brought around. They weren't impressive horses, but she could sell them and the other two for enough to cover expenses for a month. Or Caterrina might adopt them. You never could tell what a horse lover would do when presented with new animals.

It was full dark by the time everything was settled. The air was still as warm as midday, wrapping Ginnevra in the smells of animal waste and cooking meat and faint floral perfume that meant civilization. Her muscles ached from her exertions with the travois, keeping her from falling asleep in the saddle as she wanted to do. But even a paladin was a target for pickpockets in the city, so she made herself sit upright and look alert.

The streets leading to Caterrina's house were well-lit, not with ordinary lanterns but frosted glass globes containing merrily dancing flames. To Ginnevra's eyes, they cast a white haze over the cobblestones and the houses and even the sky. She wasn't sure she cared for the effect, but probably the local householders appreciated the brightness that would drive the merely opportunistic thieves away. A determined thief wouldn't give up so easily, as Ginnevra knew from having stalked and apprehended one a month ago.

She passed through a small plaza, notable for having seven streets leading away from it. A white marble fountain at the center of the plaza sent cooling sprays of water through the air, and the smell of the water made Ginnevra thirsty. She promised herself a glass of wine once she reached Caterrina's house and could put her feet up. Then the bath.

The houses here didn't share common walls, and they were each only three stories tall, with property surrounding each house that most people turned into gardens. After the heat of the day, the smell of the night gardens was cool and refreshed Ginnevra. Caterrina's house was halfway down a street that curved like a bow. While she, too, had a garden in front, a path led from the street around the north side of the tall house, beaten down and dry from a week of no rain. Ginnevra dismounted and led the horses around to Caterrina's stable.

Though the stable was out of sight from the street, it wasn't out of range of Ginnevra's sense of smell. Manure wasn't an awful smell, though, and Ginnevra privately considered it comforting, a smell out of her childhood. She sniffed again, and hesitated. Something was wrong, something so subtle only her instincts had noticed. Concerned, she walked a little faster, tugging on the horses' reins to hurry them along. It felt like something was missing, some smell that should have been there, though she didn't know why she expected to be able to smell anything but manure.

The stables filled the whole of Caterrina's back garden space, though Ginnevra had never known them to be full; Caterrina cared for horses broken down by abuse or neglect and sold them on to more conscientious owners. There were six stalls, three of which were occupied. The strange lack of smell niggled at Ginnevra more strongly. Worried now, she left the bandits' horses in two of the empty stalls and hurried to see if her horse, Dauntless, was well. It was a foolish worry, because Caterrina would sooner neglect herself than a horse, but with her instincts ringing a warning in her heart, Ginnevra didn't want to make assumptions.

Dauntless stuck his head out of his stall as she approached. The woman she'd bought him from had called him a blue roan, which wasn't a color Ginnevra had ever seen before, and although his name had been Blueberry, Ginnevra called him Dauntless and told him a paladin's horse deserved a noble name.

Now Dauntless pressed his face against Ginnevra's hand and whickered. "Sorry, I don't have a treat for you," Ginnevra said. Dauntless made a disappointed noise that made Ginnevra laugh. He was smart for a horse, a little too smart, as the seller had explained; he was a trained war horse, but he had trouble with company maneuvers, always wanting to strike out on his own. That sounded just right to Ginnevra.

She ran her palms over his neck and withers and discovered he was trembling. "What's wrong, noble one?" she whispered, and opened the door to his stall. In the next moment, she got a clear look at his water trough.

It was completely dry.

Shocked, Ginnevra reflexively continued petting the horse and stepped in to get a closer look. It wasn't an illusion; the trough was bone dry. Finally she realized what the missing smell was. "Dauntless, what happened?" she said.

Dauntless shook his head as if he understood her and wanted to communicate, if only he spoke human language. Ginnevra backed out and looked at Ginger in the next stall. The enormous gelding's name made sense, as he was a rich golden color, and was at the same time completely inappropriate, given that he was the most placid, most docile horse ever born. They'd had trouble finding a mount for Eodan, since horses knew predators when they smelled them regardless of their shape, but Ginger not only hadn't tried to bolt when Eodan came close, he'd let Eodan pet him and then mount him without a single twitch. They'd bought him on the spot.

Ginger was more placid than Dauntless, but his eyes looked dull, and his water trough, too, was empty. Just to be thorough, Ginnevra checked on the black mare in the third stall. She had her right foreleg poulticed, but the poultice had come loose as if the mare had scraped it until it fell. Ginnevra didn't know how to replace it and was afraid of hurting the horse more if she fumbled around. Here, too, the water trough was empty.

Ginnevra shut the stall door and turned to look at Caterrina's house. Four windows interrupted the smooth plaster façade, their glass gleaming in the moonlight. No lights burned behind any of them. Ginnevra circled the house and discovered it was completely dark. Thoroughly alarmed, she returned to the stable yard and tried the back door. It was unlocked. With only the faintest twinge of guilt at going where she hadn't been invited, she entered.

Old smells of bread and cooked chicken and roasted garlic filled the air, but Ginnevra already knew this was the kitchen. No windows let in the moonlight, and even Ginnevra's Goddess-enhanced sight couldn't overcome a complete absence of light. She touched her grace and said, *"By Your grace I see clearly."*

The room sprang into stark relief, white lines and dark shadows revealing a table, a wooden counter, a pump sink that drew on the same cistern as the bath house, and strings of garlic and a small sack of tomatoes hanging from the ceiling. Ginnevra had no trouble navigating the room to the door on its opposite side.

Beyond, a short hallway led to the front door and, to the right, stairs going up. Ginnevra ascended as rapidly as she dared, listening for signs that Caterrina was somewhere in the house. If she were hurt...Ginnevra couldn't think of any other reason for her aunt to be at home but not have cared for those horses.

The second floor was all what Ginnevra thought of as public

rooms: a parlor, a dining room, Caterrina's small library. All were unlit. All were empty. Thoroughly unnerved, Ginnevra called out, "Aunt? It's Ginnevra. Are you here?" The house echoed her words back at her. Ginnevra didn't open the drapes, which would have let moonlight in to interfere with the sight she'd received from her invocation. She was just superstitious enough not to want the Bright One's malevolent eye casting a curse over the house, making Ginnevra's worst fears come true.

Three bedrooms took up the top floor. Ginnevra hurried straight for her aunt's. It was empty, though the bed was made, and the water pitcher on the wash stand was as dry as Dauntless's trough. Ginnevra sniffed. The room didn't have the musty smell of a room long closed off, but that didn't tell her anything because Ginnevra had only been gone three days, and her aunt had definitely occupied the room before Ginnevra and Eodan had left for the wilderness.

Ginnevra checked the other bedrooms, but half-heartedly. Caterrina wasn't in either of them. None of them looked disturbed, not even the one Ginnevra and Eodan had used the night before they left for the wilderness.

She heard someone moving around downstairs, and her heart leaped before she realized it was Eodan. She hurried down the stairs to meet him on the second floor, outside the dining room. "Aunt Caterrina is gone," she said. "And not just for a few hours. She's been gone for more than a day, maybe more than two."

"I saw the horses," Eodan said. "There's no way she would simply have walked away and left them."

"I know." Ginnevra grabbed his hand, feeling the need for reassurance. "I know. But she's not here. Something terrible must have happened to her."

CHAPTER

FIVE

"Let's care for the horses first," Eodan said. "Or, rather, you should. I doubt any of them but Ginger will be willing to let me get close."

Ginnevra nodded absently. She was already going over possibilities in her head. Caterrina hadn't mentioned anything that might take her away from Uparde when they'd arrived four days before. Ginnevra was certain of it. So either something had unexpectedly come up, or something had happened to her. And since even if something had arisen to take Caterrina away, she would have arranged for the horses' care, that meant anything that had occurred had also ended in foul play. Ginnevra made herself take a deep breath and pushed her fears to one side. She couldn't help Caterrina by panicking.

Downstairs, she pumped water for all the horses, including the robbers' mounts, and filled the feeding troughs as well. She returned to the house to find light spilling from the back door. Eodan had lit several lanterns in the kitchen, but he wasn't there. She collected a lantern and tracked him down in their bedroom. It was small and bland, guest quarters rather than anything in use regularly, with a single bed and a washstand and a clothespress at the bed's foot. But it smelled of lavender, and it was clean, and the room's one window shone in the lantern light.

"I've been searching for any message Caterrina might have left," Eodan said. "I haven't found anything. Though if she left, intending to return immediately, there wouldn't be."

"I don't know which is more worrisome, that she left without warning or she left without thinking she needed to give warning," Ginnevra said. "I'm going to talk to her neighbors. Someone must have seen something."

"That's a good plan. It's not that late yet." Eodan took Ginnevra's hand and pulled her close to embrace her. "Don't worry. There's got to be an explanation. We'll figure it out."

Ginnevra nodded against his shoulder. "We will."

But an hour later, Ginnevra's confidence had vanished. She'd lived in cities her whole life and had always taken for granted how people knew their neighbors' business. But her family wasn't wealthy, and they'd never lived in a neighborhood like this one, with its detached houses and gardens and almost nonexistent foot traffic that wasn't the residents. She'd knocked on doors up and down the street surrounding Caterrina's house, and no one could remember seeing Caterrina more recently than three days ago.

"I remember *you*," one old man said. He lived in the house nearly directly opposite Caterrina's, and Ginnevra felt hopeful of him, because he struck her as the sort of man who would spy on his neighbors out of sheer boredom. "You and the big fellow. Aren't you staying with my lady Cassaline?"

"Yes, she's my aunt," Ginnevra said. "My companion and I had business out of town, and we're just now getting back. Are you sure you don't remember the last time you saw her?"

"I remember her leaving on foot," the old man said. "Don't know when that was, though. The days all blur together."

"That's all right," Ginnevra lied. "Did she look different than usual? Was anyone with her?"

The old man's eyes unfocused in thought. "Can't say I noticed anything unusual," he finally said. "She was alone, though. Wasn't armed, though she doesn't carry weapons much."

"And it wasn't this morning? What about yesterday morning?"

Again, the old man looked like he was digging deep into memory. "Not this morning. Could have been yesterday or the day before. It was definitely morning, though. I'm sure about that."

"Thank you," Ginnevra said. "Please let me know if you remember anything else."

She turned to go, and the old man said, "You staying in my lady Cassaline's house, then?"

"For tonight, anyway, yes."

"You think something's happened to her?"

Ginnevra considered the possibility of starting a panic centered on the disappearance of a retired paladin, thought about how difficult it was going to be to find her, and went with, "I'm not sure. She didn't leave word she was going, so I'm concerned."

"Well, good luck to you." The old man shut his door. Ginnevra trudged across the street and tried Caterrina's front door; it was barred. She'd barred the front door, but hadn't locked the back? Ginnevra wished she knew whether that meant anything.

She walked around to the rear of the house and checked on the horses. There weren't enough stalls for all seven, so she'd tied one of the robbers' horses to the end stall where it could reach food and water and hoped that was enough. Now she took time to groom each horse, though after the day she'd had she was too exhausted even to manage the bath she'd been dreaming of. Idly, she wondered where Eodan had gone, but her mind was a pink cloud of weariness and she could barely manage the currycomb.

When she finished, she returned to the kitchen and helped herself to a red, juicy tomato she ate like an apple. The food revived her somewhat, enough that when Eodan came in through the kitchen door, she didn't reflexively try to take his head off. Eodan looked as tired as she felt.

"No one saw Caterrina leave," he said, "no one to the north of here, anyway. Whatever happened to city dwellers' legendary nosiness?"

"I suppose if you're wealthy enough, you can pay for privacy," Ginnevra said. She wiped her hands on a cloth lying puddled on the wooden counter. "I need sleep. I'm exhausted and I'm not thinking straight. Tomorrow will be soon enough to search more thoroughly."

"I brought our gear up already," Eodan said. "Did you want a bath?"

"I'm afraid I'd fall asleep in the tub and drown," Ginnevra confessed. "Thank you for taking care of Pellarius. I'm glad to be rid of him."

Eodan nodded. "I'm sorry it took so long. The first two inns I approached didn't have any available rooms on the ground floor. Then I had to arrange for his care—"

"His care?"

Eodan busied himself with an old nick in the countertop, not meeting Ginnevra's eyes. "His care?" she repeated, a little more forcefully.

"Pellarius can't walk," Eodan said, a little defensively. "I had to make sure the inn would bring him food. And then I found a physician willing to check in on him next week—"

"Eodan, he hates you!"

Eodan scowled. "Yes, well, he apologized."

Ginnevra's mouth fell open. "He did not. And if he did, he didn't mean it."

"He was sincere. And he thanked me." Eodan shook his head and ran his thumbnail along the crack. "Besides, it's not about whether they deserve good treatment. It's about who I am."

Ginnevra hugged him. "You are a good man," she said. "Much nicer than me."

"I know," Eodan said with a wry smile. Ginnevra punched him lightly in the side, and he captured her hand with his. "Bed, now. Things have to look better in the morning."

"Thank you for being optimistic for my sake." She kissed him, and some of her tension melted away. "Time enough for a new plan in the morning."

"A new plan and a bath," Eodan said. "We both smell like we spent the day acting like cart horses."

Ginnevra had to admit the werewolf musk was stronger than usual. "Optimistic *and* practical," she said.

SHE ROSE when dawn pinked the horizon and tiptoed downstairs, leaving Eodan sleeping, to run herself a bath. The hot water eased muscles made sore by yesterday's exertions, but once she was fully awake, she found her desire to linger in the tub had vanished, replaced by worry over her missing aunt.

She scrounged food in the kitchen, half a loaf of stale bread, more tomatoes, a round of cheese she trimmed fuzz off, and a sack of shelled almonds, and took it all upstairs. Eodan was just waking when she entered. He smiled when he saw the food. "I'm starving," he said. "I think I forgot to eat supper last night, in all the commotion."

"All I had was a tomato, and that's delicious but not filling."

"I've never had tomato before. What does it taste like?" Eodan took one from her armful and sniffed it.

"Ah...like tomato, actually. You'll have to try it and see what you think." Ginnevra spread her bounty on the end of the bed and carved off another hunk of cheese, slightly hard but still edible.

Eodan took a bite of tomato as she had the previous night and looked surprised when juice spilled over his chin. "It's very different," he said. "I like it. Where do they come from?"

"A country far south of the Lordagne. They're really only available in the southern city-states, like Devoyenne and Paese, which are close enough for trade." Ginnevra helped herself to her own tomato and ate it more tidily than Eodan. "Did you want a bath? The cistern's still full."

"Yes, after I eat." He swiped tomato juice off his chin and took another, less messy bite. "Then what?"

"I think we should check her studio in town next. Ottavio has to know something. After that...I really do have to report in to the chapel, see if they've messages for me. That's as far as I've planned. I'm hoping Aunt Caterrina's partner will give me some direction." Ottavio Rinarzi had been a mercenary in the armies of several princes and dukes and electors before giving up the fighting life to join Caterrina in teaching swordplay to young people who were never likely to get closer to the battlefield than a tapestry illustration. Caterrina definitely wouldn't have left Uparde without telling Ottavio.

Eodan wrenched off a hunk of bread, winced at how dry it was, and ate it anyway. "Do you want me to come with you?"

"I need your help. We have to do something with those horses, the extra ones, and I can't care for Aunt Caterrina's injured mare. We'll need to find a buyer and we'll need a place that can tend an injured horse."

"I have an idea for the second one," Eodan said. "And I can ask around about a buyer." He stood, brushed off crumbs, and lightly kissed her. "I'll bathe and see about making myself smell less like a werewolf."

"*I* like how you smell," Ginnevra said with a smile.

"You're also not a horse, thank the Goddess." Eodan gathered up a change of shirt and left the room.

Ginnevra finished her meal and donned her armor. She would have preferred to go about her inquiries in ordinary clothes, but she would report to the Uparde chapel in an official capacity, which meant the full kit. She belted her pistol on and checked that it came easily to her hand, then gathered up her sword and sword belt.

For a moment, she examined the sword. Nearly five feet long from end to end, the blade over four feet of that length, the scabbard of black leather worn slightly where she gripped it to draw the sword. She slid the sword free of the scabbard a few inches to reveal the silvered steel. Her father, a blacksmith, had silvered all sorts of weapons and armor for the paladins who stopped at his forge, but she knew little of the process aside from how it coated the steel with a type of metal inimical to werewolves. It was seeing all those paladins going in and out of the smithy that had inspired Ginnevra to join their ranks. And now she had a werewolf for a companion. Life was stranger than anything she could imagine.

She trod downstairs and found Eodan leaving the bath house, which was a smallish room off the kitchen that backed on the enormous circle hearth. His hair and beard were damp, but he was fully dressed, and he smelled like flowers over the werewolf musk. "I love the way you look," he said.

"You mean, in armor? Isn't that odd? I mean, my armor can seriously hurt you." She pulled on her coif and settled her helmet over it.

"You look powerful, and dangerous, and I've always been drawn to powerful, dangerous women." Eodan smiled and carefully brushed her cheek with his fingertips, avoiding the silvered plate mail. "Maybe there's also a part of me that likes a challenge."

Ginnevra smiled. "I don't know that any man's ever found me more attractive in armor than not."

"Oh, you're even more beautiful when you're wearing nothing," Eodan assured her with a smile that made her blush.

"Well, I'll be out of this armor soon enough. Just as soon as I check in with the chapel and see if they've messages for me." Ginnevra slung her sword over her shoulder. "Thank you for taking care of the horses. Will you meet me at the chapel later? We can decide what to do next."

"Around noon, say? I can't imagine it will take longer than that to sell the horses." Eodan stepped back to let her pass.

Ginnevra crossed the stable yard to check on the horses. She wasn't a horse lover, and to her they were useful tools, but she knew how important it was to care for them properly. Her aunt wouldn't stand for someone of her family, let alone a fellow paladin, to behave as if a horse wasn't as deserving of consideration as a person. And she was fond of Dauntless. So she saddled him with extra care and some murmured reassurances before helping Eodan put lead lines on the robbers' horses. Then, with a final wave, she set out.

They'd gotten an early enough start, even with the baths, that Uparde was only just waking up when she returned to the town's main street. Uparde by daylight was a much more sedate town, though movement off the side streets suggested thriving markets where most of the foot traffic had gone. Why the markets weren't out in the open as in most cities, she didn't know, but she appreciated not being pressed on all sides by pedestrians. Even the air smelled fresher, though it still smelled of waste and human bodies as well as the hidden markets selling produce of all kinds.

She read the handbills and posters out of habit as she rode. Advertisements, notices, broadsheets titled WANTED or ALERT or MISSING covered the foundations to head height. The MISSING posters caught Ginnevra's eye now, though she didn't know if there were more of them than usual. It was just her heightened awareness and her fear for Caterrina that made them seem to be everywhere.

Caterrina's studio was down a side street too narrow for the sun to illuminate it fully. Without the sun's rays, it was unexpectedly chilly, and lanterns still burned at intervals along the street. Signboards bearing pictures of what could be bought or sold or traded within advertised the shops that lined the street. Most of them bore no writing; despite the many broadsheets and advertisements plastering the walls of Uparde, vendors didn't count on their patrons being able to read. The smells of the market had vanished, and Ginnevra didn't even smell food being prepared. The hotter the day became, the more noxious the odors of waste and human bodies would be, but for now, it was a pleasant morning.

Ginnevra brought Dauntless to a halt outside a door beneath a painted sign depicting two crossed swords and the word CASSALINE. She dismounted and pounded on the door, hard enough to rouse Ottavio, who Ginnevra knew was a late sleeper. The sound echoed off the sides of the narrow canyon of a street.

She was aware of people slowing to pass her and heard their whispered conversations that might as well have been shouting to her Goddess-enhanced hearing. She did her best not to listen, but she was drawn by the nearest conversation: *you go...no, you do it...dare you...dare you back...*

She turned to see a couple of children, maybe no older than

ten, pressed against the wall in the scant shelter of a door frame and regarding her with wide eyes. "Good morning," she said.

The children's eyes grew wider, and they backed away a pace, but they didn't flee.

"Do you two live around here?" Ginnevra continued. One of the children bobbed his head—her head? Ginnevra was terrible with children—in assent. "I've got to visit a friend here. I'll pay you to watch my horse while I'm inside."

The other child's mouth fell open. "I'm better at watching," he said. The first child elbowed him in the stomach.

"I meant both of you." Ginnevra dipped into the pouch she wore below her cuirass and pulled out a couple of copper larins, which she flicked at the children. Both snatched the coins out of the air with the expert dexterity that said this wasn't the first time. "Twice again as much when I'm back, all right?" She fastened her sword to the horse's saddle and thought about warning them not to touch it, but that would only have made her more likely to do so when she was a child.

The first child accepted Dauntless's reins with an awed expression. Ginnevra patted her horse a final time and banged on the door again, louder and more forcefully. Finally, she heard footsteps on the stairs inside. The door flew open.

"I ought to—oh, Ginnevra," Ottavio said. He was shirtless and held his trousers up with one hand. His other hand was raised in a fist, but lowered as he realized who she was. "Is she back?"

Ginnevra's heart sank. Part of her had hoped this was all a mistake, and Caterrina was here and had an explanation for everything. But Ottavio's hopeful expression brought that fantasy crashing down. "I thought you'd know where she was," she said.

Ottavio ran a hand through his thick brown curls. "You'd better come inside," he said.

CHAPTER

SIX

G innevra followed him inside, past the door that led to the ground floor sparring room and up the narrow stairs to his apartment. It was a single room the size of the sparring room below, furnished on one side with a rickety bed, a table and two chairs, a couple of mismatched wooden cabinets, and a rack where Ottavio stored his weapons. The only bright spots about it were the heavy, multicolored carpets strewn across half the floor, piled over each other with no regard for clashing colors or décor. The other half of the room was empty, the floor bare and unvarnished wood.

Ottavio waved Ginnevra to a chair and walked to the bed, tying his trouser laces as he moved. He grabbed a shirt draped across its foot and pulled it casually over his head, then ran his fingers through his curls to straighten them—a futile gesture, as his hair defied any attempts to tame it. "When did you arrive?" he asked.

"Late last night. Ottavio, how long has Aunt Caterrina been missing?"

Ottavio opened a cabinet and removed a bottle of brandy. He poured a splash into a dirty glass cup, brandished the bottle at Ginnevra in invitation, and put it away when she declined. "Last I saw her was three days ago. Nights. Goddess help me, I can't think straight." He tossed back the brandy, shuddered, and set the glass down as carefully as if it were a precious gem. "She left here three evenings ago like she always does. Then she didn't come back the following morning. I didn't start to worry until that evening. I went to her house and nobody was there. Looked like it was locked up tight."

"Why would she leave and not tell you?" Ginnevra asked. She gripped the back of the chair, but didn't sit—she could sit in her armor, unlike the paladins of a hundred years ago, but the cuisses dug into her thighs.

"That," Ottavio said, jabbing a finger at Ginnevra, "is the question, isn't it? I spent yesterday tracking down all her friends, thinking either she'd be with one of them or would have told one of them what she intended. No one had seen her after the night she left here. I'm out of ideas, Ginnevra. I hope you've got something in mind."

Since Ginnevra had hoped *Ottavio* would offer her a lead, this discouraged her. "She didn't say anything before she left? I mean, in the days before she left. Nothing about leaving town, or wishing to see an old friend, or family trouble...?"

"Wouldn't her family trouble be your family trouble, too?"

Ginnevra sighed. "Probably. But she's in closer touch with our family than I am. Think, Ottavio. Anything might be a clue."

Ottavio shook his head. "I went to the justiciary to report her missing yesterday evening. Not that they'll do any good. She's not the only missing person in Uparde. Justiciary's got their hands full."

Ginnevra's mind immediately flashed on all those MISSING notices. "People missing?"

"All over town," Ottavio said. "No warning, no clues. They just up and vanish. The upper crust is starting to make a stink about it, but I think the problem's worse than they realize. For every rich man goes missing, five poor people disappear and nobody notices."

"But...someone must have some idea. Usually if someone goes missing, at least in the big cities, it's only a matter of hours before a body shows up. It doesn't sound like that's the case here."

"No bodies," Ottavio said with a shrug. "A definite lack of bodies. And everyone's got a theory. Abductions. People running off to Devoyenne or Fayonne to start a new life. Monsters devouring their victims so nothing's left."

Ginnevra made a face. "I don't know of any monsters who consume their prey that thoroughly."

"That's just one of the theories. I didn't say I believed it." Ottavio poured himself more brandy and swilled it down. Counter to sense, his stance and diction were becoming clearer the more he drank.

"Well, what *do* you believe?"

"About the disappearances, or about Caterrina?" Ottavio let out a deep breath. "Something happened to Caterrina. She'd never just walk away from her responsibilities. Either she was kidnapped, or she had an accident..." He gestured in a futile way with the bottle. "But a kidnapper would have asked for ransom by now, and an accident wouldn't make her disappear this thoroughly."

"True." Ginnevra pushed off the chair. "I have to report in at the chapel, but after that I'll go to the justiciary and see what I can learn. If there are a lot of people suddenly going missing, it doesn't make sense that they're not all related somehow. And maybe someone at the chapel has an idea."

"I don't much think of anointed as criminal investigators, Ginnevra."

"They aren't, but if people came to them looking for help, they might have information. I'll find her, Ottavio. I promise." Ginnevra wasn't sure that was the sort of promise she should make. She wasn't an experienced investigator. But this was her aunt, and she couldn't bear the thought of not knowing what had happened to her.

Ottavio nodded. "I'll go on searching out her friends," he said. "I'll let you know if I learn anything."

On the street outside, Ginnevra paid her little helpers and pretended not to notice the small, grimy fingerprints on the smooth black leather of the scabbard. She mounted and rode back toward the main street. Her errand at the chapel now made her impatient. She reminded herself that a paladin's duty was more important than her personal life, but that didn't stop her urging Dauntless forward faster than she likely should through the crowded streets.

The main road wound through Uparde and into a more affluent part of town similar to Caterrina's neighborhood, where the houses didn't share walls and the cobblestones gave way to pavers made of concrete and edged with ridged granite, separating the walkways from the street so people could avoid the muck that gathered there. Though no greenery fronted these houses, Ginnevra smelled fresh grass and flowers and guessed the owners could afford private gardens behind. Her own family hadn't been poor, but gardens were above their touch, and Ginnevra and her brothers had gotten into trouble more than once from sneaking into other people's gardens and stealing fruit or fresh peas. She couldn't help wondering where her horse minders had gone and whether they, too, liked a little unautho-rized gardening.

Eventually, Ginnevra came to a plaza paved in pale gray granite streaked with white where pigeons had passed over. The fountain at the center drew Ginnevra to it like a hook reeling in a fish. Its black basalt made the granite seem paler by comparison, and the brass fittings shaped like trumpets shone like gold in the sun. Water spurted from each trumpet, making an intricate pattern of liquid arches and splashing loudly into the basin, where lay a scattering of coins. Ginnevra didn't need to see the black building opposite the fountain to know she'd reached the chapel of the Goddess. This was the only place in Uparde where no one would steal loose coin.

She didn't know what the chapel was built of beneath its black marble facings, but as this was a chapel and not a sanctuary, holiest of holies, she guessed it was of more ordinary stone or even wood. Its high lintel carved with a scene of the Goddess blessing humanity radiated an aura of sanctity over anyone enter-ing, while its windowless walls bore lanterns shaped like inverted tulips in brackets of gleaming brass. Every chapel looked different, but they all spoke to Ginnevra of home. Surprisingly, the door to this one was shut. Chapel doors were never shut in daytime, not even in stormy weather. Ginnevra couldn't think why this one would be different.

She dismounted and led her horse around to the back of the chapel, where a lone acolyte in knee-length robe and sandals leaned against the hitching post in front of the stable. A couple of horses peered out over stall doors. The acolyte straightened when she saw Ginnevra and said, "My lady, welcome. Let me care for your animal."

"Thank you," Ginnevra said. She handed Dauntless's reins over and then walked back to the chapel door. When she pushed on it, she discovered it was locked. Strange. It was mid-morning, too early for a meal even if going home for a meal was something anointed did.

She knocked on the door, which was wood and not marble. No one responded. Frowning, she banged harder. Almost immediately, the door swung open, and someone said, "What?" in tones of such profound irritation Ginnevra felt angry.

"Ginnevra Cassaline, paladin—prime of the Goddess," she said. "Is there some reason this chapel is locked?"

The woman's irritated expression became horrified in a flash. "Goddess save me," she breathed. "My lady, I apologize. Please, come in. I didn't know Abraciabene would act so quickly."

Ginnevra almost asked what she meant by her strange remark, but in time remembered it was always smart not to give away one's ignorance, even to someone who presumably wasn't an enemy. She followed the woman inside. The door swung shut, leaving the hall in near darkness, lit only by warm, gleaming specks of fire in brass baskets near the ceiling. Ginnevra's eyes instantly compensated, and she observed the entrance chamber, which was carved all over with images of the Goddess's creations.

"*By Your grace the fire burns bright,*" the woman said, and the sparks in the baskets grew to be fist-sized globes. By their light, Ginnevra saw the woman wore the midnight-blue cowled tunic of a Dedicate, the first rank of anointed beyond acolyte. She wore her brown hair coiled at the base of her neck, nestled into her cowl. Her face was round and plump, but sharply angled eyebrows saved her from looking like a child playing dress-up.

"I'm Feora Mantovane," the Dedicate said. "Welcome to the Uparde chapel. Please, let me escort you to meet the Revered Agostino Abbate."

"You have a man as your Revered?" Ginnevra said.

Feora's round cheeks reddened. "He—my lady, he's not—weren't you told?"

"I should speak to him first," Ginnevra said, sidestepping the question. Her curiosity grew by the moment. Of course men could hold rank, even Revered rank, within the Goddess's Faith, though Ginnevra knew of none who'd achieved the highest rank of Hallowed. It was just odd to find one in charge of a chapel or sanctuary. Something strange was going on. Combined with the mystery of the missing people, it keyed Ginnevra's nerves almost to breaking.

Three doorways led off the entrance chamber. The one opposite the front door led to the sanctum proper, as Ginnevra knew because regardless of differences in construction, the sanctum always opened directly off the front door. Feora led them down the left-hand hall, which was wide enough for both of them to walk side by side and still allow two other people to pass going the other way.

They walked past a number of doors on the left, all closed, and a blank wall on the right to another doorway at the hallway's end. This one had an arched rather than square top and was rimmed in black marble carved with abstract curves that suggested the dark moon. Though the hallway was unlit, lights from beyond the doorway cast the carvings into relief, making them look even more as if the moon's thin crescent glowed with its own light.

As they reached the doorway, a handful of acolytes emerged. They came to a stop when they saw Ginnevra, making a few more acolytes bump into them in a comical way. Ginnevra kept her expression stern, enjoying the awestruck way they looked at her —not at her, though, but at a paladin of their Goddess. She didn't like being stared at on her own behalf, but she liked the idea of being a living representative of the Dark Lady.

After a moment, the acolytes recovered, continuing forward.

Each bowed to Ginnevra as they passed. That was less amusing, but she reminded herself they were offering respect to the Goddess and not to her and nodded back. When the doorway was clear, Ginnevra followed Feora through.

The room looked like the instructor's hall at the sanctuary where Ginnevra had received her training. Globes of fire illuminated plain wooden pews varnished a glossy black, their low backs and seats unpadded. Niches on the back sides of the pews held unadorned books bound in black leather, gospels and handbooks for the instruction of acolytes or paladins. The floor was pale gray granite similar to what paved the plaza outside, and it was scuffed by the passage of thousands of feet over hundreds of years. Even the smell was the same, the smell of varnish and chalk and old paper and woody incense. Ginnevra turned to the front of the hall, half expecting to see her old instructor Dedicate Mastarcce with her iron-gray hair and the walking stick she never hesitated to use on trainees whose attention wandered.

The man at the end of the hall did have iron-gray hair, but he stood erect, taller than Dedicate Mastarcce would have been even if her back problems had let her stand up straight. His hair was cut very short, shorter than Ginnevra's own, and framed a somber face with thin lips and heavy black eyebrows that seemed to have a life of their own. When he looked up from the large wooden table covered with books and inkwells, those eyebrows raised nearly to his hairline. "I didn't expect a response so soon," he said. His voice was as deep and resonant as Eodan's, but there was a nasal tone to it that set Ginnevra's nerves on edge.

"This is Prime Ginnevra Cassaline," Feora said. "My lady, the Revered Agostino Abbate."

Ginnevra saluted the Revered with her left fist over her heart. "Revered."

"I welcome the Blessed in your person here," Agostino said.

Ginnevra's heart thumped hard, just once, before settling on a slightly faster than normal rate. She had only heard that salutation once before, and it had not then been addressed to her. It meant Agostino believed she was there in an official capacity, as the Blessed's direct representative, and something was seriously wrong.

"I think we have a misunderstanding," she said. "I am one of the Blessed's primes, yes, but I was not sent by Abraciabene in response to whatever request you made. However, since I *am* here, perhaps you can tell me what's wrong?"

Agostino's mobile eyebrows furrowed like a couple of mating caterpillars. "I don't know...this is a rather sensitive issue, and perhaps—"

"Revered," Ginnevra interrupted, "if your problem is so severe you sent to the holy city for help, I'm sure the Blessed would send someone. At the very least, she will contact the sanctuary at Devoyenne to see which of her primes is nearest. Since, at the moment, that prime is me, I might well be the someone she sends. So there's no reason you can't confide in me. Or am I wrong, and your problem can wait until someone else arrives?"

Agostino's expression relaxed, and the caterpillars retreated. "You make a good point," he said. "Please, have a seat."

Ginnevra sat on the front pew. There was a chair behind the cluttered table, but Agostino didn't take it. Instead, he paced in front of the table, clenching and unclenching his hands as if forcing feeling back into them. "I'm sure you're wondering why a man is the Revered of this chapel," he said.

"I was, a little," Ginnevra said, "but of course a man is as good as a woman in the Goddess's sight."

Agostino smiled slightly, and Ginnevra reviewed her words in her head and felt uncomfortable at having been unintentionally condescending. "The truth is, I'm not the ranking Revered. That would be Revered Massina Parenogne. I am her second in matters pertaining to the chapel."

"Oh." Ginnevra shot a quick glance at Feora, who stood nearby and looked increasingly agitated. "Then...is she ill?"

Agostino shook his head. "We don't know," he said. "Massina Parenogne has been missing for three days."

CHAPTER

SEVEN

"Missing?" Ginnevra said. For a moment, his words made no sense. It was Caterrina who was missing, not the Revered. "How does a Revered go missing?"

"I wish I knew," Agostino said. "Three mornings ago I arrived at the chapel to find it still locked. Normally the Revered arrives early to open it. I visited her home to see if perhaps she was ill. She wasn't there, and the servants hadn't seen her that morning. They assumed she'd left earlier than usual for the chapel."

The whole situation was starting to sound surreal. "Was that likely?"

Agostino shrugged. "The Revered is a creature of habit. If she went somewhere else that morning, some errand, it was in her religious role, because her robes were missing. But I don't know of any religious duty she had that would take her away from the chapel. Even so, that's what I assumed—that she had gone to instruct someone in the Faith, or to perform a ceremony or sanctification. It was odd, but nothing to be alarmed about. I didn't start to worry until around noon, when she was scheduled to lead the worship service."

"That makes sense." Ginnevra shifted her sword into a more comfortable position. "She's not the only one who's gone missing in Uparde."

"No. We've had all manner of supplicants asking for our help in locating their lost loved ones. I hate turning them away, but of course it would take the Hallowed at the sanctuary in Devoyenne to perform that level of magic." Agostino looked genuinely distressed. "I'm afraid the worst may have happened, to them and to Revered Parenogne. It's hard to believe anyone might wish a Revered harm, but I have trouble imagining anything else, after three days."

Ginnevra made herself stay focused. Logic. Reason. It was easier to stay detached when she was considering the fate of someone she didn't care about. Not that she wished harm to the Revered, but it wasn't the same as her worries for Caterrina. "She might have left Uparde. Did you send to Devoyenne? I know it would be odd for her to have left for the city without word, but—"

Agostino shook his head. "The sanctuary and the chapels in Devoyenne haven't seen her, either. I sent word there the day after she disappeared. Yesterday I sent to Abraciabene with my report and a request for help."

Ginnevra thought about this. "There are any number of other places the Revered might have gone, including Devoyenne—she might have had a reason not to report in to the sanctuary there. Did you ask the sanctuary to perform a seeking rite?"

"I did, but you know how unreliable those are when it's a living creature with even a modicum of free will," Agostino said. "They confirmed Massina is still alive, which is a comfort, but they had no idea where she might be."

"That's still good news. For them to learn anything about the

Revered's condition or location, she has to be within a certain distance of the seeking, no more than fifty miles. She might even still be in Uparde." Ginnevra stood. "If you sent word to Abraciabene yesterday, it will be most of a week before a reply arrives. That reply might come in the person of another prime. Until then, I'll search for Revered Parenogne." It wouldn't take much more work to look for two people than for one, yes? And for all Ginnevra knew, the two disappearances were related.

"Thank you," Agostino said. "I'm sure I don't have to ask you to be discreet. We don't need people believing a Revered is vulnerable to assault, or kidnapping."

"Discreet?"

Agostino flapped a hand distractedly. "No one knows the Revered is missing. It would lower morale if people were to learn of her disappearance."

"Maybe, but if she's in danger, isn't it better to do whatever it takes to find her? Secrecy might not be our friend, Revered Abbate. And it's not as if she's the only person who's disappeared in Uparde recently."

Agostino's lips pinched tight shut. "You must do as you see best, my lady," he said. "But the Revered is punctilious about her duties. She would never leave without making thorough preparations for her absence. And we had her residence searched thoroughly. We found no mislaid note of explanation. That's why I'm sure the Revered's disappearance has nothing to do with all the other missing people."

Ginnevra almost challenged him, but decided in time that getting into an argument over why a Revered was too special to partake of the fate of others was pointless. Besides, she could understand Agostino's distress. He'd been thrust into a role he'd probably never expected to fill, in the most uncertain of circumstances. That would be enough to make anyone uncertain. Well, not Ginnevra. She wasn't an experienced investigator, true, but she'd been taught by the best and she would do her utmost. Caterrina might be counting on her.

Agostino walked with her back to the entrance, with Feora trailing behind. "We're at your disposal, of course," he assured Ginnevra. "Anything you need...I'm afraid I don't know what this kind of investigation entails."

"I'll need to talk to all of the anointed here, and the household servants at the residence. You're probably right that something happened to her, but I can't rule out the possibility that she left for perfectly innocent reasons and was accosted or something." All the things she would do to find Caterrina. The two disappearances were so similar, and in the same time frame, Ginnevra couldn't help wondering if they were connected. Ginnevra didn't know what her aunt's relationship with the chapel and its anointed was.

"I don't suppose you know my aunt? Caterrina Cassaline?" she asked.

"Of course. I should have recognized the name," Agostino said. "She attends services at least once a week, though she never draws attention to herself. She and the Revered are good friends. Perhaps she knows something of the Revered's disappearance?"

Agostino's innocent helpfulness made tears well up in Ginnevra's eyes as nothing else had. She blinked them away and said, "Aunt Caterrina disappeared recently. Three days ago. I'm searching for her, as well."

"Oh," said Agostino, looking deflated. "You don't think..."

"I don't know why they would have gone off together," Ginnevra said. "It's possible, and I won't rule it out immediately. But it's more likely to be coincidence." Despite her words, she felt more hopeful. Coincidences happened, but they weren't the only possibility.

"You'd know best," Agostino said. He came to a halt at the entrance chamber. "The acolytes have instruction until noon, when we have worship services. You're welcome to attend."

"Thank you, I will. And I'll want to question the acolytes afterward."

Agostino's eyebrows did their mating dance again. "Surely you don't think they know anything useful?"

"I won't know what they know until I ask. It's possible one of them noticed something important." The one prime Ginnevra had ever met, Dolcea Lupare, had said most of digging out the truth involved talking to a lot of people until you found one who knew something. Ginnevra's company had escorted Lupare to one of her assignments, and she and Ginnevra had talked often on that trip. Most of what Ginnevra knew about investigation, she'd gleaned from Lupare's comments.

"Then I'll prepare them to speak with you. And the Revered's residence is three streets down from the plaza off the main road. You'll know it when you see it." Agostino saluted Ginnevra the anointeds' way, briefly touching his hairline with his right hand and making a swooping arc away from his head, symbolizing the crescent moon. Ginnevra returned him a paladin's salute and left the chapel.

The acolyte was still at the stable, sweeping out the unoccupied stalls. On a whim, Ginnevra approached her. "What's your name?"

The acolyte stopped sweeping, but continued to hold her broom. "Saneddra, my lady."

"Saneddra, how much contact did you have with Revered Parenogne?"

Saneddra's eyes widened. "*Me*, my lady? Almost none. We acolytes don't speak to the Revereds much. I saw her at instruction and presiding over worship services, and she once told me to straighten my robe."

"And did you like her?"

Saneddra's cheeks turned rosy. "It's not my place to say."

That was an unexpected answer. "You mean you didn't like her."

Saneddra blushed harder and said nothing.

"Look, Saneddra," Ginnevra said, "the Revered is missing. Something bad might have happened to her. I've never met her, so I need to know everything I can learn about her. If you're not honest with me, it could mean danger for her—and I think, even if you didn't like her much, you don't want harm to come to her, right?"

Saneddra shook her head. "Of course not." She drew a breath as if steeling herself against what she was about to say. "It's not about liking or disliking," she said in a low, confidential voice like she was afraid of someone overhearing, though the two of them were the only ones in the stable. "It's more that the Revered is strict, but not always. Sometimes she comes down hard on someone for the littlest misstep, and other times she ignores something big—never anything sinful, just things that are against the rules. So you never know how she'll react. It made her unpopular with the acolytes."

"I see." Ginnevra didn't know if that had anything to do with the disappearance, unless one of the acolytes had gotten fed up with the Revered's behavior. Too soon to make judgments. "When's the last time you saw the Revered?"

"Four days ago, at noon worship," Saneddra said promptly.

"And she didn't request a horse after that? There wasn't a horse missing from the stable the next morning?"

"Oh, no, nothing like that," Saneddra said. "The Revered only

rode for special occasions, like processionals or official delega-
tions to the lord mayor's office. She preferred to walk."

"I see. Thank you, Saneddra."

Saneddra unwrapped Dauntless's reins from the pole, but
didn't immediately hand them over. "Are you going to find the
Revered, my lady?"

"I'll investigate, yes. I hope I'll find her."

"That's good. In truth, my lady, Revered Abbate is nicer than
Revered Parenogne, but it's not right, having a man in charge of a
chapel, is it?"

Saneddra's confiding, trusting tone reminded Ginnevra of how
she'd accidentally called the man's qualifications into question.
The memory sharpened her words. "The Goddess loves us all
equally, Saneddra, and if She is willing to extend Her power to male
anointed, it's not our place to say where those anointed should or
should not serve. I hope you're respectful of Revered Abbate."

Saneddra blushed again and gave Ginnevra the reins. "Of
course I am. I'm sorry I said that."

"Just don't say it to his face, and you'll be fine." She felt hopelessly stuffy at having delivered that lecture, but it was true, and
Ginnevra needed to hear it as much as Saneddra had.

She rode slowly across the plaza, lost in thought. Caterrina
missing. The Revered missing. Goddess knew how many other
men and women missing. Something was going on in Uparde, and
she intended to find out what—not just for her aunt's sake, but
for the sake of all those missing people.

She heard her name being called and came out of her reverie
to see Eodan approaching on Ginger. He'd rewrapped his forearm
in a clean bandage, but showed no sign the injury bothered him
aside from holding that arm a little stiffly. Smiling, she altered
course to meet him. "Did everything go all right?"

"I found buyers for the horses, at better than average prices," Eodan said. "One of the women told me horses are in demand right now, but she didn't know why. And I didn't much care, since they weren't our horses to begin with. What about you?"

Ginnevra told him what little she'd learned, ending with the news of the Revered's disappearance. "I know I shouldn't get my hopes up, but they *did* both disappear on the same day...and, yes, probably half a dozen other people did too. But that has to work in our favor. People don't just vanish for no reason, and it's too much of a coincidence if they all go missing at the same time for completely unrelated reasons."

"So, where first? The justiciary, or the Revered's home?" Eodan asked.

Ginnevra rapped her knuckles on her left vambrace, making a dull metallic clank. "I'm still in my robes of office, so to speak, so maybe the residence first? I'm hoping if I learn something important there, it will lead to Aunt Caterrina as well. Will you help? We'll need to talk to all the servants, and it will go faster if there are two of us."

"Of course. Do you know what the Revered looks like?" Eodan asked.

"That would be another thing to ask the servants. It sounds like she left in her religious robes, which would be helpful if I could be certain she still had them on."

Eodan drew closer as they left the quiet plaza for the main road, where traffic had increased slightly. "That sounds like you think she was abducted. But why would anyone kidnap a Revered?"

"I don't know. Right now, I think she left the residence without telling anyone she was going and then either sneaked away to some other city, or a hidey-hole in this city, or was taken off the street and concealed somewhere. That means I need to know who saw her last and whether that person knows anything useful."

"That still doesn't tell you why."

"No, it doesn't, and that's where I come up blank." Ginnevra pulled up on Dauntless's reins to keep him from running over a child who came out of nowhere to dart in front of the war horse's enormous hooves. "It's the same as with Aunt Caterrina. Either they ran away, or they were abducted, and neither of those things make sense, particularly if they disappeared together."

"You don't suppose it was a romantic tryst? That Caterrina and the Revered were involved?" Eodan looked like he hadn't considered the possibility until just then.

"I doubt it. Aunt Caterrina is very fond of men, particularly younger ones who are impressed by a paladin's scars." Ginnevra sighed. "I've decided not to worry about 'why' until I've exhausted the possibilities of 'how.'"

Eodan nodded. "That's smart. I take it we're going to the residence now?"

"We are. It's just ahead."

The street they were currently on was narrow enough that there wasn't much room for them and the pedestrians using it. Ginnevra could tell the tall, narrow buildings with their stone pediments and painted plaster exteriors were all houses because of the palm-sized obsidian mirrors hanging beside almost every door. The mirrors were symbolic of commitment to the Goddess, a reminder of the dark moon, and were popular among city dwellers. Some people thought they provided magical defenses, but to Ginnevra's knowledge none of them were ever blessed by the anointed to have magic powers.

While most of the doors were painted bright colors, red or blue or purple, one door stood out in stark blackness against the creamy plaster of the wall. Black marble panels the size and shape of ordinary bricks formed the doorposts and lintel, gleaming even in the indirect light that shone into this canyon of a street.

Ginnevra and Eodan stopped in front of the black door. "Is it normal for a Revered to live in such an ordinary location?" Eodan asked.

"It's different in different cities," Ginnevra replied. "In smaller towns, the ranking Revered often lives above the chapel, or in a house nearby. I don't know how they make the decisions. I was more wondering what we'll do with the horses." She dismounted and knocked on the door. The knocker was a plain iron ring with a knot at the bottom that made a metallic crack against the iron door plate.

After a moment, the door opened silently, and a tall, thin man peered out. He didn't seem surprised to see a paladin on the doorstep. "Yes, my lady?"

"I'm Ginnevra Cassaline, prime of the Blessed," Ginnevra said. "I'm investigating the disappearance of the Revered Massina Parenogne. This is my companion Eodan. May we enter?"

The man looked past her at Eodan, the slight widening of his eyes the only sign he found Eodan's physical form impressive. Then he examined the horses. "If you'll wait, I'll summon a footman to watch your animals," he said, and shut the door.

Ginnevra and Eodan exchanged glances. "So were they expecting you, or is that man just extremely self-contained?" Eodan asked.

"I'm sure they were expecting *someone*," Ginnevra began, and then the door swung open again and a young man clad in brown breeches and a white shirt with a black jerkin that all together looked like a uniform emerged.

"I'm to take your horses, my lady," he said. There was an eager look in his eyes Ginnevra suspected meant he didn't have much to du most days, and certainly never had the opportunity to serve a paladin. Ginnevra and Eodan handed over their reins.

The tall, thin man stood in the doorway. "Please, follow me," he said, and gestured politely into the dark interior of the residence. Without hesitation, Ginnevra entered, Eodan at her back.

EIGHT

" I am Lanberto," the man said. "Majordomo of the Revered's household." He led the way down a small, dimly-lit hallway that smelled of soup and cabbage. Its walls were painted a dark brown into which a couple of doors blended almost perfectly. The smell of soup became stronger as they passed the second door. Four small sconces held lanterns whose light wasn't enough to do more than raise shadows. Ginnevra had never seen a house whose main door opened so directly on the kitchen and offices. She wondered if the Revered ever entertained here, and if so, whether she felt embarrassed at guests traipsing through this part of the house. It would be like showing one's unclad backside to the world.

Stairs at the end of the hall rose up out of the netherworld into a more brightly-lit hall, one where windows provided the illumination. Even the walls were brighter, painted a pale pink and trimmed with white carved moldings at the ceiling. Lanberto caught Ginnevra looking around and said, somewhat defensively,

"The residence is not owned by the Revered or even by the Faith. It is as the owners made it."

"It seems quite comfortable," Ginnevra said. She thought about complimenting him on the household's frugality in not redecorating, but decided that might seem patronizing. For all she knew, the Revered's residence represented a profligate use of resources—she had no idea whether it was more common for the Faith to buy houses for its anointed—and she would just make herself look foolish.

Instead, she said, "I'd like to talk to you about the Revered, if you don't mind."

"I have already told Revered Abbate everything I know," Lanberto said, still somewhat icily.

"Yes, and I'm sure your time is valuable," Ginnevra said. She was tempted to browbeat the man, but she decided to try the nice way first. "But it's better for my investigation if I hear what you know directly from you. I'm sure you understand. And while we're talking, Eodan will meet with the rest of your staff. That will make everything go much faster."

"I won't be too disruptive," Eodan said with his most pleasant smile.

"Well..." Lanberto eyed Eodan speculatively, as if questioning whether a man his size could be subtle enough for an investigation. Ginnevra would have been annoyed at the assumption that Eodan was too big to be intelligent if she didn't know it amused Eodan to be underestimated. "All right," Lanberto said. "My lady, if you'll wait in the parlor, I'll take your...companion...to the servants' hall and arrange for the others to join him there."

By the look of him, Lanberto was angling for a hint as to Eodan's relationship to Ginnevra, whether "companion" meant associate or sexual partner or possibly both. Ginnevra smiled brightly at him and didn't flinch. After a moment, Lanberto opened a door for Ginnevra and bowed her inside.

When the door closed on her, Ginnevra took a moment to examine her surroundings. The room was as bright and pale pink as the hall, with roses carved into the moldings at the corners of the ceiling, and was mostly empty of furniture. There was a credenza in one corner, ornately carved and with panels in which bits of different colored wood made pictures of lilies in vases, next to a bench seat with a tall back and wooden canopy. The back, but not the seat, was upholstered in a tapestry pattern echoed in two other benches, these with low backs, placed at the middle of the room. Ginnevra wandered over to look at the tapestry. It was too worn to make out details, but she thought it might depict a hunt. She amused herself pretending it was paladins hunting monsters and moved on.

The two large windows looked out on the street. Ginnevra looked down on Dauntless and Ginger and their attendant, who was petting Ginger and didn't notice Ginnevra watching him. Heavy black brocade draperies hung open over the windows. Ginnevra judged they would put the room in near-total darkness if they were closed.

She took a closer look, and found signs that this room could be used for religious purposes. A small, spindly-legged table between the benches held a brass bowl with a scattering of ashes, mounted in a base of ebony; Ginnevra sniffed the ashes and smelled incense beneath the scent of old fire. Brass fixtures held unlit lanterns similar to the ones at the chapel, ready to be lit with a match or an invocation. By the doorway, she found a couple of ritual knives in sheaths hanging from the wall and a black walnut box that, when opened, proved to contain obsidian graces in wire settings, but without chains or leather thongs to turn them into necklaces. Ginnevra wasn't sure why Revered Parenogne might perform sanctifications here rather than at the chapel, but it wasn't important. She hoped.

The door opened again, and Lanberto entered. "How can I help you, my lady?" he said.

Ginnevra nodded. "There are things I need to know," she said. "To start, who was the last person to see Revered Parenogne?"

"That would be Letta, the upstairs serving girl," Lanberto said. "She turned down the Revered's bedclothes the night before the Revered went missing. As she left the room, the Revered entered and bade her good night."

Eodan would no doubt question this Letta in more detail. Ginnevra forged on, hoping these were the right questions. "And when did you see the Revered last?"

"At supper. The Revered eats a very small meal in the evenings, and eats late." Lanberto's chin was raised high in a superior attitude, and his tone was as icy as ever. "I oversaw the meal service, and the Revered thanked me as she always does. Then she entered her study. I have not seen her since."

Ginnevra didn't like Lanberto's excessive formality. It felt like he was mocking her rather than giving her the respect most people gave a paladin. She thought about calling him on it, but decided to match him politeness for politeness until that stopped being useful. "Revered Abbate told me they'd searched the residence for evidence of a note or anything that might say where the Revered had gone. Did she mention anything to you? A late errand, or being called away to a religious rite?"

Lanberto shook his head. "The Revered is of the opinion that while the Faith is open to all, people should not come to think of the anointed as dispensers of religion, on call at all hours. She would not have left the residence for anything but funeral rites, and even then, she is likely to ask Revered Abbate to perform those duties."

That seemed odd. "Why is that?"

"It's not my place to divine the intentions of the Revered." Lanberto sounded so smugly prim Ginnevra longed to pinch him.

"You mean she never said why she abrogated her duties?" she said, deliberately provocative.

It got the desired reaction. "The Revered always performed her duties more than satisfactorily," Lanberto replied, somewhat hotly. "There is no law that dictates what rites a Revered must give her time to. I'm sure she had a good reason for wanting Revered Abbate to officiate at deathbeds. It might give him experience and provide opportunities to demonstrate compassion."

Ginnevra thought privately that Lanberto had strong opinions for someone who didn't want to read the Revered's mind. "I'm sure you're right," she said. "What *does* the Revered do, as a matter of course? That is, are there duties she takes on more frequently than others?"

"The Revered is committed to the religious education of the young," Lanberto said, "and she takes a personal interest in their sanctification and their acceptance of their grace. She teaches daily at the chapel and presides over the noon worship. She feels strongly her responsibility to the people of Uparde."

"So is there any chance she might have gone somewhere for a sanctification, and had something befall her?"

Lanberto shook his head. "Sanctifications happen in this room or at the chapel," he said, with a look that suggested Ginnevra should have known this. "The Revered believes strongly in sacred spaces. She does not hold with this newfangled notion that rites can be performed anywhere."

Ginnevra, whose sanctification as a young adult had been performed in a field behind her father's smithy, forbore to comment. "What kind of guards do you post at the residence?" she asked.

That startled Lanberto. "Guards? We have no guards. They're completely unnecessary."

"So someone could have entered this house and abducted the Revered—"

"Oh, no, not that either," Lanberto said, returning to his usual slightly smug self. "We are always aware of entrances and exits, and we have wards on the front door to prevent anyone entering or leaving between the hours of midnight and five o'clock in the morning."

"Anyone? Including the Revered?"

"Of course, even the Revered..." Lanberto's voice trailed off. "That is...in truth, my lady, I don't know if the Revered had a way to bypass the wards. It would be unnecessary. Why would anyone leave the residence at that hour?"

"That's a good question, Lanberto." And one Ginnevra wished she knew the answer to. She was increasingly convinced the Revered had walked away from the residence of her own free will sometime between...well, Eodan would learn what time the Revered had last been seen. Between that time and— "Lanberto, what is the Revered's usual morning schedule? When does she rise?"

Lanberto fell back on comfortable ground. "She rises between five-thirty and six o'clock. Breakfast is served at six-fifteen precisely. Then she—"

"I beg your pardon for interrupting, but does that mean the first anyone knew she was missing was at five-thirty in the morning three days ago?"

"More specifically, we expected to see her at six-fifteen and did not."

What next? "And...was anything else missing besides the Revered's robes of office?"

"Nothing that shouldn't be missing, my lady." Lanberto's eyes unfocused, as if he was going over memories. "Her robes, her shoes, her grace. Her gospel was gone as well, but she takes it everywhere. I understand it was given her upon her seminary graduation."

"So..." Ginnevra chewed her lower lip in thought. "There's nothing to say the Revered didn't just leave early, or go out late the night before." The same night Caterrina had disappeared.

"But why would she?" Lanberto said.

"I don't know," Ginnevra said, "but if I can figure that out, I'll be closer to finding her. One last thing—would you describe the Revered?"

"She is of average height, plump, and wears her hair, which is streaked with white, cut short," Lanberto said promptly. "I believe she is fifty-seven or fifty-eight years of age. Her complexion is unusually pale, and she has a mole at the right corner of her mouth."

"Thank you, that's very detailed," Ginnevra said. She eyed Lanberto, but he still showed no sign that this conversation mattered to him beyond whatever it might do toward bringing the Revered back. And yet he'd been quick to defend Massina Parenogne, and that description had been unusually on-point. If he was the Revered's lover, he was doing an excellent job of concealing it.

She left the parlor to see Eodan coming up the stairs. The sight of him cheered her. She managed not to hurry to join him, feeling Lanberto's eyes on her from behind. Her relationship with Eodan wasn't secret, but she didn't like the idea of the majordomo turning it into something unseemly, even in his own head.

"I've gotten everything I could think to ask out of the servants," Eodan said. He glanced over her shoulder, presumably at Lanberto, and added in a lower voice pitched for her ears alone,

"We can discuss it elsewhere. It's close to noon, and I'm getting hungry."

"I told Agostino Abbate I'd return for noon services. Can you wait a little longer?"

"My people believe delaying the gratification of a physical impulse makes the eventual indulgence sweeter." Eodan led the way back down the stairs. "Personally, I think that's what our mothers tell us when they just don't feel like cooking. But yes, I can wait."

They accepted the horses' reins from the young man and made their way back to the main street, which was busy now with pedestrians and a number of riders. All of them gave way to the paladin and her companion, and Ginnevra and Eodan made good time returning to the chapel. "So, what did you learn?" Ginnevra asked.

"I'm not sure," Eodan said. "I discovered the last anyone saw the Revered was between ten and ten-fifteen the night before her disappearance, or at least before she went missing. The girl who makes up the Revered's room, Letta, couldn't be more specific than that."

"That's good enough. Anything else?"

Eodan shrugged. "None of them liked the Revered much. A couple of them are secretly glad she's gone and hope someone else will take her position—not that they wanted harm to come to her," he hastily added. "None of them are the sort to plot revenge for some slight, and none of them know more than they're saying."

Ginnevra didn't ask if he was sure. Eodan had very good instincts for when someone was lying. "That matches what the acolyte at the stable told us. I wonder if the Revered behaved as erratically to her household as she does to the acolytes?"

"Possibly. All of that is inference. None of them were willing to come out and admit to disliking a missing woman who might be in trouble." Eodan nudged Ginger closer to Ginnevra. "Among my people, that kind of dislike might be enough to get someone accidentally-on-purpose killed."

"Except we know the Revered is still alive." Ginnevra sighed. "I don't understand it. Revered Abbate told me the Revered and Aunt Caterrina were good friends. I can't believe the Revered was as awful as we keep hearing, because Aunt Caterrina is a very good judge of character."

"She doesn't have to be an awful person to be disliked," Eodan said. "The servants were also all in agreement that the Revered was deeply committed to the Faith. People with strong convictions about something aren't always well-liked by others not similarly committed."

"That's true." Ginnevra shook her head. "I don't think the Revered's personality is relevant to her disappearance, especially if nobody disliked her so strongly as to want to get rid of her." She chewed her lower lip in thought. "So. Massina Parenogne disappeared sometime between ten o'clock in the evening three nights ago and six-fifteen the following morning. She apparently walked of her own free will out of the residence, dressed for a day of religious observances. Nobody admits to hating her, but nobody likes her. And wherever she is, she's alive."

"That's more than we started with," Eodan said when they came in sight of the chapel. A steady stream of people entered it, many of them dressed in traditional black, but several in ordinary clothes and two people wearing silks and satins. The rest gave that couple plenty of room.

Ginnevra steered Dauntless wide around the worshippers to approach the stable. "I'll question the acolytes after the service. Why don't you ask around in the residence's neighborhood, see if anyone saw the Revered? If she left in the middle of the night, it's not likely, but it will give you something to do that isn't waiting on me. And you can get something to eat. We can meet at the justiciary in a few hours."

"I like that plan. I don't want to encounter the anointed in a place where they might start a riot, since we still don't know whether the Revereds here will recognize what I am," Eodan said.

"Eodan. You know I want them to know the truth." Ginnevra felt uncomfortable every time the subject of revealing Eodan to her fellows in the Faith came up.

"And *you* know *I* think you're hopelessly optimistic," Eodan said, with a smile that took the sting out of his words. "It's all right, Ginnevra. Someday." He brushed his fingertips against hers, avoiding the silvered plate mail, before turning back the way they'd come.

Ginnevra watched him ride away until he was a tiny figure on the far side of the plaza. Then she dismounted and handed the reins over to Saneddra, who looked as enthusiastic as ever about caring for the paladin's horse. Ginnevra loved Eodan, and the knowledge that he was outcast by two religions made her burn with righteous indignation. It was unfair—but she herself had heard the Goddess say She couldn't do anything about it without breaking Her own law, and Ginnevra could hardly argue with that.

As Ginnevra walked back around to the entrance, she thought about the Revered, not as a missing person or a problem to solve but as a woman who wasn't much liked. She must have fulfilled her religious duties well, or someone would have petitioned for her to be removed, but being faithful and diligent didn't mean having friends. With Caterrina also missing, she certainly hadn't had anyone who cared enough about her to search for her, if even Agostino's concern was for the reputation of the chapel rather than the welfare of its Revered. Ginnevra didn't resent having to search for the Revered, but it was a duty rather than a labor of love —not the way it was for finding Caterrina.

Well, the Revered might not have many friends, but now she had Ginnevra. And Ginnevra was more than ever determined to solve this mystery and bring both women home.

CHAPTER

NINE

Ginnevra rode toward the justiciary later that afternoon feeling hungry and slightly discouraged. She hadn't learned much at the chapel. She'd spoken to the acolytes after the noon service, while Agostino and Feora and the second Dedicate, Rigarrda, were holding religious instruction for the public. Most of the acolytes were enough overawed by her they had to be prompted to answer her questions, though two of them, Agnella and Federigo, were forthcoming enough to admit to what Saneddra had said: the Revered wasn't well-liked by the acolytes. None of them had seen the Revered after she'd left the chapel the evening before her disappearance.

When the instruction was over, she'd talked to Feora and Rigarrda separately and gotten similar results. Rigarrda was a little mouse of a woman Ginnevra privately felt was not suited to religious life. Even low-ranking anointed like Dedicates needed forthrightness and strength of spirit to set a good example for the populace, and Rigarrda was meek and timid beyond even what

Ginnevra expected from someone facing a paladin of the Dark Lady.

Feora, on the other hand, met Ginnevra's eyes fearlessly and answered her questions with a refreshing directness. Ginnevra discovered she'd been a Dedicate for two years and was well on her way to achieving Revered rank. Feora was also the first person Ginnevra had talked to who seemed genuinely distressed at the Revered's disappearance, not because of the turmoil it threw the chapel into, but because she liked and admired Massina.

"She's so committed to the Faith," Feora had said. "She goes out of her way to make sure the children have a solid religious education. And she makes sure the sanctification rite is meaningful and memorable."

"How so?" Ginnevra had asked.

"Oh...she never does them anywhere ordinary, just the chapel sanctuary or the residence. That makes it special for the young man or woman. And she doesn't do a lot of sanctifications all at once—it's always just the one person. That makes it their special day." Feora's eyes gleamed with fervor.

"Do you know why the Revered didn't attend a lot of deathbeds?" Ginnevra asked, remembering what Lanberto had said.

"I didn't know about that," Feora said. The fervent light vanished from her eyes. "I'm sure she had a good reason."

Neither Feora nor Rigarrda had seen the Revered after seven o'clock the evening before her disappearance. Ginnevra had spoken again briefly with Agostino before leaving, but he hadn't been any more forthcoming.

Now Ginnevra wished she'd spent the time searching for Caterrina instead. It was a foolish wish, given that she hadn't known what the anointed knew about the Revered's disappearance and would have had to speak with them eventually, but she didn't feel she was making progress, and that made her impatient.

The justiciary in daylight was even more sullen and dour than it had been the previous evening, its granite blocks a weight on the landscape. Ginnevra wondered what its neighbors thought of its presence, whether they resented it or were comforted by the visual reminder of justice being served. The other buildings nearby appeared to be shops rather than residences, and they stood well away from the justiciary like ladies pinching their noses at some smelly cur sniffing their heels.

Eodan waited at the corner, well away from the door, holding a covered basket. "They wanted to roust me, but I told them I was your companion and they backed off," he said. He flipped back the cloth covering the basket, revealing a third of a loaf of bread, a wax-coated round of cheese the size of Ginnevra's fist, and a bunch of rosy purple grapes. "I also brought food."

The smell of the bread made Ginnevra's stomach rumble. "I love you," she said, fervently, and Eodan chuckled.

She dismounted and ate heartily, spitting grape seeds on the ground without caring about how uncouth it was. "So, did you learn anything?"

Eodan crossed his arms over his chest. "There aren't any shops or vendors in that neighborhood. That means no regulars on the street, at least not during the day. I don't know what it's like at night. So no one I asked was anything but a passerby, and none of them had been in the street on the night or morning in question. But I also asked the residents, and one of them said he'd seen someone in a dark cloak leave the residence the night the Revered disappeared."

Ginnevra straightened. "That's good news."

"Maybe." Eodan shook his head slightly. "The person who claimed that was...well, he's a shut-in, and I got the feeling he doesn't have much to do all day but watch the street. And while he might therefore be a good witness, he might also have made up the story, or exaggerated it, because he thought it was what I wanted to hear and it kept me talking to him."

"Oh." Ginnevra slumped. "So we're back where we started."

"We always knew that was an unlikely source of information." Eodan took a handful of grapes. "What about you?"

"I confirmed that almost no one liked the Revered, and that she was passionate about the Faith. Nothing useful." Ginnevra wiped her mouth and wrapped up the remaining food. "And now I'm going to see what I can learn from the justiciary."

"I'll wait here with the horses," Eodan said.

The guards at the door were, naturally, not the ones who'd been on duty the night before, but they were as quick to recognize a paladin as their comrades had been. They admitted her with no reservations, and Ginnevra found herself in the small, bleak antechamber she remembered without fondness. She knew its purpose was to put off petitioners with frivolous complaints, but she couldn't help thinking that was a selfish way of looking at the demands of justice. Suppose someone had a serious problem, and this room scared them away?

The clerk at the tall desk didn't look up when she entered. "Name and complaint," he said in a bored way. His pen scritched across the paper in front of him.

"The paladin Ginnevra Cassaline, here on prime business," Ginnevra said. Again, she felt uncomfortable. From the clerk's lack of interest, she had the feeling people who weren't paladins struggled to get the justiciary to take them seriously.

The pen stopped scritching. The man's head snapped up. His wide eyes and open mouth eased some of Ginnevra's discomfort because it made her want to laugh at his consternation. "My lady," he said, sounding awed. "I apologize for not...that is, I didn't realize..."

"It's all right," Ginnevra said. "I'm here about a missing woman. My aunt, Caterrina Cassaline. She was reported missing yesterday."

The man's expression lightened in relief Ginnevra didn't understand. "Of course! The disappearances! Wait here, my lady, I'll be right back." He hopped down from his stool and hurried through a door behind the desk.

Ginnevra waited. She thought about reading the paper the clerk had been writing on and decided that would be boring as well as intrusive. She adopted the parade rest stance she could maintain for hours if she had to and let her mind drift. It couldn't be coincidence that Caterrina and the Revered had disappeared on the same night, could it? Particularly since they knew each other. But Ginnevra couldn't think of any reason the Revered might call on Caterrina to accompany her somewhere, or vice versa.

On the other hand, that meant pursuing one investigation meant pursuing the other at the same time, which saved effort. She'd come up against a dead end with the Revered's movements, so maybe it was time to move on to finding out where Caterrina had gone. If none of her aunt's friends had seen her...well, someone had to have noticed *something*.

"Here you are, my lady," the man said, pushing the door open with his foot. His arms were full of documents, stacks of loose pages and half a dozen scroll cases and a fat little book the size of Ginnevra's two palms. He dumped the lot on the table and stood back, looking very pleased with himself.

Ginnevra eyed the pile in growing unease. "Here I am, what?"

"This is everything we have on the disappearances," the man said. "It's such a relief to have a prime take over. Nobody's had time to really dig into the problem, aside from the few, um, special cases."

"What do you mean, special cases?" Ginnevra's unease threatened to blossom into panic she tamped down hard. Investigate *all* the disappearances?

"Well..." The clerk wouldn't meet Ginnevra's eyes. "You know. The *special* cases. The ones who...their families are powerful, so they get..."

"I see." Ginnevra did see. It wasn't something she was thrilled about, not coming from wealth herself, this idea that having money meant you could buy justice, but it was so common she didn't know why the clerk wouldn't just come out and say what he meant. Maybe he didn't like the idea, either. "But I'm not here about all the disappearances, just the one."

Now the clerk looked at her. "You're not? Why not?"

"I'm in Uparde on my own time, not on an assignment. This is just..." Her voice trailed off in the face of the man's obvious disappointment. "I mean, I'm sure someone here will look into it eventually."

"Maybe." The clerk put a hand on one of the scroll cases, steadying it. "I'm sorry for my presumption, my lady."

"No, I understand, but..." Ginnevra sighed. Well, she'd wanted information. And maybe, if there was something sinister underlying all the disappearances, there could be something in the clerk's pile that would shed light on Caterrina's absence. "Never mind. I'm here, and I might as well take on this task, so long as I'm looking for Caterrina and the Revered."

"The Revered?" The clerk sounded startled. "Is the Revered missing? Nobody's reported it."

Ginnevra spared a brief thought for Agostino and his desire to keep this quiet and then dismissed him. "They didn't want people to worry, but it's been a few days and I think the time for secrecy is past." She examined the stack of documents. "Could you get me a sack? And I need to talk to whoever has been following up on the...special cases."

While the clerk hunted out something to put all the documents in, Ginnevra ended up in an even smaller, less pleasant room, windowless and smelling of must, talking to a justicer in the plain black doublet and hose of his office. The justicer, Ciutto Baroccius, was clearly unimpressed with Ginnevra's rank and offered no resistance to giving over even the small authority of searching for the missing people. "You won't find anything," he said. "People are probably just leaving for better opportunities elsewhere. Uparde isn't thriving like it used to."

"What kind of searching have you done?" Ginnevra asked.

Ciutto shrugged. "I asked around their neighborhoods. Talked to friends and relatives. They all said they hadn't seen their missing loved one any time close to when it turned out they were missing."

"And were the missing people dissatisfied with life here? Eager to move on?"

Another shrug. "How should I know? They're missing. It's not like I could ask them anything."

"You could have asked their friends and families," Ginnevra pointed out. "I understand you spent most of your time on the wealthier, um, victims."

"Of course. Those families have power." The justicer shifted his weight impatiently. "You've got the records. Why don't you see what those tell you?"

Ginnevra decided she wasn't going to get anything more out of the justicer and saw herself out.

Lugging the sack, she returned to Eodan's side. He was talking to a couple of children who looked awed not by Ginnevra's sword, hanging off Dauntless's harness, but by

Eodan's size. They bolted when Ginnevra approached, leaving Eodan laughing.

"I'm sorry that took so long," Ginnevra said. "It seems I'm now responsible for discovering the fates of *all* the missing people in Uparde. I wonder if they'd have been so quick to pass it all off on me if I hadn't been wearing the armor? Which, by the way, I would like to get out of, so let's head back to Aunt Caterrina's house." She tied the sack to the harness and mounted.

"I'm guessing no one else has taken the search seriously, and that's why they gave it to you, armor or not," Eodan said. He, too, mounted and led the way back down the street. "Or do justicers spend a lot of time investigating complaints?"

"Practically none, as far as I can tell," Ginnevra said. "Most people hire private agents if there's a crime they need investigated. Then the agents do the legwork and bring the evidence to the justiciary to press charges."

"That seems hard on anyone who can't afford a private agent."

"It is, but I don't see any way around it. There aren't enough justicers to pursue every complaint that comes their way. It does make me wonder how many disappearances haven't been reported because the families are searching privately." Ginnevra patted the sack. "This is a lot of paperwork for just a few missing people. It's a much bigger problem than I thought."

"But if there's a single underlying cause, anything you learn from it will help find Caterrina," Eodan said.

"That's what I told myself. Where are you going?" Eodan had turned onto a side street.

"I need to see about the mare, the injured one from Caterrina's stable. I brought her to an inn for care, and they told me to return this afternoon for more information."

"You took her to an inn?"

Eodan looked defensive. "The stable master is skilled at tending horses, and he was the only person I knew who is."

Ginnevra nudged Dauntless after Ginger. "Sorry. It just seems strange. How do you know anyone in Uparde? You've been here exactly once before for about seven hours."

"He watched the horses while I was taking care of Pellarius." Eodan pointed down the road. "The inn's just there. The Golden Sickle. It's very nice."

Ginnevra caught on. "Eodan," she said in a level tone, "did you use our money to pay for Pellarius's care?"

"Just for the doctor. And if he needs to stay longer than a week." Eodan sounded too cheerful.

"Eodan—"

"Ginnevra, if we can't prove to the world that we're honorable and generous by spending a little money, what's the point of ever expecting anyone to believe a werewolf isn't evil?" Eodan dismounted in the inn's front yard, but stood holding Ginger's reins, looking up at her.

Ginnevra opened her mouth for a retort and couldn't think of anything to say. "You said he apologized," she eventually said.

"He did. Not under duress, even."

She sighed. "I don't know why I begrudge the money. You're right, we're building goodwill one person at a time. I just wish the one person wasn't a smelly hunter with no common sense and an entitled attitude."

Eodan smiled at her, a warm, loving smile that made her wish she wasn't encased in silvered steel. "You're generous, too. Think of all those people whose loved ones you'll try to find."

"That's just enlightened self-interest." But her heart already felt lighter.

Caterrina's mare looked much healthier than Ginnevra remembered, which might just have been the new poultice but was probably also plenty of water and a good meal. The stable master was a cheerful man, small and slim, who clearly loved horses as much as Caterrina did. "You might want to leave her here for a few days," he told Ginnevra. "Not to be insulting or anything, but I doubt you've the time or inclination to give her the care she needs."

"I'm not insulted, and you're right. If you have the room—"

"Certainly." The stable master patted Dauntless. "This is quite the fellow you've got. Don't see a lot with his coloring around here."

"I hadn't ever seen a blue roan before him. I'm glad to have found him." Ginnevra patted Dauntless, too.

"Will you keep an eye on them for a bit? I need to see to something inside," Eodan said to the stable master. He ignored Ginnevra's narrow-eyed glare and walked back around to the inn's front door. After a pause, Ginnevra followed him.

The Golden Sickle was unusual in how its owner believed in appealing to all the senses when tempting a passerby to stop and stay a night or two. So in addition to the window boxes filled with petunias, scarlet and gold to echo the Devoyenne Republic colors, and the blue glass and silver chimes that hung from the eaves and filled the air with a tinkling sound, the entrance smelled deliciously of pine boughs and fresh mint. Ginnevra saw neither pine nor mint and had no idea how the owner managed the trick.

But it was effective, she thought as she closed the front door behind her. She already felt more relaxed than even talking to the stable master had managed. The Golden Sickle's entrance chamber looked luxurious, too, with its planed wooden floor that gleamed with wax and the walls painted a cheerful buttercup yellow that made the room look bigger than it was. No one waited inside to greet potential patrons, which relieved Ginnevra's mind. Relaxed or not, she was in no mood for conversation.

Stairs led up to the second floor, with a wide doorway on the right opening on the taproom, and two hallways, one straight ahead, the other to the left, leading deeper into the inn. Eodan took the left-hand hall without hesitation. Ginnevra trailed along behind him. She couldn't remember ever staying at an inn with ground-floor rooms before, but this hall, with its five doors spaced close together, clearly opened off such rooms.

Eodan stopped at the third door and knocked briskly, then opened the door without waiting for an invitation. Ginnevra hovered outside. She might be willing to go along with Eodan's mad scheme, but she hadn't forgiven Pellarius for his role in getting Eodan hurt and didn't want to behave as if she had.

"We were in the neighborhood," Eodan was saying. Pellarius sat in the bed, propped against the wall with his legs stretched out and the pillow beneath his broken leg. He looked and smelled cleaner than Ginnevra remembered and was also more alert, his eyes bright.

Pellarius caught Ginnevra's eye, and his smile disappeared. "Didn't expect to see you again," he said, somewhat gruffly.

"Likewise," Ginnevra said. "But I understand Eodan's adopted you."

Pellarius's cheeks reddened. "He's been more generous than I deserve," he said. "And so have you. I...you could have left me there."

"I really couldn't." Ginnevra took up her parade rest stance again, pretending to herself it wasn't as intimidating as she knew it was.

"I don't mean that. I know now what paladins are like." Pellarius drew in a breath. "I mean I apologize for how I behaved. You were generous with me when you didn't need to be, and I repaid that with rudeness."

Ginnevra blinked. "I don't..." She cleared her throat, feeling horribly awkward. "You were in a lot of pain, I'm sure. And Eodan *is* a werewolf."

"That's no excuse. Thank you for not dumping me on my ass even though I deserved it." Pellarius was still redder than a ripe tomato, something Ginnevra felt they had in common just then, but his gaze was direct.

"You're welcome," Ginnevra said. "I...that's not what I expected."

Pellarius grimaced. "I had a lot of time to think while you two were dragging me back to civilization. I still say you don't know how hunting works, but maybe you have a small point about the number of traps I use."

"I think I can admit I'd have cared less if you hadn't caught Eodan," Ginnevra said. "Besides, I returned to set off all the traps by the river, so you won't catch any bears that way."

Pellarius looked briefly angry, then abashed. "Guess that was smart of you, my lady," he said. "With me not in a position to deal with them."

"You'll heal quickly," Eodan said. "And then you'll be back to your usual profession."

Pellarius looked even more abashed. "I'm giving that some thought, too," he said. "Not sure I want to keep up the hunting. But we'll see."

Ginnevra almost asked what else he might do, but realized she didn't want to be drawn into more conversation than she already had. Pellarius might have apologized, and maybe he wasn't as bad as she thought, but she still didn't harbor any warm feelings for him. Besides, now that she had some direction and a pile of documents, she felt the draw of an intriguing puzzle tugging at her.

"Just remember to stay off that leg, and everything will be fine," Eodan said. "You sent word to Guinio?"

"Yes, and my friends will come for me at the end of the week, when I'm better able to travel." Pellarius hitched himself more upright. "Thanks again."

"It was our pleasure," Eodan said. Ginnevra managed a smile so she wouldn't give him the lie. "Take care, Pellarius."

In the hall, Eodan said, "See? That wasn't so bad."

"Eodan," Ginnevra said, "you may be the kindest person I know."

His lips quirked in a smile. "I won't ask how many people you know, then."

In the face of that smile, Ginnevra couldn't think of anything but how much she wanted to kiss him. "Let's get back to Aunt Caterrina's and get me out of this armor," she said.

"And read through those documents?" Eodan said, arching one eyebrow.

"Eventually," Ginnevra said.

S pread out across the library's one table, the documents concerning the disappearances looked as though they'd multiplied during their time in the sack. Ginnevra squared up a stack of papers and chewed her lip in thought. She was very aware that her experience in investigating crimes was limited, and that made the task ahead daunting. But she was also methodical and persistent, two things the prime Dolcea had said were key to solving puzzles, and this was a puzzle like no other.

She picked up the book the clerk had included and flipped it open. "I don't think this list of missing people is complete even in terms of what the justiciary knows," she said. "Somebody had the initiative to begin it with names and dates reported missing, but those dates get farther apart the longer the list gets. Which is what I told you, that justicers don't have time or inclination to pursue crimes if the victims aren't wealthy or influential."

"That really bothers you, doesn't it?" Eodan said.

"I—" Ginnevra began, then paused to think. "Maybe it does. I don't think I ever thought about it before I became a prime. It's just something people take for granted—money gets privilege, even with the law. And yet I don't think the wealthy are more deserving of justice. I know if someone in my family—my immediate family, not Aunt Caterrina—disappeared like this, no one outside the family would care enough to do anything about it. My parents aren't rich enough to afford a private agent and they're not powerful enough to rate the attention of the justicers. So it's unfair, and I hate unfairness."

"But now these people have you." Eodan tapped the nearest stack of papers.

"Let's hope it's enough." Ginnevra raked her fingers through her hair. "The justicers' clerks wrote down the basics when someone was reported missing. Name, age, description. Home address. The date the report came in and sometimes the last date anyone remembered seeing the missing person, if that was different. And this book makes it look like someone at the justiciary started out interested in analyzing all that information."

"But got overwhelmed by the number of reports," Eodan said.

"Right." Ginnevra picked up the top scroll case from the pile of seven. "These contain information about the so-called special cases. Lots more information. In addition to the clerk's report, there are pages of notes that justicer, Ciutto, made in talking to the disappeared person's friends and family and sometimes neighbors. But since he mostly didn't ask the right questions, it's all useless facts with no meaning."

She uncapped the scroll case and removed the sheaf of papers inside. "Take this one. Ranterrius Godolfo. Fifty-four years old, white hair and a large belly, lives in west Uparde about six streets north of Aunt Caterrina. Went missing ten days ago. He's the head of a large family and owner of a mercantile empire here and in Devoyenne. And that fool Ciutto didn't think to ask if anyone had sent to Devoyenne to see if he'd gone there!" She fanned out the papers on the table. "Nor did he ask anything about his mental state, or if he had enemies who might want him out of the way, or whether his family liked him. No inquiry about his finances or his will. I swear Ciutto might as well not have bothered."

"But he had to make a show of caring because Sieur Godolfo is rich," Eodan said.

Ginnevra tapped her nose and nodded. "And it's the same for the other six. I'll say this in favor of serving the wealthy, they do tend to provide more information because there are more people watching their every move. But the justicer made a hash of the investigation." She sighed. "The thought of following up on every one of these reports makes me cringe."

"So look at the bigger picture," Eodan said. "See if there's any commonalities. You're right that this is too many disappearances for them all to be unrelated. Something happened to these people, and the secret to what and why is somewhere in all this mess."

"All right." Ginnevra straightened. "Let's start by figuring out how long it's been going on. I don't trust the list in this book, so we'll need to look at the reports. You take that stack, and I'll start here."

"I'd love to help, but I can't read," Eodan said.

Ginnevra blinked. "You can't read?"

"Werewolves don't generally have a need for literacy," Eodan said. "We keep oral records instead of written ones, so reading is something we think of as a human skill."

"I see." Ginnevra still felt unexpectedly shocked. "I suppose it surprises me because among humans, physicians are always literate. But I didn't learn to read until I was about thirteen and decided to train for a paladin, since paladins have to be literate. So it's not like being able to read is a universal thing even among humans."

"I've thought maybe I should learn, given that I'm living

among humans now." Eodan sounded as casual as if he was discussing what they should have for supper. "But now's not the time."

"No, I—actually, we can make a start." Ginnevra picked up the stack of paper and pointed at the upper left corner of the first page. "The dates are written in numerals, not words—those are easier to remember. I'll make you a list. The first numeral or two numerals is the month, then there's a dot, and the next two are the day of the month, and then another dot and the four numerals of the year, which we don't care about. It doesn't look like the disappearances started before last month, so there's only two months to keep track of. And you just have to be able to count up."

Eodan took the papers from her. "Interesting. You don't have names for the months?"

"The old calendar did, about two hundred years ago before the worship of the Goddess was preeminent. That one only had twelve months of varying lengths, and I think they named the months after seasonal elements, like rain or snow or harvest. I don't know much about it. But our calendar has thirteen months, and we believe each month is a new beginning, so naming them would be...like saying one is more important than another, maybe? I don't know much about that, either."

"Interesting," Eodan repeated. "So, tell me what each of these marks represents."

Ginnevra tore a page out of the back of the book—it was surprisingly thick for a blank book, and she wondered briefly how the justiciary could afford something so expensive—and quickly wrote numerals from zero to nine, and then in pairs all the way to twenty-eight. "Why do werewolves count the way humans do, if you don't learn to read?" she asked.

Eodan shrugged. "We do have some contact with humans.

And the concept of null makes tallying easier whether you can read or not."

"I intend to be grateful that I don't have to translate numbers." She handed him the paper. "I'll go through this stack, then, and we'll see what turns up."

Despite initially having to refer to his guide, Eodan turned out to be faster than Ginnevra at sorting. Some of that was how Ginnevra was constantly distracted by the rest of what was in the reports, particularly the places the missing people lived. She wished she knew Uparde better to know if there was significance to those locations.

Finally, she sorted her pile into Eodan's and flipped through it. "Well, I was right about one thing," she said. "The disappearances start well before someone made note of them in this book. Four weeks ago almost to the day."

"But we can't know if all those early disappearances are related," Eodan pointed out. "Even if it's true that something happened to cause these people to go missing, something they all have in common, that's not the only reason people disappear."

"True. I think, since we can't know that, we have to act as if all of them are related, at least until we find some other identifying factor." Ginnevra opened the book and turned to a fresh page. "Now it gets tedious. I have to copy all these names so I can make note of what they have in common. You don't have to stay for this."

"Actually, neither should you," Eodan said. "By which I mean it's suppertime, and if we wait to eat until you finish your note taking, you'll be starving and cranky."

Ginnevra glanced out the window, which showed the ruddy light of sunset. "That's a good point," she said, laying down her pen. "And I am not ashamed to admit I'm more eager for food than usual because eating lets me delay this unpleasant task."

A quick search showed very little by way of food in Caterrina's kitchen, just the strings of garlic and the slightly squishy sack of tomatoes and the increasingly furry cheese. It didn't take long for them to decide finding a tavern was a better idea. Hand in hand, they strolled through Caterrina's neighborhood to the boisterous crowds of the main street of Uparde. Music followed them through the streets, songs building and fading as they left one set of musicians behind for another. The crowds cheered Ginnevra. Her frustration and despondency faded in the face of thousands of people all out for a good time.

They picked the first tavern they came to that wasn't over-flowing with revelers and found seats at the communal table, waving at the nearest serving girl for a meal. Shortly, a girl dressed in a colorful blue and gold skirt and a white blouse deposited plates in front of them. "Meal's on the house," she said, or rather shouted to be heard over the din. "Wart's happy to host a paladin at his tavern."

Ginnevra, startled, said, "You know who I am?" She'd left the sword at the house, not feeling in the mood to wrestle with its awkward length while eating.

"Saw you at noon services, Wart did," the girl said. "He says paladins and their companions drink free."

Ginnevra privately reflected on the drinking habits of some of her sister paladins. Wart's generosity might put him out of business if offered to the wrong lady. "That's nice of him. Please thank him for me?"

The serving girl nodded and whirled away into the crowd. Ginnevra tucked into chicken deep-fried in the northern style, sliced tomatoes drizzled with vinaigrette, and a pile of green beans that were crunchy and sweet instead of boiled into a soupy mess. "I didn't know how hungry I was," she said.

"Same here," Eodan said with his mouth full. "This is unexpectedly good for tavern fare."

Ginnevra nodded and tore into another drumstick. The crowd had gotten louder since they sat down, and now the sound of a fiddle tuning up cut across the noise. Ginnevra couldn't see the player from where she sat, but the crisp notes made her feel like dancing.

"Paladin!" A skinny man who looked like he'd been warmed over a fire and stretched thin piled onto the seat next to Ginnevra. His beery breath told her he was seriously intoxicated. Ginnevra had been appreciating the empty space and how it meant no one pressed her too closely, but she suppressed her irritation and smiled politely at the man. He slapped her on the back twice in an overly friendly manner. "Paladin, don't see many of you around without a whole mess of you. Where's your company?"

"I am a prime, sieur," Ginnevra said, again going for politeness.

The man's eyes dulled briefly. "Don't know what that means."

"It means I serve the Blessed directly, and I work alone." She opted not to complicate her explanation by including Eodan.

He still looked confused, but forged ahead anyway. "I bet you see all kinds of horrors. Monsters and hairy tics." He belched. "I mean heretics."

"You should give the lady a little space, friend," Eodan said. He, too, looked friendly, but his deep voice gave his words a warning edge.

The drunk didn't notice. "Bet you're here about that Lady Jiulliana," he said, lowering his voice to what he probably thought was a whisper. "'Snot right, her being magical all over the place and not being anointed. 'Snot proper. Don't know why the Revered hasn't run her out of town."

Despite her reservations about being drawn into conversation with this man, Ginnevra asked, "Who is Lady Jiulliana?"

The drunk belched again. "She's favored of the Goddess, *she* says. She talks in riddles that are supposed to be wise, and she helps people find things. I heard she gives prophecies, too."

"Prophecies?" That *was* heresy, and something Ginnevra was duty-bound to counter. Prophecies belonged to the Bright One, who wanted to take away people's free will by directing them down a predestined path. "Why didn't the Revered stop her?"

"I don't know." The drunk waved his hand to indicate his lack of knowledge. "Maybe it's not prophecy. But *I* think, prophecy or no, it's wrong to let someone go on cheating the public, pretending to have power when really it's what any reasonable person would think." He clapped Ginnevra on the shoulder again. "So you should—hey!"

A big, meaty hand came down on the drunk's shoulder and hauled him off the bench. "Clerrius, what are you doing bothering my guest?" the owner of the hand boomed. He was big, bigger than Eodan, with an enormous belly and arms that looked like a couple of hams. "Be off with you, and be grateful my lady didn't take your head off."

The drunk, Clerrius, looked confused, but he staggered off in the direction of the still-unseen fiddler. The beefy man watched him go. "Sorry about that, my lady," he said. "Clerrius is loud when he gets drunk, but he's harmless. I'm Wart."

"Thank you for the welcome, sieur," Ginnevra said. "Ginnevra Cassaline, and this is my companion Eodan."

"It's good to see you." Wart tugged the apron he wore over his stomach straight. "Let me know if there's aught I can do for you."

"Thank you, I—wait. I have a question. Have you heard of a Lady Jiulliana?"

Wart's face, which had been creased in a smile, stilled. "Jiul-liana Dolcebenette?"

"I suppose. Who is she?"

"Trouble, in my opinion." Wart sat gingerly on the bench next to Ginnevra, making it creak and bend alarmingly. "She's never done anything heretical, at least that's what the Revereds say, but I've heard she comes awfully close to prophecy. But people say she solves their problems, and I've known at least two whose lost property she found, so she's got magic of some kind."

"That's unexpected." Ginnevra considered this. As a paladin, she shouldn't consort with anyone whose magical powers didn't come direct from the Goddess, but if Lady Jiulliana had a history of finding lost things...it wasn't the same as finding lost people, who had free will, but it might be close enough. "What does she say about the source of her magic?"

"She claims to have the Goddess's gift, that everything she does is for the Goddess's glory." Wart shrugged. "I'm not calling her a liar, but I'm not sure I believe it."

"Neither do I." Ginnevra took a drink of her ale, which was delicious. "I don't suppose you know where I can find her?"

"You planning to investigate? That would be a relief." Wart gave her directions to a west Uparde neighborhood. "Like I said, the Revereds haven't done anything about her, but I hear as how paladins have the gift of hearing truth."

"I'd just like to talk to her." Ginnevra knew there was an invocation that would allow a paladin to hear the difference between truths and lies, but not what it was.

"Good luck, then." Wart stood and nodded politely to Eodan, bowed to Ginnevra, and walked away, parting the crowds like the prow of a ship cutting through waves.

"Do you think this Lady Jiulliana knows something, or are you worried about heresy?" Eodan asked.

"I don't know what I think anymore." Ginnevra swigged down the last of her ale and speared a few last green beans with her fork. "I shouldn't resort to a possible charlatan for help, but anything I can learn is useful. And if the Revered spoke to her, she might know something about the Revered that's relevant to her disappearance."

"Then I think we should return to the house so you can go through those notes, and visit Lady Jiulliana tomorrow morning," Eodan said. Ginnevra made a face, and he laughed. "I'm sorry I can't help."

"It's all right. I just wish I had some guarantee we're not headed off in the wrong direction. I don't need to add rebuking heretics to my list of tasks." She rose and took Eodan's hand.

"What would that look like, rebuking a heretic?" Eodan asked.

Ginnevra thought back to the few times her company had backed up an anointed who challenged a heretic. "It's never pretty," she said. "If I could prove she is practicing heresy, I'd give her a chance to recant, and if she doesn't recant, I'm supposed to take her to Abraciabene for trial. Which is unpleasant as well as, in this case, an interference with my actual task. But if the Revered didn't do it, it's unlikely I'll have to."

"Unless the Revered was waiting for a paladin's arrival to challenge Lady Jiulliana," Eodan said.

Ginnevra made another face. "Let's hope Lady Jiulliana knows something useful. And hope even more I don't have to roust her for a fraud or a heretic. That drunk made it sound like she's popular."

"Meaning we could be facing a mob," Eodan said.

Ginnevra nodded. "I don't suppose that's something you have experience with?"

"Surprisingly, no. We'll just have to avoid starting a fight."

Ginnevra smiled. "I'm good at that. The sword makes my argument for me."

Eodan eyed her skeptically. "I'd think you were more provocative than placating, with that thing."

"You'd be surprised how quickly people reconsider fighting when it's their fists versus my blade," Ginnevra said with a smile.

CHAPTER

ELEVEN

T hick gray clouds promising rain menaced Uparde the following morning, but Ginnevra still felt more sanguine than she had the previous night. Putting the justicers' notes in order had given her the sense that she was accomplishing something, even though her heart had ached when she came across the report on her aunt's disappearance. She'd gone to sleep vowing to find Caterrina and woke to a feeling that was possible.

While Lady Jiulliana lived in an upscale west side neighborhood, it didn't resemble Caterrina's except in both being very clean, as if the residents paid someone to sweep up animal waste and human rubbish. The tall buildings, all of them houses, still shared common walls but were three or four times as wide as those near the center of town. Large glass windows caught the morning sunlight, turning gold and copper like new coins. Ginnevra had become accustomed to the handbills plastering the ground floor walls, advertising inns or performances, but none of that touched these mansions. It felt like walking through the largest stage setting ever conceived.

Eodan, beside her, seemed unmoved by the strangeness. Well, it was unlikely he had enough experience with human cities to realize this was unusual. They'd left the horses at the stable, reasoning that they didn't want to have anything extra to worry about if this encounter turned ugly, and Ginnevra wore no armor, just the sword that was her badge of office. She put a hand on the strap to steady the blade and said, "I hope I'm not too provocative just walking in."

"You could have left the sword behind," Eodan pointed out.

"That would have been worse. Paladins aren't supposed to conceal what they are, and even if that wasn't the case, I don't want anyone thinking I'm being underhanded. Me going in incognito would be like saying I believe Lady Jiulliana is a criminal and a fraud."

"Then Lady Jiulliana ought to honor your openness. It's a sign of respect. And you don't have anything to worry about." Eodan nodded politely to someone who passed them going the other way. The woman's attention was fixed on the sword, and she didn't notice Eodan's greeting.

"True. And really, I have no reason to believe Lady Jiulliana is doing anything wrong. It's just a feeling, accompanied by fear of the worst. Which is unworthy of me." Ginnevra sighed. "I wonder how close we are. Wart wasn't very specific. Maybe we should ask for directions."

"I don't know," Eodan said. He pointed. "I think we may have found her."

They hadn't seen many pedestrians in this quiet, well-to-do neighborhood, but ahead, the street teemed with a crowd so eerily quiet Ginnevra's nerves twanged again. Men and women, some with children in tow, thronged one of the houses despite the earliness of the hour, leaving space immediately surrounding the door but otherwise packed in tightly. Ginnevra's keen hearing picked up on the movement of feet and bodies, but no speech, not even the ordinary complaints one heard in any large crowd of being stepped on or shoved. Even the very small children made no noise. She'd never seen a gathering like this before.

She approached cautiously, though she wasn't sure what she feared—setting off a stampede, perhaps? No large group of people could possibly be that still without being under extraordinary tension. None of the people noticed her and Eodan's approach. They were all intent on the door. It looked just the same as all the other doors on the street, intricately carved wood behind a grille of iron, the wood stained a warm brown rather than painted.

When she and Eodan were still about fifty feet away, the door and the grille swung open. As one, everyone surrounding it stepped back a pace, the rustling of their clothes sounding like whispers of conversation. The crowd obscured the rather short person who stood at the door, but Ginnevra heard him say, "Nunnia Sighere." The whispers grew louder as people added their voices to the rustle of fabric. A woman dragging two small children behind her pushed forward past the others and entered, followed by the speaker, who then shut the door. The whispering gradually faded until once more there was nothing but silence.

Ginnevra's steps slowed as she approached the crowd. Intent as they were on the door, they either didn't hear her or didn't care. She stopped a few paces away, and she and Eodan looked at each other. Eodan didn't seem any more certain about what to do than she was. The profound stillness made Ginnevra feel awkward about disturbing it with questions.

Then she came to her senses. This Jiulliana Dolcebenette wasn't an anointed, and whatever she was up to wasn't sacred. Asking questions wouldn't disrupt a holy ritual the way talking during services at the chapel would. Ginnevra could be polite and still get what she'd come for.

She stepped up behind one of the people on the outskirts of the crowd and said, "Excuse me. Is this the home of Lady Jiulliana?"

The woman jumped as if Ginnevra had goosed her backside and turned. "Why don't you—oh," she said, her initial irritation disappearing as she registered the sword. "My lady, yes, this is the holy Jiulliana's residence." Her words seemed louder by contrast with the stillness. Her nearest neighbors turned as well, though none of them spoke in protest at the disruption.

Ginnevra chose not to take issue with the woman's choice of titles for Lady Jiulliana. Suppose the Goddess had blessed the woman with Her power, and Lady Jiulliana had for whatever reason chosen not to become anointed? It was possible, though unlikely. "Could you tell me why you're all standing here?"

"The holy Jiulliana must not be overwhelmed by petitioners," the woman said, smiling as if Ginnevra had given her a tremendous compliment. "She draws her strength from pure and unsullied communion with the Goddess, and too much contact with the masses would diminish her power. We wait in the hope she will call us into her presence."

Ginnevra cast an eye over the gathering. Most of the petitioners ignored the conversation, and as the woman spoke, the ones who'd turned to listen drifted away to return to focusing on the door. The woman herself cast quick glances over her shoulder, as if she were afraid of missing the next appearance of Lady Jiulliana's majordomo or whatever he was.

Not wanting to lose the woman's attention, Ginnevra quickly said, "Have you spoken with Lady Jiulliana before?"

"I?" The woman's astonishment raised her voice, and once again their conversation drew attention from those nearest. "No, my lady, of course not. Holy Jiulliana only grants one audience to a person, ever. I've been coming for two weeks, hoping she will give me a moment of her time."

"That seems...patient of you," Eodan said. Ginnevra thought it actually sounded a little desperate. "Is there something in particular you wanted of Lady Jiulliana? Help finding something?"

The woman turned her attention on Eodan as if only just noticing he was there. "That's private," she said, but not angrily. "Holy Jiulliana is wise beyond the scope of ordinary humans. I hope she will provide me guidance."

"Surely you don't mean she foretells the future," Ginnevra said. She kept her voice even, hoping not to shut the woman up by criticizing the respected Jiulliana.

"Oh, no, my lady, not that. She simply sees to the heart of things, sees what's invisible to most." The rapt, happy look was back.

"If Lady Jiulliana's work is so private, how does anyone know about it?" Eodan asked.

That seemed to confuse the woman, who said, "Her powers are well-known throughout Uparde. People don't need to divulge their secrets to reveal that she's helped them. Even the Lord Mayor has asked for her assistance. Surely that shows how wonderful she is!"

"And she doesn't—" Ginnevra began.

The door opened, and the grille swung outward on creaking iron hinges, silencing Ginnevra. Instantly, the woman turned, intent on the majordomo. Ginnevra still couldn't see him despite her being taller than most of the crowd. His voice, however, rang out like that of a man Eodan's size, saying, "Ginnevra Cassaline."

Ginnevra blinked. All around her, people murmured to their neighbors, asking who it was Lady Jiulliana had summoned. She felt a deep disquiet at this stranger knowing her name, as if Lady

Jiulliana had access to secrets Ginnevra had never told. Then she mentally slapped herself. Holy or not, Lady Jiulliana was just a woman. Ginnevra's presence in Uparde wasn't a secret; someone had probably told Lady Jiulliana about her, the majordomo had seen the sword, and the woman had decided to see what interest the paladin had in her.

She moved forward, Eodan in her wake, gently pushing past people until she stood at the front of the crowd. "I'm Ginnevra Cassaline," she told the majordomo.

"This way, my lady," the man said, bowing and indicating the doorway.

Ginnevra stepped forward and came up short when the majordomo held up a hand. "Just you, my lady. Not your companion."

Ginnevra's eyebrows raised. "Eodan goes with me," she said. "Or I don't go."

"The Lady Jiulliana is always very clear in her requests," the majordomo said. "She said she will see you alone."

Ginnevra crossed her arms over her chest, wishing for the silent authority of her armor. "I'm afraid that's impossible." The idea of going into who knew what kind of situation without Eodan at her side unsettled her.

The majordomo's calm demeanor cracked slightly. "I...will inquire," he said, and returned inside, leaving the door open. Ginnevra thought about following him immediately, but she heard the crowd's confusion as those who could hear the conversation relayed its contents to those who couldn't. It was a sound that could easily grow ugly if the waiting petitioners believed Ginnevra wasn't giving proper respect to their holy lady. Ginnevra had no desire to turn this into a brawl, so she decided to give the majordomo a chance to resolve the situation amicably.

Soon, the majordomo returned. "The Lady Jiulliana has words

only for you, my lady," he said. "They are private, not to be revealed to anyone else. Hence her desire to speak only to you."

"Eodan shares all my secrets," Ginnevra declared. "I don't mind if he hears what Lady Jiulliana has to say. If that's her only objection, I see no problem."

The majordomo hesitated, glancing past Ginnevra at the watching crowd. He clearly was assessing the possible consequences of giving in to a petitioner's demands versus rejecting a petitioner over something so small. "Very well," he said. "Lady Jiulliana understands loyalty, and she will not deny your companion future wisdom for having partaken of what she bestows upon you, my lady."

That was a nice, diplomatic way to control the crowd. Ginnevra mentally applauded his solution even as she wondered why Lady Jiulliana would want her separated from Eodan. Or did she not know about him? That would mean her much-touted wisdom had its limits. Ginnevra suppressed the feeling of satisfaction this idea gave her. If Lady Jiulliana's wisdom came from the Goddess, it was unworthy of Ginnevra to want it to be weak or ineffectual.

Frosted glass globes set in brass bases lit the long, low-ceilinged hallway. Unlike the ground floor of the Revered's residence, dark and dour, pale blue walls caught the lanterns' light and magnified it, giving the corridor a feeling of openness despite the lowering ceiling. Ornately carved doors painted white kept the hall from feeling eternal. Ginnevra slowed to examine the carvings on one door; they were abstract rather than representative, suggesting ocean waves and rippling sand shaped by water. It was an odd choice for a house so far inland, but a beautiful one.

A stairway at the far end of the hall led up to a small, square landing, turning back on itself there and rising to the first floor. Here, Ginnevra had another surprise: instead of another long hallway as there was in the Revered's residence, the stairs came out on a grand, open space, with a high ceiling that must rise two stories tall and pillars holding up the lower ceilings on each side. Chairs with fat tapestry cushions sat in little groups throughout the room, arranged for intimate discussions, though Ginnevra observed how easy it would be to move the chairs to accommodate a large gathering. A hallway led deeper into the house, its entrance curtained by filmy drapes.

There was only one door, and it was directly opposite the stairs. The majordomo crossed the room without hesitation and opened it. "Please show respect to the Lady Jiulliana by not speaking unless she speaks to you first. And do not draw attention to anything you see. The Lady Jiulliana values her privacy and detests pity."

More curious than ever, Ginnevra walked across the plush woven carpet that bore the marks of Fayonne craftsmanship and through the doorway, where she came to an abrupt halt. Eodan, close behind her, put a hand on her waist to steady her.

The room was much smaller, less than twenty feet across, and it was lit by the same glass globes as the ground floor, but turned very low. Ginnevra's vision instantly sharpened to compensate, but she still made out very little: three chairs near the center of the room, tapestries on the walls so intricately woven she couldn't distinguish their subjects, and, opposite the door, a bed big enough for four. The pillars at its corners held up gauzy blue draperies that curtained the bed in a midnight film, obscuring its occupant further.

A woman sat in the middle of the bed, swathed below the waist in blankets. She wore the dress of a highborn lady, a rich brocaded silk stiffened through the bodice and tight through the sleeves, with a neckline that plunged to reveal the upper curves of her breasts. The bodice glimmered in the low light with hundreds of tiny gems sewn in elaborate patterns to echo the brocade. Around her neck hung a golden chain with a single prism-cut ruby as big as the first joint of Ginnevra's thumb dangling from it.

Lady Jiulliana sat placidly with her hands clasped in her lap and said nothing. Ginnevra, who hadn't planned to obey the majordomo's instructions, found herself incapable of speech. The scene was so bizarre she didn't know where to begin.

She walked forward to stand beside the chairs, but didn't sit. Eodan took up a position on the other side. That this left her sword arm unimpeded was not lost on Ginnevra.

Lady Jiulliana shifted her weight slightly, using her arms to balance herself. "Ginnevra Cassaline," she said in a low, sweet voice, "greetings. I hoped you would come."

CHAPTER

TWELVE

"Someone told you of my arrival in Uparde," Ginnevra said.

Lady Jiulliana smiled and shook her head. "The Goddess grants me Her sight, and I am aware of many things that happen in this city I love. Is that so difficult for you to believe?"

"I've never known the Goddess to bestow Her power on anyone who wasn't sworn to Her service," Ginnevra said. "And aside from you knowing my name, which anyone might have informed you of, I haven't seen any evidence that She has done so in this circumstance." She heard her language growing more formal, a sign of her discomfort, and told herself sharply to stiffen her spine. This woman was no threat.

"I understand," Lady Jiulliana said. "The anointed, and the paladins who are their good right arm, are always the hardest to convince. I don't hold it against you that you don't believe."

"What, you don't want to prove yourself to me?" Ginnevra said.

The woman let out a low, soft chuckle. "Do you feel the need to prove your identity to everyone you meet? No, your certainty in yourself speaks for you. As does that unmistakable weapon. I believe you will come to see the truth of what I claim. But, as a token..." Lady Jiulliana turned to look directly at Eodan. "Your companion's name is Eodan, and despite appearances, he is not human. He is, in fact, a werewolf."

Ginnevra realized her hand was on her sword hilt. She drew in a deep breath and released it slowly. "If you were trying to put me at ease," she said, "you failed."

"You have bound your life to his, and the Goddess has not struck you down," Lady Jiulliana continued as if Ginnevra had not spoken. "You believe the werewolves who refuse to serve the Bright One should not be treated as monsters. And you would like to share that belief with your fellow servants of the Goddess."

"You can't possibly know all that," Eodan said. He sounded calmer than Ginnevra felt.

"The Goddess knows all, sees all," Lady Jiulliana said, "and grants Her knowledge to Her chosen servants. The Goddess honors you for your courage, Ginnevra. Ask the questions that brought you here, and I will answer."

Ginnevra's heart raced. Aside from Caterrina, only the Blessed and the Goddess knew the truth of what she had learned from Eodan: that werewolves weren't inherently evil, that many of them had spurned their creator, and that only the Goddess's oath kept Her from accepting them as Hers. And yet here was this woman repeating back to Ginnevra words she had said to almost no one except Eodan. It was getting harder to deny Lady Jiulliana had supernatural insight.

"What do you intend to do with your knowledge?" she said.

Lady Jiulliana smiled. "You mean, do I intend to blackmail a paladin? Of course not. If the Goddess has not censured you, it's not my place to pass judgment. But I should warn you that your desire to reveal the truth to the anointed here in Uparde is a dangerous one. They know you only as a stranger, and they have no reason to believe you are not deviant for loving a werewolf. If you choose to tell them your secret, you should be prepared for the worst reaction."

"That's our business," Eodan said angrily. "I don't know what your game is, but so far I haven't heard anything that couldn't be explained by someone else's information and good guessing."

"Eodan," Ginnevra said. She knew him well enough to recognize when he was pretending to hostility in order to draw someone out, and she had a feeling the ploy wouldn't work in this case.

"You can't antagonize me," Lady Jiulliana said. "I bear you nothing but good will. And your devotion to your lover is laudable. I swear I will say nothing but the truth."

Eodan glanced at Ginnevra. "It's your choice, *my lady*," he said. Ginnevra recognized in his choice of words his acknowledgment that this was a paladin's responsibility.

Ginnevra let go of her sword and flexed feeling back into her hand. She didn't want to start this line of questioning by asking about Caterrina, implying that she believed Lady Jiulliana had the power to find things as she'd been told. "I'm searching for the Revered Massina Parenogne. I wondered if you'd spoken to her."

"The Revered visited me several times with the intent of proving me a charlatan." Lady Jiulliana laughed again, as if this was the funniest thing ever. "I understand, of course. A Revered needs to be alert to the possibility of heresy, the chance that a servant of the Bright One might lead innocents astray. Even if I were nothing more than a fraud intent on fleecing the populace, that is the sort of thing that opens the way to more serious deceptions."

"I was told you only grant one visit to a person in their lifetime," Ginnevra said. "And yet you spoke with the Revered more than once."

"The Goddess is the one who decides when someone deserves Her wisdom, and She is sparing with Her gifts." Lady Jiulliana clasped her hands together in her lap and examined her knuckles. "If it were up to me, I would not limit Her blessings, but the Goddess understands humanity better than I. At any rate, my conversations with the Revered were along doctrinal lines. The Goddess guided me, but She did not provide me with a blessing for the Revered."

"So you spoke of religious matters? The Revered tested your faith?" The enormous ruby fascinated Ginnevra, the way it caught what little light there was and reflected it with wine-dark clarity. She wrenched her gaze from it and focused on the woman's face. Lady Jiulliana had the kind of symmetrical beauty only Nature could grant, her skin a little darker than Ginnevra's, her face unaccented by cosmetics. Dark eyebrows highlighted her large eyes, which were fringed with long black lashes, and she wore her hair pulled plainly back from her face in a way that drew attention to its beauty. And yet Ginnevra felt unmoved by her appearance, as if she were looking at a statue and not a living woman.

"She questioned me, yes. I'm afraid my answers did not satisfy her." Lady Jiulliana shook her head ruefully. "That is, she wanted to prove me heretic and could not."

"When's the last time you saw the Revered?"

Lady Jiulliana used her hands to hitch herself forward slightly. The motion drew Ginnevra's eyes to the lump under the many blankets where Lady Jiulliana's legs were. They didn't move at all, not even when the woman scooted forward. "Her last visit was five days ago. You may ask Marcellus, my assistant, for confirmation. She was seen by any number of petitioners as well, though naturally I do not keep records of those who visit me."

She spoke so matter-of-factly Ginnevra was taken aback. Ginnevra had expected...what, exactly? Some evidence that Lady Jiulliana was complicit in the Revered's disappearance? And yet the woman spoke so casually and yet so confidently Ginnevra couldn't think what to ask next. "I...did she say or do anything during that visit that was out of character?" she managed.

"The Revered and I are not close," Lady Jiulliana said. "I don't know her well enough to know what would be out of character."

"You know how she behaved all the other times," Ginnevra pressed on. "Did she behave differently? Maybe she was softening toward you?"

"That's an interesting question." Lady Jiulliana laughed again. "I had the feeling she...oh, but it's foolishness."

"I'll decide that," Ginnevra said, clutching at this hint of a thread.

Lady Jiulliana cast her eyes down. "I had the feeling she had become attracted to me, if you must know."

"Oh," Ginnevra said, feeling foolish herself. "I...that would be different, naturally."

"Naturally," Lady Jiulliana said. "Of course, my heart is given to the Goddess, and I have forsaken more earthly loves, but I was flattered."

Ginnevra's cheeks were hot with embarrassment. "That's... nice," she said. "I don't suppose she made her interest explicit?" If the Revered had run off as a result of being romantically spurned, that wouldn't make her any easier to find, but it would mean Ginnevra was back where she started with regard to where her aunt might have gone. It was unlikely Caterrina would have accompanied the Revered on those grounds.

"Oh, no. But I am extremely perceptive." Lady Jiulliana raised her head so those enormous dark eyes fixed directly on Ginnevra.

"I wish I could tell you where the Revered is, but my insight is limited in such matters."

"That makes sense," Ginnevra said, not really hearing what she was saying. If the Revered was as perceptive as Lady Jiulliana, she might not have needed to be explicitly rebuffed. She might still have run off to nurse a broken heart. "I mean—it's too bad."

"I hope she is in no danger, wherever she is," Lady Jiulliana said.

"So do I," Ginnevra replied. She hesitated, then said, "One more thing. My aunt, Caterrina Cassaline, is also missing. I don't suppose you ever spoke to her?"

Lady Jiulliana's expressive eyes widened. "Your aunt? No, I never met with anyone by that name. And you're seeking for her, as well?"

Ginnevra watched the woman closely. "I'm charged with investigating all the many disappearances in Uparde in the past four weeks. But yes, I'm concerned about my aunt."

"I would offer to help find her, but my gifts don't extend to locating living creatures." Lady Jiulliana laughed. "And I'm not sure you'd accept my help, in any case. It might look bad for a paladin to resort to the aid of someone like me."

Ginnevra's face reddened. "If you're gifted by the Goddess, it would be wrong for me to spurn that."

Lady Jiulliana laughed again, a merry sound that grated on Ginnevra's nerves. "But you don't believe I am. It's all right, I don't mind."

The woman's subtle mockery irritated Ginnevra. She tamped down on her anger and said, "Thank you for your time, Lady Jiulliana."

As she turned to go, the woman said, "Oh, but that's not why I called you here, my lady paladin. Don't you want to know what wisdom the Goddess has for you?"

Ginnevra hesitated. This all came much too close to prophecy, which was counter to the Dark Lady's intentions for Her creations. But Lady Jiulliana had spoken with such authority, and on subjects she could not have known anything about without the insight of the Goddess, Ginnevra could not resist. "All right," she said, turning back. "What wisdom?"

Lady Jiulliana took the ruby in her right hand and leaned heavily on her left. "You are strong and capable," she said. Her voice rang out stronger and clearer than before, and her words took on a singsong quality. "But your desires will make you weak if you give into them. Do not think to challenge the Goddess's decree. She cannot accept those who have cast off the Bright One, regardless of their desires and intents. Do not try to force Her hand by enlisting the anointed in your cause. That way lies only sorrow."

Numbness gripped Ginnevra, a terrible immobility she couldn't immediately shake. "That sounds like prophecy," she said, and was surprised at how calm she sounded. "Did you want to declare yourself heretic?"

"It does not take a prophet to know how the Goddess feels about those who challenge Her. Your desire to have your lover accepted by your fellows in the Faith is a selfish one, and you are wrong to pursue it."

"It's hardly selfish to want to see justice done," Ginnevra retorted, forgetting she didn't want to be drawn into a confrontation. "You make it sound like I want this for my own sake instead of for the werewolves'. And how is it any of your business?"

Jiulliana let go of the ruby and bowed her head. "I see what I see, and I pass that wisdom on. It's your choice what to make of it. I'm sorry I offended you." She didn't sound sorry. She sounded as calm and implacable as ever.

Ginnevra turned on her heel and made for the door, slamming

through it without remembering Eodan was close behind her. Marcellus, the majordomo, stood just outside. "Please follow me," he said, bowing.

"I don't need an escort," Ginnevra snarled.

"I will show you to the exit, my lady. It is on the other side from the entrance." Marcellus didn't seem offended by her hostility. He bowed again and added, "Petitioners prefer not to be mobbed by the crowd upon leaving, but of course it's up to you."

Ginnevra closed her eyes and calmed herself. Anger did her no good. "Fine," she said, less forcefully.

Marcellus led them beyond the drapery-shrouded doorway, through passages and down a short flight of stairs to another door, this one less ornate than the front door. It opened on a garden Ginnevra was still too angry to appreciate. She stalked through the door without a word for Marcellus, followed closely by Eodan.

A stone path wound away from the door, inviting visitors to follow. Bushes with blooming yellow flowers lined both sides, with beds of gentians and other flowers Ginnevra didn't recognize growing at intervals beyond. The sight ruined Ginnevra's tenuous grasp on calmness, infuriating her with the assumption that anyone visiting might want to be soothed by the sights and the aromatic smells. She saw the garden gate in the distance and thought about making a straight line for it, wrecking the careful construction. How *dare* that woman call her selfish?

A hand on her arm brought her up short. "Ginnevra. Stop. She's wrong," Eodan said in a low, quiet voice. "You don't actually believe she's what she claims to be?"

Ginnevra closed her eyes and shuddered. "She can't be," she said. "I heard the Goddess's voice, telling me I had Her blessing. It's not possible that this woman has some true insight that says otherwise. I don't believe it." And yet a tiny doubting voice whispered *And if you're wrong?* Lady Jiulliana had known so much—

"No. She's a fraud," she declared. "She did her research, yes, but everything she said could have been discovered the mundane way. I refuse to believe she has the Goddess's blessing."

Eodan made her look at him. "So she wants you confused and doubting yourself," he said. "Does that mean she lied about everything?"

"You were there. What do *you* think?"

Eodan's brow furrowed in thought. "I'm not sure," he said. "The alternative is that she has something to do with the Revered's disappearance, and I have no idea why she would care. Unless the Revered was preaching against her, and we don't know that's true. And if Lady Jiulliana *was* responsible, what does that mean for all the other disappearances?"

Ginnevra sighed and put her arms around Eodan. "More questions to ask."

He embraced her and kissed her forehead. "You're the least selfish person I know. Come on. You should talk to the anointed at the chapel, find out what they know about Lady Jiulliana."

They followed the winding path, and despite herself Ginnevra's anger dissipated. It was a beautiful garden, and if Lady Jiulliana had been what she claimed to be, it would be a pleasant place to contemplate the words of wisdom she shared. As it was, Ginnevra could only see it as part of the ruse.

At the garden gate, Ginnevra stopped. "What's this?" A wooden box, stained dark with rainwater and covered on one side with lichen, was affixed to the stone wall next to the gate. It looked like a large bird feeder, but with nowhere for birds to perch and eat. Its slanted top had a slot in the middle.

"It opens," Eodan said, pointing to a hinge at the peak of the "roof." The steel hinge was shiny and looked far newer than the rest of the box.

Ginnevra felt along the place where the slanted top overlapped the side and found a latch. She pushed on it, and the top moved. Carefully, she lifted the lid and peered inside. "Goddess have mercy," she breathed. "There must be hundreds of aurins' worth of coin in here!" Loose coin mingled with small sacks that clinked when she prodded them. Most of the loose coins were silver dinas, but gold glinted here and there in the pile.

"So much for Lady Jiulliana not charging anything for her wisdom," Ginnevra said. "This is even more evidence that she's a fraud. She doesn't request money, but people are free to donate whatever they think is right...this isn't the first time I've seen this trick." She shut the box's lid. "I would love to go back in there and arrest her."

"You have no proof," Eodan pointed out. "And arresting a holy woman who's also partially paralyzed..."

"I know. It's impossible." Ginnevra sighed. "But I intend to keep a close eye on our friend there. And when she slips up, I'll have her."

"That could take a while." Eodan pushed open the gate.

"I may or may not be selfish, but I'm definitely patient," Ginnevra said.

CHAPTER

THIRTEEN

"Lady Jiulliana," Agostino said. His face looked pinched, as if he smelled something nasty. "I hadn't thought she might know anything, but of course..." His voice trailed off, and he looked past Ginnevra's right ear with his eyes unfocused.

"So you've had dealings with her?" Ginnevra said.

Agostino came to himself. "Not as such. The Revered forbade the Dedicates and the acolytes to have anything to do with her, in case she was a heretic who might corrupt their faith. And I was always too busy with chapel business. So it fell to the Revered to challenge her."

"Lady Jiulliana said she'd spoken with the Revered often."

"I'm sure she did. The Revered takes her duties as champion and protector of the Faith very seriously. When Lady Jiulliana first made herself known, the Revered interrogated her thoroughly. She told me she didn't believe Lady Jiulliana was a heretic, but she wasn't sure she wasn't a fraud." Agostino looked thoughtful again. "Personally, I felt if the woman wasn't a heretic, we should leave her to the temporal authorities. It's not our business to expose frauds. But the Revered disagreed."

"I can understand that." The sting of Lady Jiulliana's words had faded the farther away Ginnevra got, and with that and half an hour's distance, Ginnevra could think clearly. "I mean, you're right, that sort of thing is a job for a paladin or the law, but I can see how the Revered might have taken Lady Jiulliana's abuse of the people personally."

"Indeed." Agostino nodded. "What did Lady Jiulliana say when you questioned her?"

"Not much. She denied having seen the Revered after her disappearance. She seemed very calm about all of it. I don't suppose you know anything about Lady Jiulliana's disability?"

"I didn't know she had one," Agostino said. "I've never met the woman."

"It doesn't matter." It really didn't matter, except insofar as being paralyzed from the waist down made Lady Jiulliana even more of a sympathetic figure and therefore more appealing to the average person. The average person who didn't know she was a fraud.

"I'll let you know if I discover anything," Ginnevra said, rising from her seat on the uncomfortable black pew in the instruction room. "You know where to reach me if anything occurs."

Agostino bade her farewell, and Ginnevra left the chapel. Eodan was seated on the rim of the black fountain, watching the sprays of water. Ginnevra took a moment to admire him. He was handsome, yes, but he was also kind and considerate and capable, and she loved him more than words could express. It *wasn't* self-ishness to want justice for his people.

It startled Ginnevra to discover Lady Jiulliana's words still bothered her. She should have shrugged them off easily, but that same tiny voice continued to whisper *She knew everything else* and

How sure are you that your motives are pure? She ignored the tiny voice and joined Eodan at the fountain.

Eodan was running his fingers through the water in the basin. "I can't believe no one steals these coins," he said. "Surely Uparde has poor people?"

"Someone would have to be truly desperate to steal from the Goddess," Ginnevra said. "Even the Revered don't collect these coins. Though I've sometimes wondered if the Goddess sees things differently. Like, if someone *is* desperate enough to steal Her offerings, She understands that? And the coins never overflow the basin, so they must go somewhere..." She shook her head. "I don't know. Fortunately, it's not my place to worry about it. I have enough worries about things that *are* my responsibility."

"Like finding your aunt," Eodan said.

"Like that, thank you so much for the reminder." Ginnevra pretended to scowl at him. Eodan pretended not to notice.

The gray, lowering sky chose that moment to rumble like a hungry giant's stomach. "Let's get back to the house, and hope we aren't caught in the storm," Ginnevra said.

The rain didn't start falling until they were three streets away from Caterrina's house, but then the sky opened up on them, drenching them in torrential rainfall that was just cold enough to be truly uncomfortable. They ran like mad for the house and tumbled in through the kitchen door, laughing at how soaked they both were.

"Time to change," Ginnevra said, swiping her sodden hair out of her eyes.

Eodan put his hands low on her waist. "I like the sound of that," he murmured, and drew her close for a kiss.

Ginnevra draped her arms around his neck. "You know being wet isn't nearly as romantic as you'd like it to be."

"Anything is romantic if you have the right attitude." He

kissed her again, then let her go. "But we have other things to do. Go ahead and get out of those wet clothes, and I'll see about drying them while you go over the information."

Ginnevra stripped down and dried herself in front of the kitchen fire before dressing in her spare shirt and breeches and settling in at the library table. The stacks of papers and scroll cases looked more daunting in the dreary light of the storm. Sighing, she opened the book to a new page and settled in to read and take notes.

When Eodan came in some time later, the storm had stopped, but the skies were still gray and cloudy. Eodan had a lamp in one hand and a covered plate in the other. "There's not much food," he said. "I was waiting for the storm to let up before I went out for more. But you should eat. It's nearly one o'clock."

Ginnevra stretched and flexed her right hand, which was cramped from writing. "Thank you," she said, and made room on the table for the plate. Slightly stale bread, hard cheese, and a tomato. She ate without thinking about the food, her mind still on the puzzle.

Eodan put the lamp in a wall niche and trimmed the wick so its light burned brighter. "Did you learn anything? Or is it too early to ask?"

"Based on these reports, the missing people don't have anything in common—at least, nothing that stands out." Ginnevra bit into the tomato and wiped juice off her chin. "More of them come from the west side, but not many more, and I suspect that's because that's where the wealthy live, and those people are more likely to be reported missing. Only one of them is a child, Lutzia Serrone, and I'm not sure her disappearance is part of the pattern. The rest range in age from fifteen to sixty-two."

"Why not the child?" Eodan broke off a morsel of cheese and ate it.

"She was reported missing around noon twelve days ago, and her mother, who made the report, swears she only had her eyes off the child for a moment. That's probably not true, but it's probably not that much exaggerated. The point is that all the others were out of touch with friends or loved ones for much longer than that before they were considered missing, and most of them disappeared overnight." Ginnevra sighed. "I wonder if any of them ever returned. It's not like they're required to report in to the justiciary to call off the search, what there is of it."

"So do you have to follow up on every report, after all?"

Ginnevra groaned. "Maybe? If some of these people came home, that would be more information. I was hoping I wouldn't have to knock on every door in Uparde, though." She flipped the pages of her book. "What else...All seven of the 'special cases' were older, and all of them were independently wealthy, not through a spouse or a parent. I have no idea if that means anything. And that's about it."

She pushed the empty plate away and stood. "I think you're right, and it's time to follow up. But I want to go to the Justiciary first, to see if any more reports have come in. Another thing I've learned is that for the past four weeks, there have been between one and three reports of missing people every day without exception. That's a lot of disappearances."

Eodan pinched out the lamp, leaving the room in dimness. "Maybe we'll get lucky," he said, "and most of these people just left for the big city and have written home revealing their whereabouts."

"I'm worried there's a pile of dead bodies somewhere in Uparde," Ginnevra said, and then felt terrible at her flippancy. Suppose Aunt Caterrina was dead? Ginnevra refused to consider the notion further.

A distant banging sound caught her attention. She and Eodan looked at each other. "Was that the front door?" Ginnevra said.

Eodan hurried from the room, swiftly descending the stairs. Ginnevra followed close behind him. She couldn't imagine who might be knocking on Caterrina's door, unless... She swallowed against a sudden lump in her throat. Suppose it was someone with news of her aunt?

The knocking sounded again, at the front door. The dark hall was lit only by light coming down through the staircase, but it was enough for Ginnevra's enhanced vision to make out the door. The bolts were still shot, as they'd been using the kitchen door, but Eodan slid them both free and opened the door cautiously, without standing where he was silhouetted against the opening. Then, to Ginnevra's surprise, he stepped back and opened the door fully. "Can we help you, sieur?" he said.

Ginnevra stepped forward so she could see around Eodan. Their visitor was the justicer Ciutto Baroccius. The man looked harried and out of breath, as if he'd run all the way from the justiciary. "Sieur Baroccius," Ginnevra said. "Is something wrong?"

Ciutto took a deep breath and tugged his black doublet straight. "I would like my papers back," he said. "Immediately."

Ginnevra's eyebrows climbed to her hairline. "You want...I'm sorry, but what are you talking about?"

"The papers. My investigation into the disappearances." Ciutto extended his hand as if Ginnevra held the scroll cases and could hand them over right then.

"You turned that investigation over to me," Ginnevra said, still nonplussed by his demand. "And now you want to take it over again?"

"I...made a mistake," Ciutto said. "I should not have abrogated responsibility, even to a prime. I'm sure you understand."

"So you'll be taking over the investigation again?" Eodan said, making Ciutto's gaze flick nervously in his direction. "There are a lot of missing people. Forty-three, at last count."

"Just the special cases." Ciutto's outstretched hand shook slightly. "You can handle the rest."

Ginnevra realized in that instant what was going on. "Somebody is putting pressure on you to solve those disappearances," she said. "One of the wealthy families, right? They know you were assigned to look into it and they want to know what progress you've made. But you pushed it all off onto me, and now you're in trouble and you're trying to save your skin."

Ciutto lowered his hand. "I don't know what you're talking about. I...talked to Malchio, and learned how...overburdened you are, and I thought I should assist."

"I'm sure," Ginnevra said. "Well, that's kind of you, but I have everything under control. And I think it will be more efficient for this investigation not to be broken into parts. So why don't you tell—well, anyone who comes asking, I suppose—tell them to come to me, and I'll be happy to answer their questions."

Ciutto's face was unnaturally pale, with two red spots high on his cheekbones. He looked like a marionette from a gaudy show, one whose strings had been cut. "I can't do that," he insisted. "Those are *my* notes and I insist you give them back immediately."

"Information gathered in the process of a criminal investigation by a justicer is the property of the judiciary," Ginnevra replied promptly. "That's to protect the justicer from accusations of malfeasance, but it applies in this case, too. Look," she added, relenting in the face of his obvious distress, "if it's a matter of your reputation, you can always tell those people that you couldn't refuse a prime. They'll understand."

"This is not a game," Ciutto snarled. "You come in waving your sword like some principe's banner and expect all of us to bow to your wishes—none of this is your business."

"Nobody, including you, was doing anything about these disappearances until Ginnevra showed up," Eodan said, taking a step forward to loom over the man. "I suggest you bridle your tongue."

Ciutto ignored him, which struck Ginnevra as potentially suicidal. "I have responsibilities," he said. "People to report to."

More light dawned. "You—" Ginnevra began, then thought better of accusing him of benefiting directly from the money that greased the wheels of justice in Uparde. If he'd taken bribes to ensure one or more of those families got special treatment, he might well be under pressure now to produce results or be forced to repay the money. Any sympathy she felt for him evaporated. "I'm sorry if you made promises you couldn't keep," she said, "but this is now my investigation, and unlike you, I'm in no hurry to be rid of it. Tell anyone who makes demands of you to take their problems up with me. And don't come to this house again."

She stepped back, and Eodan shut the door in Ciutto's face and slammed the bolts shut so they made an audible thump against the door frame. Then they stood in the tiny, dark entrance, listening. Ciutto didn't knock again. After a while, Eodan said, "That was odd."

"I think he took money to turn some of those disappearances into special cases. He acted like someone whose creditors have come calling." Ginnevra ran her hands through her hair. "It's his own damn fault for putting it all on me. Let's get out of here. If I have to knock on every door in Uparde, I want to get a good start."

"Justiciary first," Eodan reminded her, "unless you're afraid of running into that fellow again."

Ginnevra made a face. "If we do, I'll just have to suffer."

By nightfall, Ginnevra's feet ached, and she wished there were such a thing as a map of a city. Maps of countries, or regions, sure, but she'd never heard of anyone drawing up a map that showed streets within a city. Most people lived in one city or town their whole lives and knew that city or town well enough that such a map would be pointless. And the other people, the ones who traveled from place to place, never stayed anywhere long enough that they needed a map. It was just investigators trying to track down twoscore missing people who could use one. Preferably one that showed names of neighborhoods and prominent landmarks.

"I'm sure we've crossed this town twice and backtracked a dozen times," she complained. "There has to be a more efficient way to handle this."

"The more efficient way," Eodan said, "would be to have a native guide. But we don't know anyone like that."

"I know." She stopped in the middle of the street and threw her head back. The stars were coming out, and lights burned in windows up and down the street. They were in east Uparde, where the houses huddled close together as if for shelter from the storm, and only a few of the windows were glass. The rest were thin oiled parchment through which lamplight glowed in a fuzzy blotch of yellow.

Ginnevra observed the lamp tied to a post next to her. Its glass was cracked, and it looked as if it hadn't been lit in weeks. In fact, the whole street had a dark, rundown appearance that hinted at nefarious doings in hidden alleys. "I think we should call it a night," she said. "People will be going to sleep soon, and I'd rather not disturb anyone."

Eodan walked over to join her. "Inefficient or not, we learned things. None of our missing folk have spontaneously turned up, for one. And only two of the eight people we talked to said their lost loved one had suffered a setback of the sort that might make someone want to leave town."

"Which suggests kidnapping, doesn't it?" Ginnevra took Eodan's hand and squeezed it. "Because I find it hard to believe six people successfully concealed their unhappiness to the point that no one knew about it. On the other hand, I don't know that kidnappers can abduct this many people without being noticed."

They followed the street, which made a series of S-curves sharp enough that the end of the street wasn't visible. The houses leaned toward each other, not quite meeting above the street so a strip of sky and stars was all that was visible. No lights burned in these windows, and the street was so empty Ginnevra could imagine herself in a town populated by ghosts. A loose shutter tapped idly against a wall, *clack, clack,* drawing Ginnevra's attention. The cracked glass of the window next to the shutter caught what little light there was and reflected it strangely, almost as if there was someone behind the window—but nothing else moved, and no person could stand so perfectly still.

Eodan came to a halt, his hand tugging at Ginnevra's. "Ginnevra," he said, his tone of voice a warning.

Ginnevra turned to look at him and was caught mid-movement by the sight, ahead at the next turn of the road, of a couple of men advancing on them. Her heart sped up, not by much. "Keep walking," she murmured. "They're no trouble."

"The rest of them might be," Eodan whispered back.

"What—"

Another two men appeared from around the bend. Then three more. The same faint light glinted off the blades of long knives and gave shape to clubs studded with iron nails and long poles thick as Ginnevra's wrist. The men kept coming, walking slowly and spreading out to cover the width of the narrow street. There were fifteen in all now, Ginnevra noted with the cold, calculating part of her mind that considered things like fighting odds and which of these men to attack first.

Instinctively, she reached for her sword before remembering she'd left it behind, reasoning that she would be a less intimidating figure without it. The people she'd intended to question might be reluctant to talk to anyone, let alone a prime. Now she regretted the impulse. She let go of Eodan's hand and took a relaxed stance in the center of the street, a stance that could turn aggressive in a heartbeat if necessary. "Can I do something for you, friends?"

The first two men, one armed with a knife as long as his forearm, the other wielding an oak cudgel, stopped fifteen feet away. The man with the cudgel bounced it off his palm, once, twice. "You're out past curfew," he said. "I think you need a lesson about not disobeying what's good for you."

FOURTEEN

"Curfew?" Ginnevra said. "I haven't heard anything about that."

"Sure you haven't," the man said. His voice was unexpectedly high-pitched, making him sound like an aggressive canary. "Bet your next move will be to say you've got urgent business."

"Um, no, not really," Ginnevra said. Her gaze flicked from the speaker to the rest of the men coming up behind him. Only fifteen, though the last three probably thought they were concealed by the darkness. "But I was telling the truth about not knowing about the curfew. How long has that been going on? The Lord Mayor should post signs."

The man smiled, an unpleasant expression. "As if we care about the Lord Mayor. This is *our* part of town, miss, and we intend to see it protected. No more disappearances, not from here."

Ginnevra realized what had been bothering her—she and

Eodan had been out after dark the previous night and had encountered no one interested in enforcing a curfew. "So the curfew is just in this neighborhood," she said, partly to herself. "I'm sorry, we didn't mean to encroach," she said more loudly.

"I reckon not," the man said. "Tell you what. I hate to mess up a lady's face, so we'll just beat your quiet friend here and let you off with a warning."

Ginnevra's blood hummed with the need to fight. All her frustration with the investigation and her anger at Ciutto Baroccius and her fear for Caterrina came bubbling to the surface. She glanced at Eodan, who smiled. His smile was that of a predator who smelled hapless, ignorant prey. "That's awfully kind of you," she said, and pounced.

Swifter than thought, she smashed her fist into the man's face and felt cartilage crunch, then twisted the cudgel from his grip and slammed the weapon into his stomach, making him fold. Beside her, Eodan had disarmed the knife wielder and kicked the knife into the shadows, locking one arm around the man's throat and choking him unconscious. He let his victim fall atop the other, groaning man. "It's not even a challenge," he said.

For a moment, no one moved. Ginnevra surveyed the rest of the vigilantes and came up with half a dozen plans contingent on whether the swift dispatch of their comrades was enough to send them fleeing. Then, someone shouted, "They killed Borrio!" and the street came alive with movement as the remaining vigilantes rushed them.

Ginnevra twirled the cudgel. It was a good, solid weight, heavier than her sword, which would have been a bad idea in this fight—these men were deluded, not evil. She whacked the first man who ran at her across his hip, making him stumble, then cracked the cudgel over his shoulder so he dropped his pole. That was a better weapon, she decided, not as heavy and less likely to do permanent damage if she hit someone upside the head. She slammed the cudgel into the next man's stomach, got her toes under the staff, and flipped it up to grab it with her off hand.

Beside her, Eodan fought with the contained violence she was now so familiar with, punching and kicking and driving men to the ground with a well-placed knee or two, his injured arm not slowing him down. Ginnevra dropped the cudgel and snatched the staff with her right hand, spinning it two-handed in time to catch her next assailant's knife and thrust it back. She used the staff to trip him, then smacked his right elbow a sharp blow that made his fingers open involuntarily so he dropped the knife. He cried out, and Ginnevra struck his temple hard enough to shut him up, though she didn't think he was unconscious.

Then there was no one else within reach. The remaining men had all backed away, and as she watched, they turned and ran. "Oh, very nice, abandon your friends, why don't you?" Ginnevra shouted after them. She turned to Eodan and said, "Are you hurt at all?"

"By these fools? Hardly," Eodan said. He had a long scratch along one cheek he blotted with the back of his hand. "Now what?"

Ginnevra looked around for the speaker and found him curled on his side, his hands covering his gory face. "Looks like I broke your nose," she said cheerfully. "Come on, sit up and let's talk. Are you the one they called Borrio?"

The man eyed her, hostility oozing from every pore. Ginnevra sighed. "I am the paladin Ginnevra Cassaline, prime of the Blessed," she said, "and you can either sit up and have a civil conversation, or I can drag you by your collar to the justiciary and have them lock you up for assaulting me and my companion. I'm sure they'll understand you had the best of motives."

The man's eyes were fearful. He pushed himself to a sitting position. "I didn't know," he began.

"Like I didn't know about your so-called curfew? Didn't we establish that not knowing doesn't matter?"

The man blanched, but said nothing.

"Listen, Borrio," Ginnevra said, "I understand your desire to protect your families. Especially since it doesn't look like Uparde has much in the way of a town guard, and you have no idea how people are going missing or what else to do to prevent it. But attacking random passersby is not the way to go about it. All that does is satisfy your need for action, and that's a selfish response."

"You could've been the kidnappers," Borrio said in a mulish, resentful tone.

"And *you* could have asked more questions to establish that instead of posturing and getting violent," Ginnevra retorted. "Don't act like this was an innocent misunderstanding."

Borrio lowered his hands. Blood covered the lower half of his face, caking his mustache and beard. "Fine," he said, though his trembling hands and wide eyes belied his defiant stance. "So what are we supposed to do? Let them take us and not fight back? Easy for you to come over all high and mighty at us when it's not you in danger."

Ginnevra knelt beside him. "My aunt disappeared," she said. "I'm trying to find her and all the others. So how about you help me instead of you and all your friends taking a beating?" *A well-deserved beating*, she didn't say.

The man blinked, and his mouth slackened with astonishment. "Help...you?"

"You can start by telling me how many people have gone missing from your neighborhood." Ginnevra pulled the book out of the sack she wore slung over her back and withdrew a stub of a charcoal pencil from between its pages.

Borrio still looked like she'd smacked him between the eyes with her commandeered staff. "Thirteen," he said. "In the past four weeks."

Ginnevra flipped through pages, counting. "That's four I don't have a record of. Did you report the disappearances to the justiciary?"

"Don't know," Borrio said with a shrug. "Some families might have. It's not like the justiciary cares about what happens on the east side unless they're rousting us for theft and assault."

After what she'd seen of the investigation's records and Ciutto, Ginnevra couldn't argue the point. "I don't suppose you know the names of the missing?"

Another shrug. "I might. Most of them were friends." He reeled off a list of names. Ginnevra checked it against her list and had him repeat a few, which she wrote down.

"And...when's the last time someone disappeared from around here?" she continued.

"It's been five days," Borrio said. "So we *are* doing the right thing. The curfew works."

"Or you've just been lucky," Ginnevra said.

She glanced over at Eodan, who'd laid out all the fallen men more comfortably and was checking the eyes of one of them. "Anyone seriously hurt?" she asked.

"No, but they'll be feeling the beating for a few days." Eodan stood and came toward her victim. "Let me look at your nose."

Borrio shied away. Ginnevra grabbed his shoulders and made him hold still. Eodan felt along the bridge of the man's nose, making him whimper in pain. "It's broken," Eodan said. "I'm afraid there's nothing I can do for you here, so you'll have to take care of it yourself. Unless you think the rakish broken-nosed look is an advantage."

Borrio glared at Eodan as he removed his hand from the man's face. "Don't tell me my business," he said, but weakly. Eodan just shrugged and crouched beside Ginnevra.

"Did he say why they came up with this brilliant plan?" he asked.

Ginnevra glanced inquiringly at Borrio. Borrio sneered, then winced at how the expression jarred his broken nose. "We defend ourselves when no one else will. Lady Jiulliana said it wasn't a crime to take back our homes."

"Lady Jiulliana?" Ginnevra said, startled. "She told you to become vigilantes?"

Borrio looked away from Ginnevra. "She gave us wisdom. Nothing wrong with that. And we followed her guide."

Ginnevra turned to Eodan. "That's inciting violence. It's a criminal offense."

"Lady Jiulliana's no criminal," Borrio said. "You can't arrest her. And she didn't tell us specifically what to do. She just said, watch over what's ours."

Ginnevra scowled. For a moment, she thought she'd had something she could use. Then she reminded herself Lady Jiulliana wasn't the threat and said, "I'm sure she'd be horrified to learn how you interpreted her wisdom. Now, tell me where I can find these people—no, I'm not going to hurt them, I just need to ask some questions to help my investigation."

Borrio didn't look happy, but he gave her directions to find the four people she hadn't known about before. Ginnevra put away the charcoal and the book and stood. Then she reached out a hand to help Borrio up. He came to his feet looking surprised.

"Lady Jiulliana was right," Ginnevra said, feeling moderately annoyed at having to say those words. "You should watch over what's yours. But that is not an excuse for you to indulge your darker, more shameful desires. I'll be back tomorrow, and if I so much as feel someone giving me the stink-eye behind my back, I will arrest every one of you. And then your neighborhood will be truly defenseless. I'm sure you don't want that." She turned her back on him and, picking her way through the rest of the men, most of whom looked afraid to get up, she walked away with Eodan at her side.

They were back at the city central, surrounded by light and music and laughter, before Eodan said, "So. Lady Jiulliana. She certainly gets around, for someone who can't walk."

"And she's nosy as hell." Ginnevra stepped closer to Eodan and took his arm as a wave of celebrating men and women threatened to wash over them. "I wonder how many other people have come to her for advice about their missing loved ones?"

"She did say she couldn't locate them. So at least a few of those people left disappointed." Eodan drew her closer as the crowd buffeted them. His warm, comforting presence eased some of the discomfort she'd felt talking about Lady Jiulliana. She wasn't as confident in herself as she'd thought if the mere mention of the woman made her angry and resentful.

"It might be worth talking to her again," she said. "I'd like to know what she told the people who came looking for help about the disappearances."

"Because you want an excuse to arrest her?" Eodan said with a smile.

"No, because if she can remember the questions they asked, that might be information I can use. Information those people might not think to share." Ginnevra sighed. "And maybe I do have some small desire to arrest her. I dislike frauds."

"So do I," Eodan said, "but I'm not sure she's our responsibility, given that we're not even citizens of Uparde. Leave it to the judiciary or the Lord Mayor—what is a Lord Mayor, anyway?"

"Someone with authority from the ruler—in this case, the Elector of Devoyenne, head of its council—to manage a town or city. In the republic of Devoyenne, the Lords Mayor of its cities are appointed by the Devoyenne council. Some places choose their own. I don't remember the name of Uparde's Lord Mayor." Ginnevra steered them both toward Wart's tavern. "Whoever he is, he's not doing a very good job if he's letting the citizens get away with vigilante justice."

"He might not know about it," Eodan pointed out.

"That's almost worse in terms of how bad it makes him look." Ginnevra pushed open the tavern door, letting out air smelling of bread and warm ale that wrapped them in its warmth. "But you're right, it's not our responsibility. Let's have something to eat, and have an early night so we can get an early start tomorrow."

"An early start beginning with a trip to the market," Eodan said. "That cheese in Caterrina's kitchen is so mature it's on its way to spawning offspring."

Ginnevra's early enthusiasm soured as the morning wore on toward noon. An unusually hot day combined with the promise of another late-summer storm turned the air to soup through which Ginnevra swam. This time, she'd brought the sword but had left off the armor, but that wasn't as much of a relief as she'd hoped. Normally, she loved the heat of the sun, but this horrible sticky dampness clung to every part of her and made her long for a bath, preferably in the warm waves off the coast of Devoyenne.

The desire felt hollow, though, hollow and selfish when she considered that she still hadn't found her aunt. She shifted her sword higher on her shoulder and drew in a breath of storm-saturated air. She was making progress. She had to believe that or she would go mad.

"So, those four didn't tell us anything new," she said. "I think we've exhausted the possibilities of the east side. I was so hopeful, too. I thought we'd find information the reports didn't have."

"We did," Eodan said. "Just nothing groundbreaking. It's going to take a lot more digging—you know that."

"I do." Ginnevra sighed again. Eodan looked as warm as she felt, his skin, paler than hers, ruddy with heat and sweat darkening his hairline. "And we eliminated three names that don't match the pattern. I think we should try the special cases next. They should all be close together, at least."

"They might not be inclined to be helpful, not if they've already been interrogated by that Ciutto Baroccius," Eodan said.

"Or they'll be more helpful because they'll see I'm taking them seriously," Ginnevra countered. "We have to talk to them regardless."

"I know. I just think we should be prepared for disappointment." Eodan wiped his forehead. "I didn't realize how hot summer is in the southern lowlands. It's not nearly this bad where I come from."

"Where is that? North, I know, but how far?"

"I don't know human measurements of distance." Eodan surreptitiously fanned himself with his shirt. "In the mountain valleys."

"That *is* far north." Ginnevra consulted her mental map of the Lordagne region. "But I met you much farther south than that, south of Abraciabene and Fayonne."

"My pack lives west of where we met. West and a little north. It's one of the southernmost packs. But we travel north in summer. I never thought I'd miss it. I wish this storm would break." Eodan eyed the heavy clouds that covered the sky. "You'd think with no direct sunlight, it would be cooler."

Ginnevra wiped sweat from the nape of her neck, then wiped her hand on her breeches. "We're close to home. Let's get something to eat. I know it's a little early, but I hate backtracking."

"Which we are going to do regardless, thanks to having no native guide," Eodan said.

"I know where one of these people lives. It's only two streets over from Aunt Caterrina's house. And I was thinking we could show those people the list and enlist their help." Ginnevra put the book away in the sack strapped across her back and stretched. "It's like having a native guide without keeping an extra person around."

Eodan nodded. They'd reached Caterrina's street and were following its now-familiar curve. Even at nearly noon, the street was deserted except for housewives sweeping their stoops—or, more likely, household servants, given how well-to-do the owners of these houses were. They stopped what they were doing as Ginnevra and Eodan passed. Ginnevra smiled and nodded at them; the women regarded her silently, without returning her salutes.

As they neared Caterrina's house, Ginnevra noticed something piled on the stoop, a large bundle of some kind. "Someone's left us a gift," she said, putting a hand on Eodan's arm to slow him. "We need to be cautious. It could be anything."

"It looks like a sack," Eodan said. "Propped against the door."

"A sack of what, though? I'm worried."

Eodan's arm under her hand stiffened. "It's not a sack," he said, and broke into a run. "It's a person."

Ginnevra trotted after him, still cautious. "A drunk?" she said. "Why would a drunk be in this neighborhood?"

Eodan had already reached the doorstep and was kneeling

beside the person, straightening his—her?—limbs. "Ginnevra, get over here now," he said.

Ginnevra came to his side. "Why," she began, and then got a good look at the figure lying sprawled against the door, her face a mass of bruises and cuts, her chest barely rising and falling as she struggled for breath. "Goddess have mercy," Ginnevra whispered. "Aunt Caterrina."

CHAPTER

FIFTEEN

A s if seizing the dramatic moment, thunder rumbled across the sky. "We have to get her inside," Eodan said.

Ginnevra lifted her aunt into her arms and stood. "The front door's still barred."

Eodan nodded and hurried around the house to the kitchen door. Ginnevra followed, careful not to jog Caterrina's battered body, though she was unconscious and couldn't feel anything. She slipped past Eodan to lay Caterrina on the table at the kitchen's center. Her aunt's long arms and legs flopped down over the sides. Ginnevra backed up and let Eodan near.

Eodan examined Caterrina, checking her pulse and her breathing, feeling along her limbs and peeling back unresponsive eyelids to examine her eyes. "Her pulse is sluggish, and her breathing is shallow," he said. "But her pupils respond to light— that's a good sign. Possibly the only good sign. One of her arms is broken, and..." He checked her bare feet, one of which was purple and swollen. "Her left foot is, too. In a couple of places."

Ginnevra made her fists relax. "Someone beat her badly," she said.

"Someone tortured her," Eodan corrected her. "This all looks very deliberate, not random the way it would if she'd lost a fight."

"Torture." Ginnevra had to relax her fists again. "How is that even possible?"

"This proves she didn't disappear voluntarily. Someone abducted her and worked her over." Eodan sounded as angry as Ginnevra felt. "And then dumped her on the doorstep when they were finished."

"No. They weren't finished, and she escaped." Ginnevra fingered the rope burns around Caterrina's wrist. "Because they couldn't afford to let her go, not with her still alive. She's a paladin; she'd heal quickly regardless of what they did, and then she'd go after them."

"Retired paladin—does that make a difference?"

Ginnevra shook her head. "A paladin is a paladin for life so far as our oaths go. Retirement means leaving your company, a resumption of menses, but most of the physical enhancements stay. Including the fast healing. So...no, I think she must have escaped. Is she...will she wake soon?"

Eodan shook his head. "I have no idea. With as much damage as she's taken, probably internal damage too, she might stay unconscious for a while as her body repairs itself."

"Damn it." Ginnevra turned away, fighting for control. "I need her to wake up and tell me who did this. Whoever it is...*damn it*. That person, or group of people, they could be doing this to everyone they abduct, which means—" She slammed a fist against the wall next to the door. The blow sent a sharp pain through her hand and arm, bringing her back to the present. "Finding the missing people suddenly got a whole lot more urgent."

The sound of rain pounding against the distant roof broke through her angry words. "We should get her into bed," she said, and moved to pick Caterrina up.

"Not here," Eodan said. "She shouldn't be left alone, and you and I are going to be busy. Once I've treated the worst of her injuries, we need to take her somewhere she can be watched over."

Ginnevra stepped back. "Where are we going to find anywhere like that?"

"I have an idea," Eodan said.

"THIS IS A TERRIBLE IDEA," Ginnevra said, balancing Caterrina in front of her saddle to sprawl gracelessly across Dauntless's withers. The war horse didn't give any sign he was disturbed by the extra passenger. "We barely know him."

"Which means we know him a hundred times better than anyone else in this town," Eodan said. "And it's not as if he has anything else to occupy his time. *And* you're the one who said Ottavio wasn't reliable."

They plodded along the street to the Golden Sickle and into its stable yard. "Fine," Ginnevra said. "You've convinced me. But he'd better behave himself."

Eodan dismounted without responding and splashed through the puddles to the inn's front door. Ginnevra held her aunt around the shoulders and avoided looking at her face. Every time she caught sight of the battered wreck Caterrina was now, her throat closed up and her eyes burned with tears, and that was a stupid response. She was a paladin; she ought to respond to senseless violence with some well-placed violence to counter it. And yet she couldn't stop remembering Caterrina's constant presence in her life. How she'd taught Ginnevra to use a sword. How she'd told stories of being a paladin that Ginnevra had drunk up like honey mead. How she'd been the only one who understood how Ginnevra felt the first time she'd taken a life. Seeing her like this... it was like the unknown torturers had diminished Ginnevra's proud, powerful aunt, and Ginnevra couldn't bear it.

She wasn't sure how long she'd sat there atop Dauntless, her mind running in terrible circles, before Eodan returned. "Give her here," he said, and Ginnevra eased Caterrina off the horse and into Eodan's arms. "I've rented a room on the ground floor, just through this way," he added, and Ginnevra followed him through the airy entrance chamber and down the hall to the last door.

The room looked almost exactly like Pellarius's, windowless and furnished with two beds, a washstand, a chair, and a clothes-press, with three lamps shedding a bright glow over the scene. The beds, however, had matching cheery blankets woven in shades of pink and yellow that were far too nice for an inn, and flowers in a vase on the washstand echoed the blankets' colors. It would have eased Ginnevra's heart if she hadn't caught sight of her aunt's mangled foot, which looked worse in the well-lighted room despite the splint and bandages—or maybe because of them. She blinked back tears again as Eodan laid Caterrina gently on the bed.

"I'll be right back," Eodan said. "Are you all right?"

He gripped her hand, gently, and Ginnevra fought back more tears. "Just wishing dismemberment and death on whoever did this," she said.

Eodan squeezed her hand, then let go. "Soon enough, love," he said, and left the room.

Ginnevra sat on the bed beside Caterrina and looked her over. Again, the light showed clearly the damage her kidnappers had done. There was no question it had been deliberate, down to the pattern of cuts on Caterrina's face. Ginnevra shut her rage and sorrow away deep within her and made herself think logically. What would be the point of torture? Caterrina might have made enemies over the years she was a paladin, or maybe even after she'd retired, and one of them might have thought this was a good revenge. But that didn't make sense, not with all the other people who'd gone missing. Ginnevra couldn't believe anyone was so obsessed with revenge against one woman they'd abduct forty more people to conceal their true motive.

Eodan bumped the door open again. He held Pellarius in his arms. "Would you move that chair closer to the bed?" he asked. Ginnevra quickly did so, and Eodan seated Pellarius in it. "I'll get the other chair," he said, and disappeared again.

Pellarius and Ginnevra looked at each other. "Is this your aunt?" Pellarius said with a gesture. "I'm sorry she endured that."

"Thank you," Ginnevra said automatically.

Pellarius fidgeted with his hands in his lap. "Guess you're even more driven to find the bastard now," he said.

"I was driven before," Ginnevra snapped, then felt guilty. "You're right, though. I mean, not just because it's personal. I didn't know this is the danger those people might be facing."

"I can understand that," Pellarius said.

Eodan entered then, carrying a chair identical to the one Pellarius sat in and a down pillow. He positioned the chair near Pellarius, set the pillow on its seat, and propped Pellarius's foot on it, elevating the broken leg. "You understand what you're to do?" he asked.

Pellarius nodded. "Watch her, and keep track of if her breathing or movement changes," he said. "Give her water if she asks for it."

Eodan dragged the washstand with its pitcher and basin close to Pellarius's hand. "We'll be back as often as we can. Shout for the innkeeper if anything happens—I've asked him to drop by occasionally. And...thank you."

"It's no trouble," Pellarius said. "Good luck to you."

Out in the stable yard, Eodan said, "I hope it's enough. I hate leaving her without a physician's care, but..."

"We need to solve this mystery quickly," Ginnevra said. "She's not the only one at risk." She urged Dauntless into a trot. "We need to talk to Aunt Caterrina's nosy neighbor first, find out if he saw anything." It was too much to hope he'd seen strangers near the house, since Caterrina's kidnappers wouldn't have left her on her doorstep if they'd found her, but if he knew when she'd arrived, or how long she'd been there...any scrap of information might turn out to be essential.

She dismounted on the street outside Caterrina's house and pounded on the door of the house opposite. It felt like forever before the man opened the door. "What?" he asked, somewhat irritably. "You don't need to rouse the whole neighborhood with your knocking."

"Did you see someone at Caterrina's door?" Ginnevra demanded. "Someone sleeping on the stoop, maybe?"

The man gave her an even more irritated look. "What, you think all I do is watch my neighbors, all day long?"

"Yes, I do," Ginnevra said. "Please, sieur. What did you see this morning?"

His lips thinned in a tight, straight line. "Vagrant," he said. "A drunk stumbling through the streets who ended up collapsed on my lady's stoop. I was going to send word to the justiciary to arrest the fellow when you showed up. So I don't know why you're asking me questions you know the answers to."

"How long did the...vagrant...arrive before Eodan and I came?"

The man shrugged. "Half an hour, an hour? I have other demands on my time."

Ginnevra began to turn away, then had a thought. "What direction did she come from?"

"West," the man said. "Did you have any other rude demands?"

"Thank you," Ginnevra said absently, her mind already elsewhere.

She hurried back to where Eodan waited and hoisted herself into the saddle. "Let's stable the horses and then see if we can pick up her trail. West."

"Someone must have seen her," Eodan said.

"If she looked like a drunk, most people will have ignored her," Ginnevra said. She nudged Dauntless forward, heading toward the stable. "Humans don't like feeling uncomfortable, and anything strange or troubling makes them uncomfortable. So they ignore what they can't avoid. We just have to hope there were a few people who noticed her passing."

But the streets remained empty, the houses blank-faced and quiet. Ginnevra cursed the good luck that had made Caterrina's fortune and given her the wealth to settle in such a part of town. She kept going west, past the houses and into one of Uparde's out-of-the-way markets, still going strong at well after noon though observation had told her most business was transacted in the early morning. People stared at her sword and whispered things she ignored, though her acute hearing made the whispers clear.

She swept the market with her gaze, noting the semi-permanent stalls that said this was a more upscale place than the ones to the east and south where vendors sold from carts or the backs of wagons. She couldn't guess which of them were most likely to have seen Caterrina struggling through the streets.

Eodan pointed discreetly to one side, at a stall draped in bolts of fabric, Fayonne silks and exotic printed cottons from beyond the

Lordagne. The vendor's attention was so ostentatiously elsewhere he had to be watching Ginnevra. Ginnevra nodded once and crossed to that stall. "Excuse me, sieur, may I have a moment of your time?"

The man looked up in exaggerated surprise. "My lady, welcome!" he exclaimed, making a dramatic bow. "I'm honored to welcome you. Please, how may I help you? I sell the finest fabrics in all of Devoyenne's many wonderful cities."

Ginnevra thought briefly of how ridiculous she would look fighting monsters draped in finest silk. "Your wares are lovely, but I'm afraid I'm not shopping today. I'm actually looking for information. Did you see a woman pass through the market a few hours ago? A...a drunk woman?" She sent up a silent prayer that the Goddess and Caterrina would forgive her lie, but she had no intention of stirring up more trouble by revealing that someone had captured and tortured one of Uparde's leading citizens.

The man's expression grew cooler. "I'm afraid I don't notice such things," he said, "and the justicers wouldn't allow such behavior to go unpunished. Not here."

"You, not notice?" Ginnevra put on a demeanor of astonished respect. "But someone with an eye for detail such as yours—your selection is far too good to be that of someone who doesn't notice things. Please, sieur, this is important. Her family is quite wealthy and worried for her. I'm sure they'll be grateful to anyone who can provide information." She hoped she was right about the man's pride being more powerful than his greed, and that she hadn't just pushed so hard he would lie to her out of a desire to prove himself worthy of her compliments.

"I don't understand. Who is this woman?" the man said.

"I'm afraid her family has requested strict anonymity," Ginnevra said, lowering her voice to confide this secret. "You did see her, didn't you? What direction did she come from?"

The man hesitated. Ginnevra dipped a hand into her purse and palmed the first large coin she touched. Holding the golden aurin between two fingers, she made a lazy gesture so the coin caught the wan post-storm light. "Or I suppose I could ask across the way," she said.

"That's unnecessary," the man said quickly. "That is...I saw a woman behaving strangely, just a few hours ago. She might have been drunk—I only noticed that she avoided the stalls, but she ran into more than a few people. I, of course, did not stare, as I did not wish to reward her bad behavior with the attention I'm sure she craved. But she passed my stall and headed east."

"So she came from the west? From which street?"

"I only noticed her when she neared Vitorria's stall. The rug merchant." The man said "merchant" as if it tasted foul. "It's that way." He inclined his head, clearly too refined to point.

Ginnevra laid the coin on the stall. "Thank you, sieur, I appreciate the help. As will her family." She smiled politely at the man and turned away.

"But...why don't you want to know where she went?" The man sounded confused. Ginnevra looked over her shoulder at him. The coin had disappeared.

"Don't trouble yourself with paladin business, sieur," she said, putting an edge on her words. The man gulped and backed away into the depths of his stall.

Eodan had moved a few stalls away and was talking to a woman selling leather items, mostly belts and purses. He clasped the woman's hand briefly and turned away as Ginnevra approached. "She says she saw Caterrina run into one of her customers before continuing east," he murmured. "She didn't see where she came from."

"West, at least as far west as the rug vendor," Ginnevra said.

"We have to move more quickly. Wherever she escaped from, they'll have taken steps to hide."

"You don't think they'll have moved on?"

Ginnevra shook her head. "Not if there are still captives. They'd risk discovery if they...oh, Goddess have mercy, unless they decided to cut their losses and kill the rest of them."

Eodan's look of horror mirrored hers. "Let's go," he said.

They moved westward, retracing Caterrina's steps as best they could. The farther they proceeded, the fewer people they found who would admit to seeing a woman staggering drunkenly through the streets. Past the market, the street narrowed again, branching off and branching again until the streets were a warren of businesses and homes. The business owners met her inquiries with polite indifference and no useful information. Ginnevra pounded on doors and got no responses from any of the house-holders.

Finally, she leaned against the wall and closed her eyes. "I have no idea which of these houses Aunt Caterrina might have been held in. I don't even have enough information to calculate how far she could have gotten in her condition."

"It couldn't have been very far. She was in bad shape." Eodan settled beside her and took her hand. "We don't know that the other missing people are dead. That is, we don't know that they were killed because Caterrina escaped. They might not have been kept alive in the first place."

"You are *not helping*," Ginnevra said.

"I'm sorry. I'm just saying, since we don't know their intentions, we have no way of knowing what happened to the rest of the missing people. Which means it's pointless for us to jump to conclusions." He squeezed her hand lightly. "On the other hand... did you notice where we are?"

Ginnevra opened her eyes. "West Uparde."

"Specifically, we're two streets over from Lady Jiulliana's house."

Ginnevra took a closer look at her surroundings. "That doesn't have to mean anything. West Uparde isn't all that big a place, not like the east side. We'd be close to her house from nearly anywhere on this side of town. And why would she have anything to do with the missing people?"

Eodan drew her close. "I love you even more," he whispered in her ear, "when you make a superhuman effort to be even-handed with someone you detest."

Ginnevra sighed and kissed him. "Was it that obvious?"

"Only to me." He kissed her back, his lips warm and soft on hers. "I think we should talk to her—or maybe to her household. We have to be close to wherever Caterrina was held, and maybe they've noticed something."

"It's worth checking," Ginnevra said. "But even I can't picture Lady Jiulliana as a filthy kidnapper. Spreader of rumor and innuendo, maybe, and a corrupter of the faith, and—" She sighed again. "She'd better not have any more 'advice' for me. My abilities to be fair and even-handed only go so far."

"If she's so insightful, she probably knows that," Eodan said.

SIXTEEN

The crowd surrounding the brown door and its grille was smaller than before, Ginnevra guessed because of the rain. But the petitioners, as she thought of them, were as intent on the door and as oblivious to everything else as they had been the last time—at least, oblivious right up until Ginnevra pushed her way through the crowd. To her surprise, their angry protests didn't die away when they saw the sword. Ginnevra didn't like the tone of the muttering. Suppressing visions of having to put down a riot, she turned when she reached the door and said, "I'm not here for personal advice from Lady Jiulliana. This is an official investigation."

That made the muttering grow louder and angrier. Ginnevra realized how her words must have sounded. It was impossible the people of Uparde didn't know Lady Jiulliana and the Revered had been in some kind of conflict, and Ginnevra's presence probably looked like an escalation of that conflict. Inwardly, she groaned. Making her investigation public might be a mistake, but if the alternative was turning the people against her...

"Have you heard about the missing people?" she said loudly. "I'm tasked with finding out what happened to them and putting a stop to the disappearances. I have to ask Lady Jiulliana some questions."

Beside her, Eodan tensed, and Ginnevra wanted to kick herself. That sounded worse. She ran over other possibilities, things she might say to keep from appearing to threaten their beloved wise woman, but to her surprise the murmuring stopped. A young, very pregnant woman at the front of the crowd said, "You're asking the holy Jiulliana for her insight? I didn't think the Revered believed in her gift."

That was better than these people assuming Ginnevra thought Jiulliana was somehow complicit in the disappearances. "I can't discuss my investigation," she said. "But I promise I don't intend to interfere in your time with Lady Jiulliana."

Behind Ginnevra, the door and the grille opened, and the short majordomo, Marcellus, stepped out. "My lady," he said, not sounding surprised. "Please, follow me, you and your companion."

"Thank you for your patience," Ginnevra said to the waiting petitioners, and entered the house.

"Lady Jiulliana has been expecting you," Marcellus said over his shoulder as he led the way down the passage.

"It's actually you I've come to talk to," Ginnevra said. "You and the rest of the household."

Marcellus came to an abrupt halt and swiveled on his heel to face Ginnevra, who nearly ran into him. "You...want to talk to me?"

"I'm investigating a number of disappearances in Uparde in the past four weeks," Ginnevra said. "One of the missing people was seen in this area before she disappeared. I'm asking everyone here if they've seen anything strange." None of that was strictly true, but it was close enough to make sense to Marcellus.

The majordomo's eyes were wide. "Disappearances?"

"Yes. So, if you don't mind, I have some questions."

"But...Lady Jiulliana is expecting you." Marcellus looked like Ginnevra had jolted him out of a familiar rut and now he didn't know where the road went.

"This won't take long. Someone told me Lady Jiulliana is a recent arrival in Uparde. How long ago did she come here?"

"Just over three weeks," Marcellus said. "Really, I—"

"And in that time, have you observed any strange behavior in any of your neighbors? People taking deliveries at odd hours, or houses where you never see anyone coming or going?"

"Nothing like that. We keep to ourselves." Marcellus clasped his hands together, restlessly rubbing them. "Lady Jiulliana wants us to be good neighbors."

Ginnevra eyed his hands. "Good neighbors?"

"Well, yes. Not intruding on others...you've seen how the people throng our door. Lady Jiulliana is conscious of how the neighbors might feel about that." His hands continued to move. "So we do our best to be unobtrusive otherwise."

"Surely someone goes out for food, though?" Eodan said. "Or receives deliveries?"

"That would be Salvia, the cook," Marcellus said. "But she's very busy."

"I won't take up much of her time. Unless there's some reason I shouldn't speak to her?" Ginnevra kept her voice calm and polite, but she shifted her weight to loom over Marcellus more directly.

"Of course not. But I doubt she knows anything." Marcellus walked a few paces down the hall and opened a door on the right-hand side. Delicious smells of roast pork wafted from the open door. Ginnevra followed the majordomo into the kitchen.

The room bustled with activity, men and women chopping vegetables and stirring pots and communicating with each other in loud voices. None of them looked up when the door opened. It seemed unusually busy for a single household's kitchen. Ginnevra was reminded of her uncle's household near Vaniere, a thriving farmstead where the kitchen served a hundred farmhands a day. This room was much smaller, but still overflowing with workers.

"Salvia," Marcellus said, pitching his voice to be heard over the noise. "Salvia, this paladin would like a word with you."

A fat woman, red-faced from the heat of the stove she stood over, wiped her hands on a towel thrust into her apron's waist-band and came slowly toward them. "My lady," she said, not sounding very friendly.

Ginnevra decided immediately she wasn't going to appear weak by inviting the woman to talk to her outside in the cooler, quieter hall. "You're the one who does the marketing?"

"I am." Salvia's hair straggled over her forehead, sweaty and lank, but she bore herself like a queen.

"I'm investigating the disappearances of several people here in Uparde. We've traced one of them to this neighborhood. Have you observed any strange behavior in your neighbors? Anything that might suggest they're hiding something?"

"I don't pry into other people's business," Salvia said.

"I'm not suggesting you do. But you must observe things all the time." Ginnevra smiled politely. "Do you go to the market yourself, or do you arrange for deliveries?"

"No deliveries. I go daily to the market."

This was like pulling teeth, dragging information out of the cook. "And you must have come to know your neighbors. Are there any who are reluctant to talk to you? You know how it is at the market—that's where you make the acquaintance of those who live nearby."

Salvia looked thoughtful. "I can't say anyone stands out as being what you're looking for," she said. "But there *is* one fellow who never talks to anyone. I don't even know his name, that's how secretive he is. I think he lives two streets over, nearer the market."

Ginnevra kept her expression polite. "That's very helpful, thank you. I won't keep you any longer."

Salvia nodded and retreated to the kitchen, shutting the door behind her.

"I'd like to talk to—" Ginnevra began.

"*Please*, my lady, Lady Jiulliana shouldn't be made to wait," Marcellus said. "She will see no one until she's spoken to you, which means all those people will have to wait longer."

Ginnevra scowled. She wasn't inclined to obey Lady Jiulliana's summons, but Marcellus had a point about the petitioners. "All right, I can question the others after I've seen Lady Jiulliana."

Marcellus wrung his hands a final time, then wiped his palms on his breeches, not seeming to notice either restless gesture. "This way," he said, bowing.

The antechamber seemed more brightly lit than before, as if someone had trimmed the lamps in response to the storm. Marcellus opened the door to Lady Jiulliana's room and bowed again. Ginnevra ignored him and settled her sword more firmly over her shoulder.

Lady Jiulliana still sat in the middle of the enormous bed, making Ginnevra wonder if she spent her whole life there. How awful, if that was the case. Ginnevra took a few steps forward, next to the chairs, but didn't sit. "How did you know I was coming?" she asked.

Lady Jiulliana folded her hands in her lap. "I didn't. That is, I did not predict your arrival at this time on this day. But I had a feeling you would return for more information. You said you were tasked with investigating all the disappearances. You must know some of those who come to me for advice asked about their missing loved ones. It does not take the wisdom of the Goddess to know you would like to learn what information I have on the subject."

"I actually came to talk to your household servants," Ginnevra said. "To see what they can tell me about the neighbors. But if you have information to give, I'm listening."

"I know very little about my neighbors." Lady Jiulliana cast her eyes down and made a gesture across her inert legs. "I don't ever leave this room. But the Goddess in her generosity shows me much. And I see the world through the eyes of those who come to me for advice."

"You said your gifts don't extend to locating missing people."

"That's true." Lady Jiulliana touched her ruby pendant. "I wish it were otherwise. Those who approach me for news of their missing loved ones grieve terribly, and I grieve with them. I can only reassure them that the Goddess knows the truth, and that the opportunities She gives them in life allow them the chance to choose their paths."

"And that...satisfies them?" Ginnevra was a paladin and committed to serving the Dark Lady, and even she would have been annoyed by an answer like that. Or maybe she disliked Lady Jiulliana enough that she would resent any answer the woman gave her.

Lady Jiulliana laughed. "Sometimes. But I am also granted insight into their hearts, and for those for whom that answer isn't sufficient, I give them advice on how to prepare for their loved ones to return and to protect themselves against future misfortune."

"So you promise the missing will return?"

"You're determined to catch me in heresy, aren't you?" Lady Jiulliana still sounded amused. "I can't tell them their loved ones will come back, because I don't know that they will. But I believe the Goddess provides them comfort by giving them something active to do that isn't mourning. One must have hope, after all."

Ginnevra glanced at Eodan, whose gaze was fixed on the woman in the bed. He stood with his hands loosely clasped behind his back in a relaxed pose Ginnevra knew could instantly turn into battle readiness. "I suppose that's true," she said. "What does your...insight...tell you about your neighbors?"

"I know these houses hold secrets, but that's true of everywhere." Lady Jiulliana touched her pendant again. "Are you looking in this area for your villains? Because it would not surprise me to learn that someone in west Uparde has been abducting citizens. The wealthy have more to hide than most."

"I can't discuss the details of my investigation," Ginnevra said automatically. "Did you have anyone specific in mind?"

"I don't see that clearly. I'm sorry, I realize that's not much help. But—" Lady Jiulliana's hand closed around the ruby. "Ginnevra Cassaline, the Goddess has words for you," she said in a clear, calm voice. "You seek the missing because you can't not serve. Not all those who are missing are gone forever. Have faith."

"Lovely platitudes," Ginnevra said, hanging onto politeness with both hands.

"Do not dismiss wisdom so flippantly, Ginnevra." Lady Jiulliana's voice had the singsong quality Ginnevra remembered and hated. "If you choose to ignore my words, you choose a terrible path. The werewolves know to whom they must look for salvation, and it is not your place to choose for them. You must follow your own path, because if you do not, you will be outcast yourself, just as the Goddess teaches."

Ginnevra's fingers felt numb with shock. "That's...interesting," she said. Her voice seemed to come from very far away.

"It's my privilege to be the Goddess's mouthpiece," Lady Jiulliana said. She lowered her hand to her lap. "Was there anything else?"

"Not at the moment, but I may have questions later," Ginnevra said. "Thank you for your time." She turned and left the room, flexing her hands to work feeling back into them.

Marcellus was standing there, but Ginnevra walked past him, heading for the exit without waiting on his escort. Eodan, striding quickly behind her, said, "Is there—"

"Not a word until we're out of here," Ginnevra said in a low voice.

She crossed the garden in silence, not deviating from the path, and exited through the garden gate, then kept going until she reached the corner. There, she leaned face-first against the wall and let out a deep breath.

Eodan put a hand on her shoulder. "She can't possibly speak for the Goddess," he said.

"And yet she hasn't ever said anything heretical," Ginnevra said. "Eodan, what if I'm wrong?"

"Why would the Goddess speak through someone who isn't of the anointed?" His hand closed more tightly on her shoulder. "If Lady Jiulliana truly hears the word of the Goddess, shouldn't she make her connection to the Faith explicit? Become an anointed? Ginnevra, what happened to her being a fraud?"

Ginnevra breathed out again, wishing her body wasn't trembling. "She has to be a fraud. I've never known any of these so-called wise women to be truly touched by the Goddess." But Lady Jiulliana's words rang in her memory, touching her heart in places she'd never thought to defend. She believed completely in the Goddess's teachings about free will and the blessing of choice, and now that tiny voice was back, demanding *what makes you think the werewolves want your intervention?*

"You have to go back to the chapel," Eodan was saying. "She may not be preaching heresy, but she just claimed to hear the voice of the Goddess, and you know that's a lie. There has to be something the anointed can do about her."

Ginnevra pushed upright and nodded. Then she embraced Eodan. "Thank you."

"For what?"

"For being who you are. For speaking reason." Her trembling was subsiding. "I didn't know my faith was on such shaky grounds."

"It's not." Eodan hugged her. "But you are facing a challenge no one's ever considered before, and it's not like there's any precedent to guide you. And, for what it's worth, I am grateful you care so much about a race not even your own."

Ginnevra laughed. "Even though I'm doomed to failure?"

"Just because I lack your faith is no reason to call your cause doomed." Eodan kissed her lightly and released her. "Back to the chapel, and then I want to check on Caterrina."

The street they were on crossed Lady Jiulliana's, and Ginnevra cast a glance at the waiting crowd. "It's not right, what she's doing," she said. "Making them believe in her 'gift'."

"One more reason to find a way to stop her," Eodan said.

"It will have to be Revered Abbate and the others who do it. I can't afford a distraction. People are still going missing. And that cook, Salvia—she suggested one of their neighbors acted suspiciously, did you notice?"

"I did. Awfully convenient that she had a candidate in mind that exactly matched what you were looking for, reasonable but anonymous and without enough details for you to track him down." Eodan slowed as Ginnevra did. The young pregnant woman was just being ushered inside.

"That's exactly what I thought. She couldn't have sounded more guilty if she'd tried. And yet it doesn't make any sense for her or anyone else in Lady Jiulliana's household to try to steer me away from investigating them for the disappearances." Ginnevra quickened her pace. "I don't understand what she was thinking. Lady Jiulliana wasn't even in Uparde when the disappearances started."

"Unless Salvia's loyalty to her employer means she wants you too busy to harass Lady Jiulliana," Eodan said. "She might not have thought beyond the moment."

"Or Lady Jiulliana is up to more than just fleecing the populace," Ginnevra said.

"What?" Eodan asked. "You don't think she's involved with the disappearances?"

"Not that. But it doesn't matter, because I just don't have *time*. I have to figure out what happened to those missing people, and pursuing Lady Jiulliana's crimes will have to wait." Ginnevra's resentment of the kidnappers increased. What she wanted was to march into Lady Jiulliana's house and arrest her, and never mind the social and political fallout. But she had a duty that trumped desire.

The square surrounding the chapel was busy with people passing through, going about their lives, talking and laughing as if nothing bad ever happened in Uparde. The noise cheered Ginnevra despite her discouragement and her fear for Caterrina. It meant not everything was terrible. She dreaded the day when the cheerful conversations were replaced by hushed mutterings and suspicious glances.

The thought slowed her steps. Between investigating what little information she had and worrying over Caterrina, she hadn't given much thought to wondering *why* someone, or a group of someones, would be abducting random citizens. But what if fear was the point? It seemed the most obvious result of news of mass abductions, people's fear that they or a loved one might be next to vanish.

Very well. Suppose this group wanted to incite fear or even panic in Uparde. The next question was: to what end? Fear was a powerful motivator, and Ginnevra had seen mobs destroy homes and even parts of cities out of fear. But she'd never seen anyone deliberately start a riot. And she couldn't guess what someone might want that they could use fear to achieve.

The clock above the chapel door told Ginnevra it was almost two o'clock, which meant the middle of the religious instruction period. Agostino and the two Dedicates would be occupied. Ginnevra didn't hesitate; she headed straight for the door, which stood open. The globes of fire burned brightly in the brass baskets, illuminating the entrance chamber with its many carvings. To her surprise, the right-hand passage, which led to the instruction hall, was dark, and no noise came from that direction. The sanctum, on the other hand, was well-lit, and Ginnevra heard voices distorted into unintelligibility by the echoes of the vast chamber. She walked forward and looked inside.

The sanctum wasn't large by absolute standards, and Ginnevra had seen many larger ones even in towns smaller than Uparde. Black, low-backed pews filled most of the space between the pillars holding up the roof. Ginnevra judged the sanctum would hold about three hundred worshippers. At the moment, all the pews were empty.

At the front of the room, near the altar, stood Agostino Abbate and the two Dedicates, Feora and Rigarrda, facing a woman with her back to Ginnevra. The unknown woman was the one speaking, her voice a low murmur and her hands gesturing to give emphasis to words Ginnevra couldn't make out. She was heavyset with rounded shoulders, and her short, white-streaked hair bobbed as she spoke.

Agostino was nodding in agreement. He caught Ginnevra's eye and startled. "My lady," he said, "you've come—this is truly amazing."

Ginnevra strode forward. "What's amazing?"

The unknown woman turned to face Ginnevra. "Is this the paladin?" she asked. A small black mole at the right corner of her mouth moved as she spoke. "Ginnevra Cassaline?"

"I am," Ginnevra said.

The woman smiled. "I'm Revered Massina Parenogne," she said.

SEVENTEEN

G innevra stopped in her tracks. "Massina Parenogne?"

"I should beg your pardon for putting you to so much trouble," the Revered said with a smile. "I feel rather foolish. I didn't realize how my departure might look."

"But...where did you go?" Ginnevra felt as if she'd stepped into a story, complete with narrator to explain everything. The Revered couldn't just walk back into Uparde after everything that had happened.

The Revered laughed, somewhat self-consciously. "I was called away to visit my sister in Guinio. Her daughter was betrothed and wanted me to perform the marriage ceremony at her home."

"And you didn't tell anyone you were leaving?" Ginnevra knew she sounded too shrill, but shock still had her in its grip.

"I did leave word, or rather I sent a message to the chapel. I suppose the runner wasn't as reliable as I hoped." The Revered shrugged. "At any rate, I am sorry if you were inconvenienced, my lady."

Ginnevra regarded her closely. The Revered's posture was erect, and yet she seemed perfectly at ease, not at all nervous or restless. Despite her words, she didn't look embarrassed, and she met Ginnevra's gaze directly. "That's...no, it was no inconvenience," Ginnevra said. "That is, I am responsible for investigating all the disappearances in Uparde, not just yours."

"More disappearances?" The Revered's eyes narrowed. "What do you mean?"

"Just that," Ginnevra said. "We believed you to be one of many. But it seems...well, obviously you weren't."

"But that's terribly distressing," the Revered said. "Have you had any luck?"

"I'm still investigating," Ginnevra said, and then wasn't sure why she hadn't been more forthcoming. "But it helps to be able to eliminate you as one of the missing."

"If there's anything we can do to assist you, please let us know," the Revered said. "Now, we should prepare for the afternoon's ceremonies, so if you don't mind..."

It was a brush-off, but Ginnevra was already on her way out the door, her mind rapidly churning over this new information. So the Revered really had walked out of the residence of her own free will, but not into the hands of the kidnappers. She'd gone on a perfectly innocent errand and it had been a mistake that no one knew where she was going. And yet every one of Ginnevra's instincts was sitting up and howling a warning. Something was wrong. She just didn't know what.

She joined Eodan at the fountain, where he was talking to a young woman carrying a basket over one arm. The young woman had a hand on Eodan's uninjured arm, and the two of them were laughing in a way that set Ginnevra's already tense nerves twanging. She reminded herself that Eodan was unlikely to be interested in a random stranger, however flirtatious and pretty she was, and said, "Can I hear the joke?"

The young woman's eyes widened. She snatched her hand from Eodan's arm and said, "Oh, my lady, I—it was nothing, really."

"Cassia here was telling me the history of this fountain," Eodan said. "Uparde's history is stranger than I imagined."

"That's true of many towns. You never know what secrets hide beneath their façades." Ginnevra smiled politely but without warmth at Cassia. "It's kind of you to welcome us to Uparde, Cassia. Perhaps we'll see you again."

Cassia correctly interpreted that as a dismissal and hurried away.

Eodan said, "That was unexpectedly harsh. You're not jealous, are you?"

"No, Eodan, I am not jealous. I'm—" Ginnevra closed her eyes and took a calming breath. "You won't believe who just walked into the chapel off the street."

"Don't tell me it was the Revered?"

Ginnevra opened her eyes. "You are a good guesser. Yes, it was the Revered. She says she's been in Guinio all this time with her sister."

Eodan looked stunned. "That can't be right."

"No, it can't. But I don't know what else to think. The Revered sounded perfectly normal, not drugged or coerced, and she didn't sound like she was lying. Which might just mean she's good at it. I don't know." She took Eodan's hand. "I want to see to Aunt Caterrina. Wouldn't it be wonderful if she was awake?"

"Don't get your hopes up," Eodan said.

"I won't. It's just that I've had enough shocks for one day, and if I have any more of them, I'd like them to be positive."

Both Caterrina and Pellarius were asleep when Ginnevra and

Eodan arrived at the Golden Sickle, though Pellarius came awake the instant the door opened. "No change," he said before either of them could speak. "She's breathing easily and she hasn't moved."

Eodan took Caterrina's wrist and laid two fingers over her pulse, then lifted her eyelids, one at a time. "She's doing well," he said. "Her pulse is stronger...she might wake at any time."

"You're not just saying that?" Ginnevra asked.

"Of course not. I wouldn't do that. Ginnevra, there isn't anything else you can do for her. Be patient." Eodan gave her a quick hug. "Pellarius, have you eaten?"

"They brought a meal a couple of hours ago." Pellarius indicated a tray set to one side. The sight of scraps of food and the lingering smell of soup made Ginnevra's stomach rumble.

"We forgot to eat," she told Eodan.

"I'll get something," Eodan said. "Wait here." He was gone before she could protest.

She looked around, but the only two chairs in the room were in use by Pellarius, and she didn't want to sit on either of the beds. So she leaned against the wall and looked everywhere but at the room's other occupants.

Pellarius cleared his throat. "Any luck?"

Ginnevra shrugged. "I don't know yet." It occurred to her that in her surprise at finding the Revered at the chapel, she hadn't told anyone her suspicions about Lady Jiulliana. She'd have to go back later. "The Revered Massina Parenogne returned, though. She wasn't kidnapped."

Pellarius let out a long, low whistle. "I hadn't heard she was missing. That's good news, isn't it?"

"Maybe." A thought occurred to her. "You're from Guinio, right? Is there a chapel there?"

"No, just a couple of shrines. We come to Uparde for weddings and sanctifications."

Ginnevra stood up. "The Revereds don't come to you?"

"Not hardly." Pellarius chuckled. "We keep hoping the Hallowed at Devoyenne will see fit to establish a chapel in Guinio, but it's much smaller than Uparde, so not much chance of that."

Ginnevra's instincts hollered at her again. She made herself consider the facts calmly. Even if Pellarius was right, the Revered had said it was her sister's child getting married, and maybe the Revered would make an exception for that. Though...what was it Lanberto, the Revered's majordomo, had said? Ginnevra couldn't remember the details...something about the Revered's responsibility to Uparde being her primary concern? Even so, supposing Ginnevra was right and the Revered's behavior was suspicious, what did it mean? She couldn't guess why the Revered would lie about where she'd been.

Someone rapped lightly on the door, and Ginnevra opened it to see Eodan with his hands full of two steaming, aromatic bowls. He handed one to her and shut the door behind him. "I had to be at my most charming to cadge these," he said. "The cook doesn't approve of people eating between meals."

"Funny, considering inns like these cater to the whims of their wealthy patrons." Ginnevra sipped her soup, which was a rich tomato-flavored chicken broth with tiny dumplings floating in it. She spooned up a dumpling and found it was filled with chopped boiled chicken meat. Her stomach rumbled again, this time in thanks.

"So why didn't the Revered tell anyone where she was going?" Pellarius asked.

Ginnevra swallowed her mouthful. "Apparently the message went astray. It still seems odd to me. She definitely left her residence at an unusual hour, and why would a simple wedding ceremony require her to sneak away?"

"You could ask her," Eodan said.

"I suppose. I don't know. She's back, after all, and maybe I should be grateful rather than pursuing a mystery that probably has nothing to do with the missing people." Ginnevra ate another dumpling. "But we have to go back for evening services. I forgot to tell the anointed about Lady Jiulliana."

"Lady Jiulliana? Who's that?" Pellarius asked.

Ginnevra scowled. "A thorn in my side. She claims to be a holy woman who hears the voice of the Goddess. But she's a fraud."

Pellarius let out a long, low whistle. "Why don't you arrest her, then?"

"Because I can't prove she's a fraud, and if I arrest her, it might start a riot. She's well-loved for someone who's only been in Uparde three weeks." Ginnevra drained the rest of her bowl and set it aside. "She's been careful not to do anything heretical, so the anointed can't touch her, but I'm going to ask them to look at her activities more closely. Even if she's not preaching heresy, if she claims to speak for the Goddess, that's something that could lead people astray."

"How do you know she doesn't speak for the Goddess?"

Pellarius's question struck Ginnevra to the heart, sending anger and uncertainty stabbing through her. "I just know!" she shouted. "You don't get to question my authority!"

Pellarius flinched. "I didn't—I meant, how can anyone tell the difference? Since it sounds like she's fooling everyone in Uparde. Sorry."

Ginnevra closed her eyes and let out a deep breath. "No, I'm sorry," she said, looking down at Pellarius. He looked genuinely contrite, and it made her feel even guiltier. "I...she's very convincing, and I don't have any way to prove she's lying. The things she's told me can't possibly be true, that's all."

"I see," Pellarius said. "And she makes people pay for her advice."

"She takes donations," Eodan said. "Which likely amount to more than she would charge anyone. It's a tidy little scam."

"I see why you think she's a fraud," Pellarius said. "And why it would be hard to do anything about it." His brow was furrowed like he was thinking about something.

Ginnevra sighed again. "We have a few hours before evening services. Let's continue to follow up on these disappearances, but focus on the west side. We might even ask around about Salvia's fake mysterious stranger—even if he's not real, Caterrina did return from somewhere in the area, and we're bound to find something."

"Spoken like a true optimist," Eodan said with a smile. He stacked their bowls atop Pellarius's plate. "We'll be back this evening to take over watching Caterrina. Thanks again, Pellarius."

"It's no trouble." Pellarius still looked like he was going over something in his head, but he smiled as they left.

"He's not at all what I thought from our first meeting," Ginnevra said as they left the inn.

"People aren't always what they seem. Of course, sometimes that means they're worse than they appear," Eodan said.

"Spoken like a true pessimist," Ginnevra said with a laugh.

THEY ARRIVED BACK at the chapel just at sunset, before the evening service began. Eodan settled on the rim of the fountain and idly unwrapped the bandage around his arm, revealing healing scabs and greenish-yellow bruises. "Maybe I should go back to the inn while you're busy with the anointed," he said.

"No, this shouldn't take long, and I want to eat before that." Ginnevra hesitated, then said, "Why don't you come with me?"

Eodan's eyebrows rose. "To holy services, in front of the Revered? Don't you think that's dangerous?"

"It's not like you'll burst into flame if you enter a chapel. You're not evil, Eodan, and you're not a monster. Please."

Eodan stood and walked to where she stood, out of the way of worshippers entering the chapel. He put a hand on her shoulder. "I love you," he said, "and I love your faith. But now is not the time. Someday, maybe."

Ginnevra covered his hand with hers. "I won't be able to travel with you without revealing your race forever. Why not now?"

"Because this is the middle of an investigation, and we don't need any distractions. Unless you think the Revereds will continue to care more about a woman who isn't overtly a heretic than they do about an actual werewolf in front of them?" He kissed her gently. "Go on, talk to them. I'll wait here."

Ginnevra scowled, but she squeezed his hand before he removed it from her shoulder. "Someday," she said, and turned to enter the chapel.

She took a seat near the back of the sanctum, not wanting to be a distraction from the service, and propped her sword beside her against the pew. There weren't as many people present as she'd expected; the sanctum wasn't more than half full. She'd thought, with the rising number of disappearances and the corresponding rise in fear, the chapel would be packed. But no one sat near her, not even the latecomers who sidled in just as the Revered took her place at the altar.

Ginnevra rose and sat with the others, made the right responses to the Revered's litany, but her mind couldn't stay focused on the service. Instead, she watched the Revered closely. The woman showed no signs of anything being wrong, nothing that might hint at her having been abducted and...what, exactly, did Ginnevra hope to find? There was no real mystery here. She didn't know the Revered at all, certainly not well enough to know if there was anything strange about her behavior. She was primed by the investigation to see conspiracy everywhere, that was all.

She bowed her head and laid her fingers against her grace while the Revered intoned the benediction, then sat while worshippers filed out in silence, their conversations beginning only when they'd left the sanctum. Finally, she and the anointed were the only ones left in the room, and Ginnevra shouldered her weapon and walked forward to greet them.

"It's good to see you again, my lady," the Revered said with a smile. "How goes your investigation?"

Since the afternoon had yielded no new information, this wasn't a question Ginnevra wanted to dwell on. "Slowly," she said. "But I now know the missing people are being abducted. My Aunt Caterrina escaped captivity, and I have reason to believe the others are still being held alive."

"Caterrina Cassaline?" The Revered's eyes widened. "I didn't know she was missing! Is she all right?"

"No, she was...hurt badly, and she's still unconscious. But I now have more of a direction in which to search."

"That's terrible," the Revered said. "She's a good friend. I can't believe anyone could be capable of overpowering her. I'll have to visit her soon."

"I hope for her full recovery. But that's not why I came. I actually wanted to talk to you about Lady Jiulliana Dolcebenette."

The Revered's expression was suddenly neutral. "What about Lady Jiulliana?"

Ginnevra glanced at Agostino, who looked grave as usual, then at the two Dedicates. Feora was watching the Revered. Rigarrda looked nervous. "I have reason to believe she's leading the people of Uparde astray."

Now the Revered was frowning. "She's not a heretic," she said.

"I have questioned her many times, and I'm satisfied she has made no claims that run counter to the Faith."

"She's not prophesying, yes, but she says she speaks with the voice of the Goddess. That can't be true."

"I'm not sure of that." The Revered shook her head to underscore her words. "True, she's not anointed, but there's no reason the Goddess might not touch an ordinary person with Her grace. And it's not as if she's deceiving anyone. Her advice seems sound."

Astonished, Ginnevra said, "But I understood you believed Lady Jiulliana was a fraud, if not a heretic." She glanced again at Agostino, who looked puzzled.

"I'm not qualified to pass judgment in that regard. I'm not a justicer." The Revered tilted her head to meet Ginnevra's eyes. "You seem very interested in proving me wrong."

"What? No, I don't—I'm sure you're—" Ginnevra caught herself. "That is, Lady Jiulliana told me things in the Goddess's name that I'm sure are false. That, to me, smacks of heresy. At the very least, she's giving bad advice people will take more seriously because they believe it comes from the Dark Lady. We have to do something about that."

"We?" The Revered raised an eyebrow in a speculative manner. "I see no reason to interfere. If Lady Jiulliana is a fraud and a heretic, she will eventually mis-step, and at that point, I will request that you arrest her. Until then, *we* will do nothing." She eyed Ginnevra, daring her to make an issue of that statement.

Ginnevra clenched her teeth to stop a harsh retort from emerging. The Revered was wrong. Ginnevra was sure of it. And yet the Revered also had more experience dealing with Lady Jiulliana, more personal contact...and what did Ginnevra have, really? A couple of cryptic exchanges and a handful of doubts. "Understood," she managed. "But I'm keeping an eye on her."

"That's your prerogative, so long as it doesn't turn into

harassment." The Revered continued toward the sanctum door. "I would have thought all your time was taken up by your investigation into the disappearances, but of course I know little of a paladin's role."

Ginnevra ground her teeth again. "It's true I'm very busy. But I should never be too busy that I lose sight of my primary responsibility to the Faith."

"That's true of all of us," Agostino said, in a tone of voice that said he wanted to send the conversation in a different direction. "My lady, is there anything we can do to help your investigation?"

Ginnevra resisted the urge to say *Do something about the heretic.* "I'd appreciate your prayers on Aunt Caterrina's behalf, of course. If she wakes up, she may be able to tell me who is responsible."

"We will gladly pray for a blessing on those treating her injuries," Agostino said. "And express our gratitude that my lady Cassaline's path brought her to safety."

"Thank you." Ginnevra headed for the front door.

"One more thing, my lady," the Revered said, following Ginnevra. "You said you have a direction for your investigation? May I ask what that is?"

Ginnevra stood in the doorway with her hand on the open door. Outside, Eodan rose from where he'd been sitting, but didn't approach. "Aunt Caterrina was seen—that is, I backtracked her to a neighborhood in west Uparde. Close to Lady Jiulliana's house, in fact. So that's where I'm searching."

The Revered nodded. "You might—"

She fell silent. Ginnevra, who'd been looking at Eodan, turned to ask her to continue. The Revered's face was frozen in an expression of horror, and her gaze was fixed on Eodan. With a shaking hand, the Revered tugged her smooth jet grace from beneath her robes and clutched it. "Monster!" she shouted. "Kill it now!"

EIGHTEEN

"No, stop!" Ginnevra shouted. She grabbed the Revered's wrist. "It's not what you think!"

The Revered's other hand, white-knuckled, held her grace as far from her body as the chain around her neck allowed. "*By Your grace the fire burns bright,*" she cried, and the fountain erupted with fire that made the water hiss. Eodan flung himself away from it and ended up in a crouch, his eyes fixed on Ginnevra.

Ginnevra felt sick with dread. "I said *stop,*" she exclaimed, wrenching the Revered around to face her. "He's not a monster. I can explain."

The Revered's eyes were wide, not with terror, but with fury. "Explain what?" she shouted, trying to tear away from Ginnevra's grasp. "It's a werewolf, come right into the middle of Uparde— come to *my chapel*—kill it now, before it attacks!"

"He's not going to attack. He's...Revered Parenogne, what you know about werewolves is mostly wrong—"

The Revered stopped fighting and stared, open-mouthed, at

Ginnevra. "You dare talk to me of heresy," she whispered. "You know that creature? And you haven't killed it? Werewolves are the pinnacle of the Bright One's creation, made to mock humanity. And yet you tell me—*me!*—I don't know a monster when I see one?"

"Please, Revered, listen to me!" Ginnevra slipped two fingers beneath her grace and pulled it fractionally away from her skin. "My grace is intact. How is that possible if I'm a heretic? I swear to you Eodan is no danger to anyone. He's not a monster. The werewolves—"

"It's gone," Agostino said. "It's loose in Uparde."

"What?" Ginnevra took her eyes off the Revered's furious face. The place where Eodan had crouched was empty. More dread filled her. Eodan had probably thought he would ease tensions by leaving, but it only made him look furtive and gave Ginnevra the lie. She pushed her fears away and said, "He just—listen, I'm telling the truth! The Blessed knows about him and she knows not all werewolves are monsters. Eodan is my companion. He's not evil. He's helped me fight monsters. He's a physician, damn it! Let go of your stupid preconceptions long enough to listen to what I say!"

"Stupid?" The Revered's voice was dangerously calm. "My calling is to serve the Dark Lady by protecting humans. So is yours —or at least I thought it was until you began spouting nonsense about werewolves not being monsters."

Ginnevra's grip on the Revered loosened, and the Revered snatched her arm away. "I don't know how you managed to trick the Blessed and the Goddess, but you are a heretic no matter what your grace looks like," she said. "I will not put up with your presence here. Agostino, send to the justiciary. They need to know a monster is loose in Uparde."

"The justicers and their guards can't fight a werewolf. They'll be torn apart," Agostino said. "That's the job of a—" He swallowed and stopped speaking, staring at Ginnevra.

"Fine," the Revered spat. She glared at Ginnevra. "In the morning, I'm sending to Devoyenne for a company of real paladins to hunt that monster. And you'd better hope they don't hunt you, as well."

Ginnevra stepped away. "You're making a mistake," she said, but her voice sounded weak and even she thought she sounded guilty.

The Revered glared at her, then shut the door. A moment later, Ginnevra heard the lock grind shut. She stared at the door until she became aware of people drawing near, their whispers awed comments on the fountain. Then she turned around. The fountain was grimy with soot through which trickles of water drew clean lines. Some of the trumpets sagged, melted by the heat of the Revered's fire, and water bubbled at their mouths without fountaining into the air. Ginnevra watched one trumpet struggle to spit water and do nothing but dribble like an infant blowing milky bubbles. Then she walked away, ignoring the crowds.

The streets teemed with people looking for entertainment, eating and drinking and cheering on performers whose music wafted from within taverns and inn taprooms. None of it touched Ginnevra. She felt she walked in a bubble of light and sound, impenetrable by anything so normal as merriment. The sword might have been responsible, but she couldn't rouse herself to care. She continued putting one foot in front of the other, letting instinct guide her, until the scent of pine and mint told her she'd reached the Golden Sickle.

She pushed open Caterrina's door as wearily as if she'd done more than cross Uparde at a leisurely walk. Pellarius was gone, but Eodan sat in the chair he'd used. Ginnevra's gaze immediately fixed on Caterrina. "It doesn't look like anything's changed."

Eodan rose. "Her color is better, and some of the bruises have faded," he said. "Ginnevra—"

"You were right," Ginnevra said dully. "She didn't want to listen. None of them did."

Eodan held her close, stroking her hair. "It's not your fault. They believe what they've been told—beloved, remember how hard it was for you to accept the truth? It was days before you trusted me. And they have no reason to believe in non-evil werewolves."

Ginnevra rested her head on his shoulder, breathing in the werewolf musk and remembering when it had represented what she hated. "It's not fair," she whispered.

"The world's not fair," Eodan replied. "Sometimes justice prevails, but that's the best we can hope for."

"I know. I just hoped I was wrong."

Eodan chuckled. "You've spent the last five years making the world a better place. Maybe you're not wrong."

Ginnevra sighed and raised her head. "I can't even figure out why people are disappearing. Some prime I turned out to be."

"It's been two days, beloved. Nobody could have done better." Eodan kissed her, sliding his hands around to caress her hips. She kissed him back, sinking deeper into his embrace until a small sound from the bed brought her back to the present. Caterrina's legs, which had been straight, were now bent at the knees as if she'd tried to stand.

With a gasp, Ginnevra flung herself at the bed only to have Eodan gently but firmly move her aside. "Don't get excited yet," he said, feeling for a pulse. Ginnevra clutched his shoulder, her heart beating so fast it hurt.

Caterrina's legs moved again, straightening. Then her eyes opened. "Aunt!" Ginnevra exclaimed.

Caterrina blinked twice, so slowly it seemed someone else was operating her eyelids. Then her eyes closed again, and she let out a long sigh.

"*Aunt!*" Ginnevra shouted, her hand closing more tightly on Eodan. "No, don't—"

"She's still alive, Ginnevra," Eodan said, straightening and letting go of Caterrina's wrist. "She's just not ready to wake up yet."

"Then what was that?"

"Her body heals faster than most people's. It makes sense that parts of it would recover faster than others. I doubt she saw you just now—that movement was just a reaction." Eodan put his arms around Ginnevra again. "This is a good sign, Ginnevra. I'm sure she'll recover fully."

His voice had a funny edge to it. "But...?" Ginnevra prompted.

Eodan sighed as deeply as Caterrina had. "There will be scars," he said. "And her foot was terribly mangled—I'm not sure how much mobility she'll have when it's healed. But she'll be alive. Hold to that."

Ginnevra nodded. "Where's Pellarius?"

"I took him back to his room. He shouldn't have to sit up all night with her. You and I can take turns sleeping." Eodan guided her to sit beside Caterrina. "I'll get our supper. You keep an eye on her. And then..." His voice trailed off. Ginnevra looked at him in inquiry. "What did the Revered threaten?"

"She's sending to Devoyenne in the morning for a company. She was going to tell the justiciary about the terrible, dangerous monster roaming Uparde, but Revered Abbate convinced her it was a bad idea." Ginnevra wished her memories didn't make her cringe. "So at least we don't have to worry about a mob. But... maybe you should leave Uparde."

"I can avoid a company of paladins, Ginnevra. I swore I

wouldn't leave you, remember?" He gripped her hand tightly, his eyes fierce. "This just means we have to work faster."

Ginnevra nodded. Far from reassuring her, Eodan's declaration just made her heart ache more. He shouldn't have to avoid her sister paladins. He shouldn't have to hide. She reminded herself that life wasn't fair and squeezed his hand in return. "The kidnappers have to be somewhere in west Uparde," she said. "We'll search there more thoroughly in the morning."

"That's the way to see it," Eodan said, and left the room.

Ginnevra sat back in her chair and thought of nothing until Eodan returned with a whole roast chicken, neatly sectioned, and a bowl of oven-roasted root vegetables speckled with herbs. He had a bottle of wine tucked under one arm and a couple of glasses held by the stems between his fingers. "We clearly don't stay at the right kinds of inns," he said at her exclamation of delight. "Drommio, the innkeeper, acted like serving us was the high point of his week. He didn't even make a fuss about how there are too many of us in this room."

"Money can buy a lot of things," Ginnevra said.

They laid out the food on the other bed and ate heartily. The wine was good without being outstanding, and Ginnevra drank more than she normally would, feeling the need for some release after the tension of the past few days. Then, at Eodan's urging, she cleared the dishes off the bed and lay down. For a while, she watched Eodan's profile as he sat beside Caterrina, for once not thinking about how handsome he was. She examined the bridge of his nose, the curves of his lips and chin, how his eyelid drooped over his one visible eye without being fully closed. There was nothing about him that said "werewolf" except the musky smell, and even that wasn't terribly strong tonight.

"Eodan," she said, "do werewolves ever try to pass for human?"

Eodan glanced at her. "Sometimes. When we need things we don't produce ourselves, we go into human cities. Often we steal what we need, but some of us pretend to be human and engage in trade. But it's never on a long-term basis, because no one wants to be isolated from the pack. Why?"

"I was just thinking...everyone we've encountered so far has believed you were human. Except the Revered, obviously. I wonder if we can't do something with that. Let people get to know you so they don't fear you."

Eodan smiled. "It's not a bad idea. If we can stay well away from paladins and the anointed, it might even work."

"It certainly worked on that young woman today," Ginnevra teased.

Eodan gave her a wicked smile. "It's nice to know I have options."

"My love, I'd have to hunt down and destroy anyone who tried to take you away from me. Do you want to condemn some poor girl to that fate?"

Eodan stood and crossed to loom over her where she lay. "That's quite the threat," he said, his smile still promising trouble. He climbed into bed and took her in his arms. "I, on the other hand," he murmured into her cheek, "would happily make disappear any man who dared try to take my place in your heart. It's werewolf tradition."

"Is it really?"

"No. Just my own inclination."

Ginnevra kissed him and warmed all over to hear him make a noise deep in his throat that was almost a growl of pleasure. "Caterrina's right over there," she said.

"I know. This is just a reminder." Eodan kissed her back. "I love you, and we will figure this out. All of it. How's that for optimistic?"

"That's very good. You must have been practicing."

"I have the best teacher," Eodan said.

SHE SLEPT UNTIL AFTER MIDNIGHT, when Eodan woke her to take his place at Caterrina's bedside. Ginnevra's body still ached with tiredness, but she quickly found herself alert and awake despite her weariness. Eodan had left one lamp burning low, just enough to give Ginnevra's enhanced eyesight a boost, and she sat and watched Caterrina sleep and let her thoughts and worries battle within her for supremacy.

Maybe it was time to involve the justiciary guards in the search for the missing people. They had the manpower to quarter the west side, searching for anywhere a lot of people could be held. *Or their bodies disposed of*, her tiny pessimistic inner voice said. She ignored it. Nothing she could do about that if it turned out to be true, and a pile of bodies might even be easier to locate. She groaned inwardly at the gruesome thought.

On the other hand, a squad of guards, or several squads, might scare the kidnappers into doing away with their captives, if the missing people were still alive. No, on the whole it was better she continue to search alone until she was closer to the truth.

The thought of squads searching the city led her back to the Revered's threat to send for a company of paladins to hunt Eodan. That wasn't as frightening a threat as the Revered probably thought, given that Ginnevra was confident in Eodan's ability to stay hidden. It was the idea of confronting that company's captain and trying to convince her Eodan wasn't evil that lowered Ginnevra's spirits. If she was lucky, it would be a company she knew and a captain who remembered her, because primes might command respect, but they didn't outrank captains except under certain circumstances. In any case, she and Eodan might be leaving Uparde at a run, without having solved the mystery.

If only the Revered had listened! Ginnevra pinched the bridge of her nose and squeezed her eyes shut. She wished she knew the woman at all, to know whether she was behaving strangely. Agostino and the Dedicates hadn't acted as if her behavior was out of the ordinary, but Ginnevra was sure something was wrong. Something the majordomo Lanberto had said...she should have taken notes the way the prime Dolcea said was essential in talking to people, but she hadn't had a way to do that and she hadn't wanted to delay her investigation for anything. Now she had only her memory to go on. Lanberto had said...he'd said the Revered was dedicated to the people of Uparde, and she didn't visit deathbeds. And she believed strongly in sacred spaces.

Ginnevra's eyes flew open. "Sacred spaces," she whispered. No ceremonies performed anywhere but the chapel and that room in the residence. And yet the Revered had gone to perform a wedding at her sister's home. Sister or no, that was definitely out of character. Which meant...what? The Revered might be lying about where she'd gone, or about why she'd gone there. And any lies raised suspicion about what the Revered was doing now.

But Ginnevra couldn't guess what the Revered might actually have done that she'd felt the need to lie about it. And it couldn't possibly have anything to do with the rest of the disappearances, because except for the Revered and Caterrina, none of the missing people had returned. They had nothing in common.

This brought Ginnevra back to contemplating her search of the west side. Mansions, upscale businesses, markets...it hardly seemed the place for a den of kidnappers, as if Ginnevra had any idea where kidnappers usually lurked. But Caterrina had definitely escaped from somewhere in that part of Uparde. Somewhere near Lady Jiulliana's house. Ginnevra dearly wished she had a reason to believe the woman was behind the disappearances. It would solve all her problems perfectly.

On the other hand...maybe it was just the lateness of the hour talking, but why *shouldn't* she investigate Lady Jiulliana more closely? True, the woman probably wasn't kidnapping people herself, but suppose it was her household? Ginnevra immediately scoffed at her foolishness. Lady Jiulliana had no reason to want to kidnap people. She certainly wasn't holding them for ransom. It was just Ginnevra's dislike of the woman that made her think such ridiculous thoughts, that and her desire to solve the mystery.

She's in the neighborhood, Ginnevra's pesky inner voice said. *You could ask around.* And she probably should, she realized. She ought to ask the same questions she'd asked Lady Jiulliana's staff of the neighbors. That wouldn't even be a distraction from the investigation. She tried not to feel triumphant at the idea.

She trimmed the lamp when it burned low and stretched. The shadows on Caterrina's face made the bruises look deeper, angering Ginnevra again. Then she realized Caterrina's eyes were open. She dropped to her knees beside the bed and took Caterrina's hand. "Aunt?" she said quietly. "Aunt, it's Ginnevra. Can you hear me?"

Caterrina blinked. She ran her tongue over her lips to moisten them. Then she opened her mouth and let out a hissing breath. Ginnevra clutched her hand more tightly, afraid to speak. Caterrina's lips moved, but no sound emerged. Tears leaked from her eyes to spill over the sides of her face.

"It's all right, Aunt, you don't have to speak," Ginnevra said. "You're badly hurt. Just lie still. Eodan is treating you, and you'll recover soon."

Caterrina's head flopped from side to side in a "no" that made the tears come faster. Her lips moved again, and this time Ginnevra heard the faintest whisper of sound emerge. "Do you know who did this to you?" Ginnevra asked. "Can you tell me where to look? It's not just you, Aunt, there are so many other people missing—"

The same "no" gesture stopped Ginnevra's speech. Caterrina closed her eyes, and once more her lips moved. The whisper was stronger this time, but even Ginnevra's enhanced hearing still couldn't make out words. Then Caterrina sagged, relaxing back into unconsciousness.

Ginnevra realized she was crying, too. She let go of Caterrina's hand and wiped her eyes. It was good news, really, but she couldn't help wishing Caterrina had been able to communicate something that would help Ginnevra find her kidnapper. She settled back into the chair and prayed, not to find the kidnapper —that would be asking for a given future, which was blasphemous—but that her skills and strength would be enough to carry her through this challenge.

When she started feeling hungry, she left the room and went to the kitchen to request breakfast. The cook was remarkably helpful, given that it probably wasn't his job to wait on inn patrons, and provided her with rolls and fruit and cold sliced ham and a small cask of new ale. The air smelled fresh and cool outside, with the promise of summer's end, and despite her various concerns Ginnevra felt more sanguine than she had in days.

Eodan was stirring when she returned and accepted an apple with thanks. "How is she?" he asked.

"She woke an hour or so ago. She was conscious and aware, but she tried to speak and couldn't. That's still good, right?"

Eodan nodded. "She just needs to rest. She'll be fine, Ginnevra." He stood. "I'll go see if Pellarius wants to join us for breakfast. Then we can settle him in to watch her while we investigate."

Ginnevra, her mouth full of ham, just nodded.

She expected him back immediately, given that Pellarius's room was just next door, but a long time passed before Eodan returned. He was breathing heavily and looked worried. "We have a problem."

"Don't tell me Pellarius's injuries have gone bad?" Ginnevra said.

"Worse than that," Eodan said. "Pellarius is missing."

NINETEEN

"He can't be missing," Ginnevra said. "He can't walk. Where would he go?"

"He can walk, after a fashion," Eodan said. He came fully into the room and shut the door. "I found him a crutch yesterday after...the chapel. I thought it might be good if he could get around, enough to get help if Caterrina woke up."

"Even so, he wouldn't just leave," Ginnevra said. "Maybe he's getting breakfast."

"I asked in the kitchen. They hadn't seen him. Neither had anyone in the private parlor where they serve meals to patrons." Eodan shook his head. "If he left—"

"It had to have been this morning," Ginnevra cut in. "He has to know he's especially vulnerable to robbery or attack in his condition, and going out at night would be dangerous. So he's only been gone an hour or so, and we can track him. He's not exactly inconspicuous."

Eodan gave her a level stare. "If he was kidnapped, none of that applies."

"We don't know he was kidnapped." It sounded weak even to her, but she pressed forward. "It's more likely—"

"Ginnevra. This is exactly the pattern we've seen in all the other disappearances. Late night or early morning, and the person gives no hint that they intend to leave the city." Eodan put a hand on her shoulder. "And he knows we're depending on him to watch Caterrina. He wouldn't walk away from that."

Ginnevra nodded. "You're right. But that means we have to move quickly. All the evidence says that the others weren't taken forcibly. No one saw anyone suspicious in the neighborhood when they disappeared. So Pellarius left this morning, or last night even, for some unrelated reason, and he was snatched. But as I said, he's conspicuous. If we go now, we might be able to find people who saw him."

"I need to find someone to sit with Caterrina. Wait here," Eodan said, and left the room.

Ginnevra stood looking down on her sleeping aunt. She looked less restless than she had an hour ago. Ginnevra hoped that was a good sign. When Eodan returned, ushering in a wide-eyed serving girl before him, she said, "What if she wakes up while we're gone?"

"Anatolla knows what to do," Eodan said. "If she wakes up, tell her what I said, all right?"

Anatolla swallowed nervously, but her nod was firm and certain. "Thank you," Ginnevra said, and hurried after Eodan.

Outside the Golden Sickle, she cast her gaze up and down the street. "You go that way," she said, pointing, and headed off in the other direction.

There were any number of businesses along the road, most of them street vendors selling food to the many passersby who hadn't had time for a real breakfast. No one had seen a man with a crutch hobbling past that morning. Ginnevra was about to accost yet another vendor when someone took her elbow. "He went this way," Eodan said. "Hurry."

She ran with Eodan back the other way, heading west. Almost immediately, they came out in one of Uparde's marketplaces, not a big one, but it might as well have sprawled across half the city so far as finding one man went. The noise of hundreds of people carrying on transactions and conversations filled the air, along with the scents of sausages and fruit and hot bread. "We're never going to find him in here," she said.

"Don't give up yet," Eodan said. "The woman I talked to said she saw him stop at—there." He pointed at a cart piled high with apples and pears.

They ran, dodging pedestrians, and came to a flying halt at the cart. The elderly man standing beside it eyed them suspiciously. "You in a hurry to buy my wares?"

"Sieur, we're looking for a man," Ginnevra said. "About so tall, full beard, walks supported by a crutch. Did you speak to him?"

The vendor's eyes narrowed further. "Speak to a lot of people," he said, rubbing the fingers of one hand together.

Ginnevra rolled her eyes and dug in her purse for a couple of dinas. She slapped them into his hastily outstretched hand. "Was he one of them?"

The man handed her a rosy pink and yellow apple and tossed one to Eodan. "Sure," he said. "Asked me directions."

"Where to?" Ginnevra shifted her grip on her sword belt, making the hilt bob above her shoulder. "Come, sieur, this is important."

The man stared at the sword as if he'd only just noticed it. "He asked me directions to some woman's house. Lady Jiorgia, or Jiutta."

"Jiulliana?" Eodan said.

"That's the one." The man tapped his nose in acknowledgement. "I couldn't help him. Never heard of her. Told him he could ask Petrocchus over there." He smiled unpleasantly. "Petrocchus knows everyone in Uparde."

Ginnevra didn't have time to press the old man on his odd reaction. "Thank you, sieur," she said, and pushed through the growing crowd to the stall he'd indicated. The mouthwatering smell of sausages rose from the little stove perched atop the stall, and many men and women crowded around it and the sausage vendor. He was a big man with beefy arms and a large stomach, the very picture of a jolly street merchant, down to his hearty laugh. Ginnevra shoved through the crowd, snarling at the one woman who protested and making her back up a step.

"Sieur, a moment of your time," she shouted over the din.

Petrocchus looked her way briefly, then focused sharply on the sword. "My lady, interested in a sausage? On the house. Anything for a servant of the Goddess."

"Thank you, no, sieur, just—"

"No? Are you sure? I sell the best sausages in Uparde. Only the freshest meat, nothing added." He pulled a steaming sausage out of the little stove and slapped it into a roll sliced lengthwise, then offered it to her.

"Sieur, truly, I need information—"

Petrocchus' eyes narrowed. "Are you suggesting I tell my customers' secrets? Not even for a paladin, say I! Never in my life would I give away—"

"*Sieur.*" Ginnevra stopped his flood of words with a sharp glare and one hand on the sword. "Did you serve a man with a crutch earlier? Small man, thick beard? He's in danger and I must find him."

Petrocchus' expression turned startled. "In danger? That little fellow? Why, I wouldn't have thought it, but I suppose if he's gimpy, he can't run away. Is that what it was, he's fleeing justice? Because I can't see why a paladin would be tasked with finding such easy prey, but—"

"Just tell me where he went!"

The big man jumped. "You don't have to yell," he said. "He bought a sausage and asked directions to Lady Jiulliana's house. He was polite enough, so I told him."

Ginnevra snatched the sausage out of his hand. "Thank you, sieur," she said, and pushed her way back out of the crowd.

She broke the sausage roll in half and handed half to Eodan. "Why would he go to Lady Jiulliana's house?" she said, taking a bite.

"I don't know, but maybe things aren't as dire as we believed. He might still be there, and if he had to wait outside, that would explain why he 'disappeared'." Eodan bit into his roll. "This is really good."

"At the very least, we can check there, and if that Marcellus person didn't see him, we'll know he disappeared from the very small area between here and Lady Jiulliana's street." Ginnevra stuffed the rest of the roll into her mouth and hurried on.

Past the market, the streets were less crowded, and they made their way westward with ease. The city was more familiar now that Ginnevra had spent days walking all over it, and she recognized the streets near Caterrina's house. Maybe she could be the one to draw the map of the city she'd wished for.

At the small plaza with seven streets leading off it, they ran into another crowd, but a smaller one, centered on the fountain at the heart of the plaza. Ginnevra glanced up at it as she hurried past. White marble fish shot jets of water from their mouths through hoops of brass. She remembered the ruined fountain outside the chapel, and a sick feeling washed over her. The

Revered would have sent to Devoyenne at first light, and it was only a day's travel from Uparde to that city, which meant in two days Ginnevra would have to face a company of paladins and try to convince them Eodan was no threat. She pushed the thought away. No time for distractions.

"My lady! My lady Cassaline!"

Ginnevra stopped a few feet from the fountain and searched the crowd for whoever had addressed her. A moment later, she saw a couple of men dressed in justicers' robes hurrying toward her. With dismay, she recognized one of them as Ciutto Baroccius. Ciutto looked smugly pleased; the stranger looked concerned.

Eodan, who'd kept going, returned to her side. "We don't have time for this," he muttered.

"I know, but maybe we can get it over with quickly," she replied.

The two justicers, breathing heavily, slowed as they approached. "My lady, I'm sorry to disturb you," the unknown justicer said. "I'm Piettro Veltranne." He bowed low, lower than was strictly necessary. "I'm afraid there's been a misunderstanding."

"Has there?" Ginnevra said. She glanced once at Ciutto, whose smile was positively blinding with malice, and then ignored him.

"Yes, I'm afraid...you see, the investigation of the missing people...you should not have had that forced on you." Piettro's nervous smile and his clasped hands made him look like a supplicant and grated on Ginnevra's nerves. "I'm afraid one of our clerks misunderstood the situation. Ciutto Baroccius is responsible for that investigation."

"I see," Ginnevra said. "Then when Sieur Baroccius gave the documentation to me—"

"I did no such thing," Ciutto said hotly. "That clerk was the one who usurped my authority. I demand you return that documentation to me so I can carry out my sworn duties."

Ginnevra felt like screaming. "Sieur Baroccius, you must have forgotten our conversation at the justiciary. You were very clear that you believed this investigation beneath you."

"You're mistaken." Ciutto glared at Ginnevra. She returned his look with her best steely-eyed stare and was pleased to see him falter briefly.

It was a short-lived moment. Piettro stepped forward, breaking Ginnevra's line of sight, and said, "Come, sieur, my lady, surely reasonable people can come to agreement? This really isn't something we expect of a paladin and a visitor to our city. The justiciary is honored that you have been willing to give your valuable time to our service, but legally, it's the duty of the justiciary to carry out such investigations. I'm sure you understand."

Eodan laid a hand on Ginnevra's arm. "We understand, don't we?" he murmured.

Ginnevra ground her back teeth together. "Fine," she said. "Come to Caterrina Cassaline's house this evening—"

"Now," Ciutto said. "This is an important investigation that should not be delayed." He sounded so triumphant it took all Ginnevra's discipline not to punch him in the face.

She took a deep breath, let it out slowly, then turned on her heel and walked to the far side of the plaza, to the street leading to Caterrina's house.

The two justicers trailed behind her, while Eodan paced beside. "We don't have time for this," he said.

"I know. You should go to Lady Jiulliana's. I'll meet you there."

"Is it a good idea to separate?"

Ginnevra shook her head. "It's a worse idea to lose Pellarius's trail. Go on."

Eodan turned and ran back the way they'd come.

"Where is he going?" Ciutto demanded.

"That's none of your business," Ginnevra shot back over her shoulder.

A hand fell on her shoulder. "He'd better not—" Ciutto began.

Ginnevra grabbed Ciutto's wrist and spun him around, twisting his arm painfully behind his back. "Did you just touch me without my permission?" she hissed.

"Now, my lady, my lady, there's no need—it was a misunderstanding—" Piettro said in a whining, pleading voice that made Ginnevra even angrier.

"You people seem to have a lot of misunderstandings," she said, and released Ciutto with a shove that sent him stumbling several feet away. "The next 'misunderstanding' is going to be resolved by my sword, understand?"

Ciutto glared at her, but rubbed his wrist and said nothing.

Ginnevra led the way around the house to the kitchen door, but stopped the men when they would have followed her inside. "My aunt isn't here to welcome you, so I'm not at liberty to let you in. I'll be back."

She stormed up the stairs to the library and shoved all the documentation into the sack. For a moment, she considered keeping the book where she'd taken all her notes, but reminded herself that information gathered in the course of an investigation belonged to the justiciary and thrust it in on top of the scroll cases.

Downstairs, she handed the sack to Ciutto, who looked briefly dismayed. Ginnevra thought it might be the prospect of carrying a sack through the streets like a common laborer that offended his patrician heart. "That's everything," she said. "Now, if you'll excuse me, I have business elsewhere."

"That 'business' had better not be searching for the missing people," Ciutto said. "That's no longer your concern."

"You can't stop me looking," Ginnevra said.

"Actually, my lady," Piettro said, still in that whining, placating voice, "you don't have authority over the investigation anymore. Sieur Baroccius is in charge. And two investigators, well, you'd interfere with each other, and there would be confusion in the public mind..."

Ginnevra stared at him. He smiled back at her, a weak smile, and she could almost hear him thinking *please don't force the issue, Goddess help me, that sword is taller than I am.* "Fine," she said. "No more investigating the missing people."

Piettro's smile became more genuine. "Thank you for your assistance to date, my lady."

"Yes, thank you," Ciutto said. His smile looked positively vulpine.

Ginnevra ignored both of them and walked away. When she reached the main street, she ran.

She turned the corner onto Lady Jiulliana's street and saw the crowd, larger than usual, with Eodan hovering on its outskirts. He came to meet her. "Pellarius was here," he said. "Some of the petitioners said Marcellus let him in about half an hour ago."

Ginnevra sagged. "What a relief. Should we go around back to meet him when he leaves? I'd really like to know why he came here."

Eodan looked grim. "He entered, but I didn't see him leave."

"Well, the back door is concealed. He might have gone another way."

"Something's not right here," Eodan said. "It's possible I just didn't see him, but I don't know."

Ginnevra glanced at the crowd. "I don't understand. Why would he still be inside? Unless he and Lady Jiulliana really hit it off and they're having tea and cakes together."

"This isn't funny," Eodan said. "I don't have an explanation.

Just a really bad feeling. And now you're no longer authorized to hunt for the missing people, so you can't burst in on that house demanding Lady Jiulliana release Pellarius."

"I'm not looking for the missing people. I'm looking for an injured friend who may need help." Ginnevra watched as the door opened and another person was led inside. "Let's go around back, just to be sure. And then we'll have to return to the inn, because if Pellarius left without you seeing him, that's where he would go."

Eodan looked like he wanted to protest, but he merely nodded and followed Ginnevra.

A woman passed them as they walked around the corner. She was crying and didn't pay any attention to them. On a whim, Ginnevra stopped her. "Excuse me. Did you visit Lady Jiulliana?"

The woman nodded. "It's private," she said dully. "Let me go."

"Sorry," Ginnevra said. When the woman was out of earshot, she told Eodan, "That confirms somebody else entered after Pellarius. And I don't see him anywhere." Ahead, the garden gate hung open slightly. Ginnevra walked over to it and looked inside Lady Jiulliana's garden. "And he's not here."

"Let's hurry," Eodan said. "If I'm right, and he's still in there—"

"We'll look stupid if we burst in on that house and it turns out he just returned to the inn." Ginnevra broke into a run. "But you're right, we have to hurry."

Pellarius's room at the Golden Sickle was empty. Ginnevra pushed open the door to Caterrina's room, startling the serving girl whose name Ginnevra had forgotten. "Has anyone else stopped by?" she asked.

The girl shook her head. "And my lady paladin hasn't moved or woken at all," she said.

"Thank you," Ginnevra said. She waited for Eodan to check Caterrina's pulse before stepping outside with him.

"He's there," Eodan said. "I don't know why, and I don't know what might have happened. But I'm sure he's there."

"Then we have to go back," Ginnevra said.

"But you don't have authority to walk in without an invitation anymore." Eodan pursed his lips in thought. "What do we do if she won't see you?"

"Use our initiative," Ginnevra said.

CHAPTER

TWENTY

They ran through the streets, dodging pedestrians and a couple of riders on a matched pair of beautiful black horses, until they came within sight of Lady Jiulliana's door. Ginnevra stopped Eodan at the corner when he would have gone on. "We have to think about how to approach," she said. "I can't lie outright about my purpose for being there—the Goddess doesn't like Her paladins misrepresenting their authority."

"I've heard you tell lies before, though," Eodan said.

"It's not so much the lying as it is telling people I'm authorized to act in Her name when I'm not. The Goddess has been known to punish Her servants for doing that because it can lead to paladins or anointed elevating themselves instead of honoring the Dark Lady." Ginnevra looked past Eodan at the waiting crowd. "But we have to get inside."

"Hmm." Eodan followed the line of her gaze. "Let's try a different approach."

Ginnevra followed him to the rear of the crowd, where as usual no one paid them any attention until Ginnevra began pushing her way through to the front. Dire mutterings rose up and subsided as the waiting people registered the presence of the sword. Ginnevra smiled politely and thanked those she pushed gently to the side. She and Eodan reached the door just as it shut on Marcellus and a petitioner. Eodan took a few more steps forward and faced the crowd.

"How many of you are here because your loved ones have gone missing?" he called out, his voice carrying to the far side of the street even though the crowd was quiet as usual.

No one moved for a few moments. Then someone near the center of the mass of people, someone too short for Ginnevra to see, answered, "My mother disappeared seven days ago. I've been coming here for five days, hoping Lady Jiulliana has an answer for me."

"And I," said a man tall enough to stand out among his neighbors. "My brother is gone."

A few more people spoke up, some waving hands in the air to get Eodan's attention. Eodan waited until the responses ceased, then said, "Lady Jiulliana told my lady paladin she cannot find missing people. But you shouldn't give up hope. The justicers are investigating, and you're encouraged to report any missing people to Ciutto Baroccius."

Ginnevra stared at Eodan. She had no idea what he was up to. Encouraging people to report to Ciutto wouldn't get her and Eodan inside Lady Jiulliana's house.

The short person in the middle of the crowd, a woman Ginnevra still couldn't see, said, "What do you mean, Lady Jiulliana can't find missing people? She has the Goddess's sight!"

"I'm afraid her gifts just don't reach that far," Eodan said, his voice low and sad. "I hope you weren't informed otherwise."

"But...no one else can help me!" the tall man said. Tears shone in his eyes. "My brother is only fifteen, and I know something bad has happened to him. Lady Jiulliana is my only hope."

"The justicers—" Eodan began.

"Damn the justicers," the tall man shouted. "They don't care about anyone who doesn't have hundreds of aurins to pay them off. And I think *you* are lying about Lady Jiulliana."

"It's not a lie," Ginnevra said. "She told me herself she couldn't find my aunt, that she didn't have that gift. It's you who've been lied to."

The murmur of the crowd redoubled. Somewhere in the back, a scuffle broke out and was stopped by men hauling the combatants apart. Someone else, possibly the short woman, burst into noisy tears. Ginnevra, still at a loss for what Eodan's plan was, shouted, "Calm down, everyone! I'm sure the Lady Jiulliana has wisdom for each of you."

"I don't want wisdom, I want my Enreo back," another woman shouted. "I'll make Lady Jiulliana tell me where he is!"

The crowd surged forward, forcing Ginnevra a step back. Swiftly, she drew her sword, casting aside the scabbard, and took up a defensive position. "That's enough," she roared, and the first rank of people stopped and were piled into by those coming up behind. "It's true Lady Jiulliana can't find missing people. I'll attest to that—unless you want to call a paladin a liar?"

The murmuring subsided. Ginnevra caught the eyes of as many people as she could, fixing them with a steady gaze most of them couldn't meet. "If you were led to believe otherwise, that's something you should take up with Lady Jiulliana. I'm sure she'll be happy to explain her gifts. *If* she chooses to speak with you. Some of you have come back day after day and never seen the lady. You can certainly go on doing that—or you could speak to the anointed at the chapel. You know, the anointed who have served Uparde faithfully for years? I realize it's always exciting when someone new comes to town, but didn't it occur to any of you that Revered Parenogne and Revered Abbate and the Dedicates do everything Lady Jiulliana does? Hanging on the words of a stranger...not exactly the nicest thing to do to them, is it?"

She had no idea where the words came from, but they poured out of her as smoothly as if she had a script in front of her. To her astonishment, the muttering began again, but this time, it sounded abashed. "The Goddess gives Her gifts where She will," she continued, "and she may or may not have given them to Lady Jiulliana, but She has most certainly bestowed Her blessing on the anointed of Uparde's chapel. And they don't pick and choose who they'll pass that blessing on to. Everyone is entitled to a moment of their time, as I'm sure those of you who received your graces at their hands know."

Hands flew up to touch chests, the spots where their obsidian graces lay beneath their clothes. Men and women looked at each other, then looked away. Two people at the back of the crowd turned and walked away, their heads bowed. Then it was five people. Then, like a clump of earth dropped into a river, the crowd dissolved, men and women and children dispersing in all directions. Some of them glanced at Ginnevra and Eodan before walking away, looking ashamed.

When the street was empty except for them, Eodan let out a deep whoosh of breath and said, "That's not what I expected."

"What did you expect?" Ginnevra asked.

"I was hoping a few of them might decide to go to the justiciary to report their missing loved ones. I didn't think you were going to clear the crowd. How did you know what to say?"

"I...don't know." Everything she'd said had felt right and perfect, leaving her with a warmth inside her chest. She gathered up the scabbard and sheathed her sword, slinging it over her shoulder. "It just came out that way. Maybe...sometimes the

Goddess gifts us with wisdom in the moment, and maybe that's what it was."

"You mean you spoke with the Goddess's voice?" Eodan sounded alarmed.

"I don't think that's how it works. I didn't feel compelled or overridden, just...right. But I don't know for sure that it *doesn't* work that way. It's not something I ever expected to happen to me." Ginnevra turned to face the door. "Marcellus might still not let us in."

"If Lady Jiulliana is as insightful as she claims, she'll know what happened and she'll want more than ever to speak with us," Eodan said, turning with her.

They waited, not speaking, for several moments that felt stretched out into an hour, though Ginnevra judged it wasn't more than ten minutes. She examined the grille and the door. Abstract carvings covered the door, but the wrought iron of the grille obscured the details. The bars were gently twisted rather than smooth, and the top arched to match the top of the door. Ginnevra examined the lock with her eyes rather than her hands, not wanting to make herself look like trouble for interfering with the grille, and saw it had both an integrated lock and a padlock. Between the locks and its weight, the grille would protect the house door well.

She startled out of her reverie when the door creaked open and Marcellus swung open the grille. His eyes widened. "Where did they all go?"

"Prior commitments?" Eodan said blandly.

"They didn't say," Ginnevra said. "May we speak to Lady Jiulliana?"

Marcellus swallowed. "It was...you are not the ones summoned."

"No, but we are the ones here," Ginnevra pointed out, not

smiling in case he decided she was mocking him and closed the door on her permanently.

Marcellus swallowed again. "I...will confer with my lady," he said, and shut both doors.

"So she didn't know they'd all left," Eodan said in a low voice.

"That's good news. She doesn't know everything." Ginnevra tamped down on the surge of satisfaction this gave her. She didn't need to be distracted by feeling unreasonably vindicated.

They waited again. This time, Ginnevra watched the street in both directions. If more petitioners showed up, that might result in Ginnevra and Eodan's visit being put off again. But no one appeared, not even anyone just interested in passing through. No one entered or left any of the other houses on the street. It had just occurred to Ginnevra to wonder if the other houses were even occupied, they were that quiet, when Marcellus reappeared and bowed them inside.

It felt as if the lights in the hallway glowed more brightly, making the hall feel bigger than before. More delicious smells, these of roast mutton and warm cream, filled the air. Ginnevra eyed the white doors with their elaborate carvings and wondered what rooms lay beyond. They looked too fancy for ordinary household offices or pantries. On the other hand, they gave the ground floor an elegant appearance, and maybe the owner had simply wanted guests to feel they weren't being made to pass through the most utilitarian parts of the house. The hall certainly felt more welcoming than the Revered's residence.

They rose out of the stairwell into the grand chamber with its tall ceiling. The chairs with their tapestry cushions had been rearranged since the last time Ginnevra had been there, spread out into a semicircle with Lady Jiulliana's chamber door as its focus. Ginnevra reflected on how she'd considered this possibility and asked, "Are you planning a large gathering, then?"

Marcellus glanced over his shoulder at her. "Lady Jiulliana hosts readings on occasion. She has cultivated the acquaintance of many poets and fabulists in Uparde and beyond. One such gathering happens tonight."

"That sounds interesting." In truth, the only interesting thing about it was how Lady Jiulliana attended such gatherings. They couldn't fit that bed through the door, and Ginnevra had trouble imagining any of Lady Jiulliana's servants doing anything so intimate as carrying her to a chair.

Marcellus opened the door and bowed again. Ginnevra nodded in return and entered the bedchamber.

Her eyes instantly adjusted to the light, which was so low as to shroud the room in perpetual twilight. Lady Jiulliana sat as usual in her bed, the blanket pulled up over her motionless legs. She held the ruby pendant between her fingers and rubbed it idly as Ginnevra and Eodan took up their now-customary places beside the chairs. "I don't suppose you can explain where everyone went?" she asked. Her voice was as pleasant and non-threatening as if she'd asked for a report on the weather.

"I don't know where they went," Ginnevra said, perfectly truthfully.

"I hope you didn't scare them off," Lady Jiulliana said. "Those people are in need of the Goddess's guidance."

"I agree, and that's what I told them." Ginnevra smiled. "Perhaps they decided they could find that guidance elsewhere."

Lady Jiulliana's pleasant expression didn't fade. "Influenced by you. My lady, have I done something to offend you, that you want to prevent me sharing the Goddess's wisdom with the city?"

"I believe in accepting what the Goddess gives regardless of the source," Ginnevra said, "and if you are that source, I won't stop you. I simply question whether that's true."

Lady Jiulliana hitched herself slightly forward. "I am no heretic."

"That's what the Revered says, and I'm sure I believe her." Ginnevra stepped forward one pace. "Have you heard? The Revered Massina Parenogne has returned. She wasn't missing, after all."

Dark brows rose in a pale face. "How wonderful! That must ease your mind considerably, my lady."

"It would if I weren't so concerned about everyone else who *is* missing." Ginnevra kept her voice calm. "They disappeared from this neighborhood, did you know that?"

"I was unaware of that." Lady Jiulliana turned the pendant so the ruby caught the low light and reflected it back at Ginnevra. "Did the Revered say where she'd been?"

"Visiting family in Guinio." Ginnevra took another step. "The message about her trip went astray. But I wonder."

"Oh? Wonder what?"

"The Revered is very strict about the places she's willing to perform sacred rites. And yet she says she traveled to Guinio to perform a marriage in someone's house. That seems out of character."

"I wouldn't know," Lady Jiulliana said, still toying with the ruby pendant. "But you sound as if you've drawn some conclusions."

"I'm getting there," Ginnevra said. "But I have a few questions for you."

Lady Jiulliana's dark eyes widened. "Surely you don't suspect me of foul play?"

Ginnevra smiled again. "Where is Pellarius Schiatte?"

She half expected Lady Jiulliana to deny knowing the name, but the woman said, "Has he gone missing, too? I spoke to him not an hour ago—surely that's not enough time to consider him missing?"

"Then you did speak to him. May I ask what he wanted to know?"

Lady Jiulliana laughed. "Oh, my lady paladin, you must realize I can't give away my visitors' secrets. I can tell you Pellarius left satisfied with my answer. Perhaps you should ask him yourself."

"I would if he weren't missing," Ginnevra shot back. She glanced at Eodan, wondering why he hadn't spoken yet. His eyes were fixed on Lady Jiulliana, and he stood very still, poised to attack. "Very well. I appreciate that you won't violate your visitors' privacy. Will you tell me why you chose to speak to him? That is, why him out of all those people waiting for your wisdom?"

"That's a different question, yes." Lady Jiulliana looked thoughtful. "The Goddess's wisdom is like a small voice whispering in my ear, but in thoughts and feelings rather than audible words. And with those thoughts come the names of those for whom the wisdom is intended. I assume the Goddess knows who is most in need of wisdom, or who is prepared to hear Her words at this time."

As Lady Jiulliana spoke, Ginnevra looked again at Eodan, more closely this time. He looked ready to leap at the woman on the bed, leaning slightly forward, his hands clenched at his sides. "That sounds like predicting the future," she said, not looking away from Eodan.

"Not at all. It feels more like a recognition of where a person is on their life's journey at the moment I receive wisdom for him or her." Lady Jiulliana ran her finger over the ruby's largest surface. "And I have wisdom for you—if you're willing to humble yourself to accept it."

Ginnevra still didn't take her eyes off Eodan. "You've given me wisdom before. Once to a customer, isn't that right?" She took a few steps toward Eodan. He didn't move, didn't turn his head. He wasn't blinking. Swiftly, Ginnevra grabbed his arm and tried to make him look at her. He swung around like a marionette on a string, his eyes glassy and his expression vacant.

"What is this?" Ginnevra demanded. "Eodan, what's wrong?" She turned on Lady Jiulliana, whose pendant glittered in the low light, drawing Ginnevra's eye. Dread suspicion crept over her. "You've entranced him—let him go!"

Lady Jiulliana laughed. "I don't think so. Bad enough having you snooping around, I certainly don't need a werewolf joining you."

Ginnevra drew her sword and pointed it at Lady Jiulliana. "Free him, or I'll kill you," she said.

"If you kill me, who will free him?" Lady Jiulliana smiled, a friendly expression that showed no hint of fear or anger or even smug triumph. "You have it all wrong, though."

"Do I?" Ginnevra grabbed Eodan by the shoulders and shook him. He didn't respond. "Free him, damn you!"

Lady Jiulliana snapped her fingers. Eodan shook himself like someone coming out of a deep slumber and drew in a breath. Ginnevra, feeling utterly relieved, said, "Eodan, she's—"

Eodan grabbed Ginnevra around the throat.

She gasped and clawed at him, unable to breathe. Eodan's expression was perfectly neutral, and his eyes were still glazed over, not focused on her. Desperate, Ginnevra punched him low in the chest, sending all the breath whooshing out of him. His grip loosened, and Ginnevra wrenched away, coughing. She turned on Lady Jiulliana. "I will kill you," she said, her voice hoarse. "Let him go. Now."

"He is free," Lady Jiulliana said. "Free to act on his true nature. And you...you'll just be another one of the missing."

A silver glow surrounded Eodan, and in an instant, he was gone. The big, black-furred werewolf stood in his place, breathing heavily, Eodan's clothes in tatters around him. A deep growl that triggered all Ginnevra's most primal instincts to flee issued from his throat. Ginnevra only had enough time to bring her sword around in a guard position before Eodan sprang at her.

CHAPTER

TWENTY-ONE

Ginnevra threw herself backward, away from the jaws that tried to close on her throat. "Eodan, stop!" she screamed. She dropped her sword and backed away farther, terrifyingly aware of how vulnerable she was, no armor, no weapon she could use against him without killing him.

Eodan advanced on her, still growling. She snatched up one of the chairs and brandished it, her heart pounding and her hands shaking. "Don't do this," she warned him.

He paused, just for a moment, then lunged at her. Ginnevra stepped aside and smashed the chair over his head. It splintered into half a dozen pieces, and Eodan swayed, temporarily stunned. Ginnevra found herself holding two short lengths of wood. She cracked them both over his skull, but Eodan simply shook his head and turned on her again. She rolled away from him, coming to her feet in a crouch, and threw the remains of the chair away.

They circled each other now, each looking for an opportunity to strike, though Ginnevra's thoughts were madly occupied with figuring out how to knock Eodan unconscious without hurting him too badly. Fury surged through her at Lady Jiulliana's treachery, but she had no attention to spare for considering what else the woman might have done with the pendant that had to be the source of her power. No time to wonder what Lady Jiulliana had sworn to the Bright One in exchange for that power. For half a breath, she did wonder why Lady Jiulliana hadn't entranced *her*, but then Eodan snapped at her again and she had to dodge, coming back to the present in a flash.

She rolled again, trying to get behind Eodan, and nearly ran into the bed. Lady Jiulliana hadn't moved—well, of course not, she couldn't exactly run away—but Ginnevra didn't dare take her attention off Eodan to see what the woman was doing. Eodan swiped at her, his claws nearly taking her arm off, close enough she felt the wind of their passing. Ginnevra pushed her hair out of her eyes and assessed him. They were both strong, they both had tremendous endurance, but Eodan clearly intended to kill her, and that put Ginnevra at a disadvantage because she had no desire to kill him.

Eodan paused, his legs akimbo and his back arched. Ginnevra feinted right, and when Eodan lunged in that direction, she moved, not left, but forward, up and over his broad shoulders like he was a fence to vault. She spun and got an arm around his throat, choking him. "I'm sorry," she muttered in his ear. "You'll thank me later."

Eodan staggered backward, but didn't fall. Ginnevra tightened her arm around his neck. Then she cried out as Eodan flung himself into the wall, crushing Ginnevra and making her lose her grip. Gasping for breath, she darted out of reach of another swipe of his enormous clawed paw.

She heard Lady Jiulliana laughing, and the sound infuriated her. Eodan didn't look at all hurt, or tired, and Ginnevra was suddenly convinced this fight would go on for hours until one of them was overwhelmed. And Ginnevra was determined she wouldn't be that one. Which meant she was going to have to hurt the man she loved in order to save him.

She cast about the room, then dodged left, ducking under Eodan's next attack and coming up with her sword. Eodan withdrew, wary of the silvered steel. Ginnevra advanced on him. Eodan snarled and lunged. Quicker than thought, Ginnevra stepped to one side and thrust the blade deep into Eodan's body, below his left shoulder.

Eodan howled in agony, a sound that cut Ginnevra to the heart. She withdrew the sword and took a guard position again, but Eodan collapsed, landing hard on his left side. In the next instant, he was in human shape again, moaning as blood poured down his chest.

Ginnevra didn't dare stop to help him. She strode to the bed and laid the sword, still gory with Eodan's blood, against Lady Jiulliana's throat. With her other hand, she grabbed the pendant and yanked on the chain until it broke. Lady Jiulliana gasped as the chain cut into her neck.

"Free him. Now," Ginnevra said. "Or we'll see how creative I can get with this sword."

Lady Jiulliana said nothing, just stared at Ginnevra's fist, holding the pendant.

"This is the key, isn't it?" Ginnevra said. "You entrance people who come here, don't you? Trick them into giving you money. What do you do with the others? The ones who go missing?"

To her surprise, Lady Jiulliana laughed. "You really don't know anything, do you? All your guesses are wrong."

Ginnevra examined the ruby, which glinted black in the low light. Then she looked again, more closely. "This is glass," she exclaimed. "How—" With an oath, she dropped the pendant on the floor and crushed it beneath her boot heel.

Behind her, Eodan let out another moan. Ginnevra turned to look at him. He hadn't made any attempt to stop the bleeding, and even in the dimness he looked far too pale. Ginnevra lowered her sword and hurried to his side. She gathered up the largest scraps of his clothing and wadded them up, then guided his hand to hold them against the wound.

"You'll never get him back," Lady Jiulliana said. Ginnevra turned to watch her. Her neck bled slightly from where the chain had cut it. "What I take is mine, now and forever."

"Your power is gone," Ginnevra said. "Now, tell me where the missing people are."

Another laugh. "Ginnevra Cassaline," Lady Jiulliana said, "your desires make you weak. You spare one whose people will always be your enemy, and you spurn the wisdom of the Goddess when it is offered to you. You believe yourself superior to all around you. Be warned, paladin—your strength will yet be as naught, and your blessings will be revoked."

Ginnevra's hand shook again, making the sword vibrate. "No," she said. For a moment, fear surged through her—fear that she was too prideful, too arrogant, and that everything she knew was wrong. She closed her eyes and drew in a deep breath. Then she stood and fixed her gaze on Lady Jiulliana.

"I don't know who you really are, and I don't care," she said, pointing the sword at the woman. "But I know who I am. The Goddess spoke to me, and She believes I am worthy. I know you don't speak for Her. I know you are a liar. And I know you want me doubting myself because that's the only way you can win. Well, let me tell you something. *You have already lost.*"

With a sour, bitter smile, Lady Jiulliana shrugged. "It was worth trying," she said, and rose from the bed.

Ginnevra's eyes widened as the lumps beneath the blanket shifted and slid, displaced by the massive snake's tail that rose from where it had been concealed. From the waist up, Lady Jiul-liana looked the same as always, but below that, purple and gold scales glinted in the lamplight, their vibrant colors making every-thing around them pale and dull by comparison. The serpent's body uncoiled, bringing Lady Jiulliana closer to Ginnevra. Ginnevra stood frozen, sword by her side, as the creature approached.

"Lamia," she whispered. "Goddess help me. You're a lamia."

"I told you everything you believed was wrong," Lady Jiulliana said with a pitying smile. "Starting with thinking I needed that glass trinket to work my magic. Such a pity paladins are immune to my charms. I would have killed you on your first visit here, but you had to bring the damn werewolf with you, didn't you? It took me some time to discover how to enthrall one of his kind." Her smile widened. "That was quite the challenge. Almost as great a challenge as Caterrina Cassaline."

"You tortured her," Ginnevra said. She knew Lady Jiulliana couldn't entrance her, but she felt as if the lamia had succeeded regardless, her body numb, her hands shaking.

Lady Jiulliana shrugged. "Oh, only a little. She's tough. And yes, I regret not killing her outright, since she managed to escape. I'm guessing she made it back to you? Then I'm doubly regretful. She was never going to be a useful tool, not like the Revered."

Ginnevra's hand closed more tightly on her sword. "So that's what was wrong. You corrupted the Revered. She never went to Guinio—she came here."

"Is this the part where I reveal my plan?" Lady Jiulliana's smile was teasing, as if she and Ginnevra were engaged in a coy flirta-tion. "I don't think so. You'll have to live with your ignorance. Or... well, not *live*, obviously, because I intend to kill you, but you take my meaning."

Her smile, and her teasing, mocking expression, sent fury

shooting through Ginnevra, dispelling her numb fear. She stepped back from the monster. "You can try," she snarled, and swung her sword at the lamia's head.

Lady Jiulliana darted back, but not quite fast enough; the tip of Ginnevra's sword scored a line across the side of her face. Lady Jiulliana hissed in fury. "That will cost you," she said. Ginnevra threw herself back to avoid the crack of the lamia's tail as it whipped toward her. She struck, but the sword glanced off the scales as if they were steel.

Ginnevra circled, looking for an opening. Lady Jiulliana's gown wasn't more than a bodice, and her serpent half began just below her waistline. The scales might be impervious to a blade, but her human upper half certainly wasn't. Ginnevra thrust for her chest and dodged the tail as it curled around to protect the vulnerable parts of the lamia's body. She dodged again, rolled, and came up behind Lady Jiulliana, bringing the sword around in a great sweeping arc aimed at taking the lamia's head off.

Lady Jiulliana ducked as if she saw the blow coming, then twisted to face Ginnevra. "Really, you have no chance," she said. Ginnevra felt something brush her leg just as the tail coiled around her body and squeezed.

Ginnevra screamed, a thin, faded sound because the tail coiled around her chest cut off her air. She beat ineffectually at the scales with her fist and her sword, then slashed at Lady Jiulliana's upper torso when that did nothing. Lady Jiulliana dodged her blows, laughing. Ginnevra's vision tunneled, and the laughter sounded far away. Her sword was far too heavy, and she wanted to drop it, but some faint memory told her paladins never gave up and they died with sword in hand.

A loud *thwack*, the sound of wood hitting flesh, brought her back to herself—but that blow hadn't struck her. The coils around her chest slackened, letting her draw beautifully restorative air into her lungs. Before her, Lady Jiulliana swayed, shaking her head dizzily. Without another thought, Ginnevra thrust her sword deep into the woman's chest, feeling the blade scrape across bone and striking her to the heart.

Lady Jiulliana screamed, a terrible sound that seemed more furious than pained. "You dare," she said. "You *dare*. I will drink your blood—"

Ginnevra drove the blade deeper. This time, the scream was agonized. Ginnevra didn't say a word.

She held her position until she was sure the monster was dead. Then she looked at Eodan, who stood behind Lady Jiulliana's body, holding the shattered remains of another chair. He was ashen and sweaty and blood still flowed from the deep wound in his shoulder. "Sit," she said. "You're going to collapse."

Eodan nodded. He threw the pieces of chair away and sank to the floor, still upright, but only just. "Did I attack you?" he said. His breathing was labored, and it slowed his speech, but he sounded in his right mind, which relieved Ginnevra.

"Don't you remember?" she said.

"I remember entering this room, and you saying the Revered had returned, and everything after that is hazy until you stabbed me." Eodan felt around for the bloody cloth and pressed it to his shoulder again. "The pain cleared my mind enough for me to realize you were in danger. I'm sorry I couldn't attack more effectively, but I hurt too much to change shape."

"Hitting her with a chair was enough." Ginnevra freed herself from the inert coils and shoved the lamia's body aside so she could crouch next to Eodan. "And you're alert now? You don't feel hazy?"

"Whatever she did to me is gone. It looks like her death released me." Eodan put a bloody hand on Ginnevra's arm. "I need clothes. Did I change shape while I was dressed?"

"You did."

"Damn. I wonder how many other people she entranced or killed?" Eodan managed to get to his feet, where he swayed but didn't fall. Ginnevra got her shoulder beneath his other arm to support him. "I'm fine. I—" He tried to take a step, and his legs gave out. Ginnevra lowered him to the floor again, her heart aching.

"It's the silver," she said. "Eodan, I'm so sorry. I didn't have any other options."

"It's all right. I just need to sit for a while." Eodan closed his eyes.

Ginnevra hurried to the bed and collected one of the sheets, then used her sword to slash cuts in it so she could tear it into strips. She folded one into a pad and made Eodan hold it in place over the wound while she bound it to him with more strips of fabric. Eodan's color still didn't look good, but his eyes were focusing now, and when she finished bandaging him, he took her hand in a strong, firm grip. "I didn't hurt you, did I?" he asked.

"No. Thank the Goddess. We don't need both of us wounded." Ginnevra put her arms around him, not caring about the blood.

"We should get out of here. It's possible some of her victims are alive." With Ginnevra's help, Eodan got to his feet. This time, he managed to stay upright. He whipped another sheet off the bed and wrapped it around himself.

Ginnevra didn't feel nearly so optimistic. Despite Lady Jiulliana's words about her ignorance, she was sure she had some of the pieces in the right place. The lamia had enthralled the Revered and probably a lot of other people, too, sent them out into the city to spread the news about the wonderful Lady Jiulliana—but what about the ones who disappeared? The ones Ginnevra was convinced had never left this house? She couldn't think of any reason for the lamia to have left them alive, even if she did enjoy torture.

Marcellus was gone when they emerged from Lady Jiulliana's chamber. Sword in hand, Ginnevra led the way down the stairs and into the hallway, following the sound of voices. The delicious smells still emanated from the kitchen, along with the smell of something burning, but the door opposite shook with several people pounding on it and muffled shouts for help. Ginnevra tried the door and discovered it was locked.

"Stand back," she shouted, and with a couple of well-placed boots to the latch smashed the door in. A dozen people tried to emerge at the same time, all of them crying or swearing. Ginnevra couldn't believe her sense of relief at seeing Pellarius stumbling at the head of the crowd, holding the door frame so he didn't fall over.

"What happened?" he said, hopping to her side to get out of the others' way. "I spoke to that Lady Jiulliana, who I doubt is a holy woman, and next thing I know I'm crammed into that dark room with a dozen people I've never seen before and my crutch is gone."

"It's a long story, and we'll tell it to you once we're out of here," Ginnevra said. "Wait here while I check these other rooms."

The kitchen was empty, though pots still sat on the hot stove, one of them boiling over and sending up great black clouds that smelled of burned pasta. Ginnevra moved them all where they wouldn't set anything on fire and proceeded down the hallway. In the room where they'd found Pellarius, Eodan had the captives sitting down so he could examine them, moving as calmly as if he wasn't injured and wearing nothing but a sheet that wasn't all that opaque. Trust Eodan to care more about other people's injuries than his own.

The next door was also locked. Ginnevra kicked it in and let her eyes adjust to the darkness. Bags and stacks of coin lay neatly against one wall, while against the other were boxes stacked high with miscellaneous things, pencils and notebooks and a couple of expensive-looking magnetic compasses, the kinds of things people carried in their belt pouches. One box piled with jewelry all tangled together looked like a pirate's treasure trove. Looking at all of it gave Ginnevra an uneasy feeling. The coins clearly came from that "donation" box in the garden, but the rest of it...

The room across from the storage room was empty. Ginnevra regarded it in silence for a while, then shut the door and returned upstairs. This time, she brushed aside the drapes shrouding the hallway and walked slowly through the passages Marcellus usually hurried her through, looking into every room she passed. A drawing room and a study, both dusty with disuse. A room filled with ranks of wooden chairs facing an empty dais Ginnevra guessed was for musical performances, also smelling as if nobody had entered it for months. And another locked door. Ginnevra rapped her knuckles against it, making a dull thud that suggested it was heavily insulated. Feeling uneasy, she kicked the lock in and opened the door.

The smell of blood washed over her, making her gag. She took one look inside and closed her eyes, breathing slowly so the stench wouldn't overwhelm her. Then she made herself examine the room, though she wanted to vomit and then run far away from the scene of the lamia's tortures. She told herself it was fortunate there wasn't anyone there, dead or alive, and shut the door.

She reached the back door and hesitated. There wasn't anything left to see, if all the donations had been removed to the treasure room, but thoroughness had always benefited her in the past. She opened the door and exclaimed as Marcellus lunged through it, a knife upraised.

Ginnevra gasped and dodged left. The knife whistled past her right ear. Marcellus's eyes were dull, as if he didn't recognize her. Ginnevra grabbed his wrist and slammed his hand against the door frame, forcing him to drop the knife. "What are you doing?" she exclaimed. She spun him around and shoved him face first into the wall, knocking his head against the plaster.

Marcellus stiffened for a moment. Then he sagged, nearly pulling free of her grip with his slight weight. Ginnevra adjusted her hold on him. "Your mistress is dead," she told him. "Whatever plot she had in mind is over. Give up now, and I'll see you receive justice."

Marcellus's shoulders began shaking, and he burst into anguished sobs. "What have I done?" he cried. "So many deaths...I remember now, I remember everything, what she made us do. The others ran, but I was trapped..."

Ginnevra didn't let go. He was probably faking. "Don't lie to me. You served a monster—"

"I didn't, I swear. I was trapped inside my head, I saw—" He sagged again as his legs stopped supporting him. "I brought them to her, I watched her drink their blood, I buried—I am damned, damned beyond redemption! My lady, kill me now, I beg you!"

Ginnevra let go of him. Marcellus curled into a tight, weeping ball and buried his face in his knees. If he was faking, he was an excellent actor. "Are you saying she enthralled you? She's dead, and that magic died with her. Why did you attack me?"

"She warned me when I let you in. Said you shouldn't leave this house alive. I remember—I am so sorry, my lady. Now it all feels like a terrible dream, except—oh, Goddess have mercy, I cannot forget what I've seen."

"Then you swear you didn't help her intentionally?"

Marcellus shook his head. "Does it matter, if there was a part of me aware of the evil that didn't fight back? I deserve death for what I've done."

Ginnevra stared down at the weeping man and made a decision to believe him. "Marcellus, what happened here?"

Marcellus drew in a deep, sobbing breath. "She made them love her. Sent them out into the city to spread the word of how wonderful she was. But some of them, she killed. It was…it was how she fed, strangling them, or torturing them, and drinking…" He gulped again. "And some, she saved for…for feeding on later. They're across from the kitchen."

"What happened to the bodies?" But Ginnevra cast an eye over the beautiful garden and felt sick. "They're buried here," she said. "Marcellus, how many?"

"Thirty," Marcellus sobbed. "Thirty lives, thirty deaths…why do you not kill me?"

Ginnevra hauled Marcellus to his feet. "Look at me," she said, grabbing his chin and holding his head steady. "The lamia made you do this. It's not your fault."

"But I didn't fight back," Marcellus said. "I—"

"You couldn't fight back. The lamia is the most evil of the Bright One's creations because she takes away the Goddess's gift of free will. And she wronged you more than anyone because she made you complicit in her crimes." Ginnevra hesitated, then put her arm around the small man's shoulders. "I'm sorry I didn't know. I should have stopped her. I don't want to know how many people she killed after I first spoke with her. Those deaths are on my conscience."

"Surely not, my lady," Marcellus whispered.

"If I can bear it, Marcellus, so can you." Ginnevra released him. "We'll need your help locating the bodies for their families. It's something you can do that might ease your soul."

Marcellus nodded. He wiped his eyes and said, "The others... you freed them?"

"Yes. And they'll go home to their families. It will be all right someday, I promise." Ginnevra looked out over the garden again, and her heart constricted painfully. That wasn't a promise she had any right making, not when there were thirty people and their loved ones for whom it was a lie. But the alternative was giving in to shame and guilt and letting the lamia win. Ginnevra closed her eyes and prayed silently: *Dark Lady, I know I shouldn't play the game of might-have-been, but if I'd been faster—*

A flash of memory, not of Lady Jiulliana or the captives or anything she'd seen recently, but of Caterrina's battered body. Caterrina, too, had been fooled by the lamia. If she'd been able to fight her way free, Ginnevra would have returned to an Uparde free of the lamia's evil. *There are always paths not taken,* she thought, and wondered if it had been her thought or someone else's. Either way, it was true: there were always other possible endings, and it was the Bright One who tried to trick humanity into dwelling on the ones that hadn't happened. But for every might-have-been that made this disaster better, there were ten that made it worse.

Ginnevra steadied Marcellus, who looked up at her with reddened, teary eyes. "We make things right not by dwelling on the past, but by looking to the future," she said. "Let's see how we can make that happen."

Marcellus nodded. "Yes, my lady," he said. "And...my thanks."

TWENTY-TWO

G innevra sent Marcellus to the justiciary for guards and a couple of justicers before returning to the house. In a corner of the great room, behind a sofa, she found Pellarius's crutch. She carried it down the stairs and handed it over. Pellarius thanked her, but remained seated. He looked remarkably well, but then he'd only been a captive for a couple of hours.

Ginnevra sat beside him and watched Eodan bandage someone's wrist. She was beginning to feel the aftereffects of the fight —both fights—but despite her weariness, she didn't feel sleepy, just exhausted. "Why did you come here, anyway?" she asked Pellarius.

"I was sure from what you said that Lady Jiulliana was a fraud." Pellarius stretched his broken leg out in front of him, grimacing in pain. "I figured, if she got all those donations, she probably didn't pay taxes. So I pretended I was an Uparde tax inspector to get her to confess to whatever she was doing. I guess it didn't work."

"It might have saved your life," Ginnevra said. "She couldn't enthrall a city official without risking your behavior becoming so odd someone might run into her in the course of investigating it. And she couldn't kill you, because your disappearance would also stir up notice. I bet she locked you up until she could figure out what to do with you."

"Well, I feel stupid," Pellarius said. "It's not as if the investigation has anything to do with me. I just wanted to help."

"You *did* help. If you hadn't come here, we might not have figured out the truth for several more days. I certainly didn't know Lady Jiulliana was responsible."

Pellarius nodded. "Where is Lady Jiulliana, anyway? Did you arrest her, after all?"

Ginnevra's exhaustion redoubled at the thought of how many people she'd have to tell the story to. "It wasn't at all what I thought," she said. "She was a monster. A lamia. And now she's dead."

"A—" Pellarius stared at her, wide-eyed. "Then...you saved our lives."

Ginnevra resisted the urge to point out how many lives she hadn't saved. Her memory of what she'd thought in the garden was too close for her to feel inappropriate guilt. "The guards will be here shortly to take care of the rest of this business. There are a lot of bodies buried in the garden, and I think Lady—the lamia looted them before she had them disposed of, if that pile of treasure is anything to go by. Someone will need to return that property to their next of kin."

She looked up as Eodan approached. He sat heavily beside her and leaned his head on her shoulder. "Can they go home? Some of them have been here for days, and they're in bad shape. Maybe we should send for their families."

"I'm going to let the guard handle that." Ginnevra twined her fingers in his. "I sent for them, and for some justicers. The lamia is dead, so it's not as if these people's testimony is needed, but it might help clear up some loose ends." She closed her eyes and cursed. "According to Marcellus, the city is full of people the lamia enthralled, not least of whom is the Revered. I wonder what will happen to them."

"They should break free of that control, if what happened to these people is any guide," Eodan said, gesturing at the people thronging the hall and the formerly empty room across from the treasure room. Ginnevra guessed none of them had wanted to go back to the scene of their captivity, even if they needed somewhere to rest. Eodan yawned, and added, "Though it might take time. Some of these captives are still a little unclear on what happened to them, like their minds aren't yet their own. I imagine anyone enthralled for much longer than a day or two might need time to shake off the effects. But I'm sure they'll all recover eventually."

"That's what happened to Marcellus." She decided not to tell Eodan the details of what she'd learned from the majordomo. Weariness had caught up with her, and that conversation felt like it might drain her completely. Then she realized he'd fallen asleep and wouldn't have heard her anyway.

She stood, careful not to disturb Eodan where he leaned against her, and walked to the front door. She half expected to find more petitioners outside, but the street was empty except for a young couple walking past on the far side. Ginnevra propped the grille open and stood outside, her mind a white blank, until she saw purposeful movement at the corner. Then she walked to meet the newcomers: a couple of squads of guards, led by Marcellus, and two justicers, one of whom was Ciutto Baroccius. Ginnevra felt wearier just looking at him.

She hoped Marcellus's feelings of guilt hadn't prompted him

to confess to what Lady Jiulliana had made him do in front of a room full of justicers, but he didn't look like he was there under duress, so Ginnevra felt confident everything would be fine.

Ciutto saw her and advanced more rapidly, outpacing the others. "You," he said in a low, furious voice. "You were told to leave this alone. I'll see you prosecuted—"

Ginnevra grabbed his arm and squeezed so her hand grated against bone, making him yelp. She pulled him close so she could speak into his ear. "There are thirty bodies buried in the back garden," she said, speaking even more quietly than he had. "If you want to make this a matter of jurisdiction, I'll be happy to testify as to how many of those bodies got that way while you had charge of this investigation. Nearly four weeks, wasn't it? Or you can shut up and look official while you proclaim the mystery solved. Now, get inside and do your job. If you remember how."

She released him and gave him a little shove toward the door. "I'm glad to see you," she proclaimed to the street at large. "It seems the Lady Jiulliana was a lamia—"

The guards all came to a stumbling stop in front of her. Most of them looked confused, like they didn't know what a lamia was, but two of them looked suddenly terrified. "She attacked me and my companion, and we killed her as is a paladin's duty. The rest is up to you. I'm confident you'll be able to sort things out with Marcellus's help."

The guards still looked slightly confused, but they hurried past Ginnevra into the house, followed more slowly by Ciutto, who refused to look at her. Marcellus stopped at her side. "Is that really all, my lady?"

Ginnevra shook her head. "But it's the beginning of the end," she said.

SHE EXPLAINED matters as best she could to Ciutto and the guards and endured their questions until she felt she might go mad. Finally, she decided she'd had enough and told them they could inquire at Caterrina's house if they needed anything else, found Eodan and Pellarius, and headed back to the Golden Sickle. She didn't mind going slowly to match Pellarius's limping gait; she felt ready to lie down and sleep for a hundred years even though it was barely past noon.

Eodan had found clothes that almost fit him among the belongings of Lady Jiulliana's servants. Marcellus had assured them no one would begrudge him the loan. "They might not even come back," he'd said with a frown.

"They're not guilty of anything but being enthralled," Ginnevra had said.

"It's hard to remember that when all our memories are of the evil she made us do," Marcellus had said, and Ginnevra had decided not to push.

Now the three of them walked through the streets, letting Ginnevra's sword clear them a path with its presence. The sounds of talking and laughing eased Ginnevra's heart. There was a city full of people who hadn't been touched by the lamia's evil, and the monster was dead now and couldn't hurt anyone else. She skirted the fountain in the plaza near Caterrina's home and said, "I hope Aunt Caterrina recovers soon. I'd like to be able to tell her what happened."

"She could wake at any time," Eodan said. He was moving more stiffly than she, and his eyes were glassy again, as if he didn't see much beyond his immediate surroundings. Ginnevra kept a close eye on him in case he collapsed. She could carry him back to the inn if necessary, but it wouldn't be a pleasant trip for either of them.

Pellarius, on her other side, hopped along on his crutch

without speaking. Ginnevra felt profound gratitude whenever she glanced his way. Whatever ill he'd done Eodan with his traps, he'd more than made amends. Even if going to Lady Jiulliana's house had been risky and foolhardy...but that, too, was in the past, and there was no sense dwelling on it.

As they approached the Golden Sickle, Ginnevra's gaze was caught by someone familiar headed up the path to the front door. In her tiredness, it took her a moment to recognize the Revered. She called out the woman's name, but despite how close she was, the Revered didn't stop or turn around, just walked through the inn's front door.

A crawling sense of dread crept over Ginnevra. She walked faster, her stride turning into a trot and then a full-out run. She burst through the door to find the innkeeper, Drommio, just heading up the stairs. "My lady!" he exclaimed. "The Revered was just asking after you."

"Did you tell her where my room is?" Ginnevra demanded.

"In truth, I didn't know you'd left. I sent her—"

Ginnevra swore and ran down the hallway, flinging open the door to the room where Caterrina lay. The Revered stood beside Caterrina, holding her hand. In her other hand, she held a short-bladed but very sharp knife.

"No!" Ginnevra shrieked. The Revered half-turned. Her eyes were dull and heavy-lidded as if she'd just woken from a deep sleep. Ginnevra threw herself at the Revered, grabbing her wrist and forcing her hand open so the knife fell to the floor. With her other hand, she shoved the Revered into the wall, cracking her head against the plaster so hard it made a dent.

The Revered cried out in pain and struggled vainly to get free. "What are you doing?" she exclaimed. Then she froze. Her eyes were wide and clear now, and she looked horrified. "What am *I* doing?" she whispered. "Goddess help me, where is this place? And who are you?"

Ginnevra released her and stuck the knife through her belt. "How much do you remember?"

The Revered blinked and looked down at Caterrina, who still slept undisturbed. "Dear Goddess have mercy," she breathed, extending a hand to touch Caterrina's bruised face but letting it fall before making contact. "Who...did the monster do this? Oh, Caterrina!"

"Then you know what Lady Jiulliana was," Ginnevra said.

The Revered nodded. "I intended to confront Lady Jiulliana Dolcebenette," she said. "I believed her to be an agent of the Bright One. I asked Caterrina to join me—I thought I might need a paladin's sword." She put a hand to her head. "It was late, but Lady Jiulliana admitted us to her house. We spoke, and she revealed herself to be a monster, and then...everything is distant, like a dream. I know I've seen you before, but I don't remember who you are."

Ginnevra felt a moment's relief that the Revered didn't remember their fight before recalling that she would have sent word of Eodan to Devoyenne at first light, and the Revered's memory loss didn't change anything. "I'm Ginnevra, Caterrina's niece," she said. "I'm afraid the rest is going to be hard for you to believe."

"What happened to Caterrina?" the Revered asked, touching Caterrina's wrist with a shaky hand. "She's badly hurt."

Movement at the door drew both their attention. Eodan stopped in the doorway, holding on to the frame like he needed its support. "I'm worse off than I believed," he said, somewhat breathlessly.

The Revered shrieked and backed into the wall. "Monster!" she screamed. "Kill it! It will kill us all!"

Ginnevra felt suddenly so weary she wanted to crawl into the other bed and close her eyes until everything went away. "I can't do that," she said. "Eodan is Aunt Caterrina's physician."

"It—what?" The Revered was breathing heavily and her hand was reaching for her grace. "That's a werewolf!"

"I know. But he's not evil. Please, Revered Parenogne, let me explain." Ginnevra helped Eodan lie on the spare bed. He was shaking and looked even paler than before, his lips almost white and his eyes rimmed with darkness.

Movement from Caterrina's bed stopped the Revered saying whatever else she might have said. Caterrina laid a hand over the Revered's and whispered, "He's not...what you think, Massina... listen to Ginnevra."

Ginnevra dropped to her knees beside Caterrina's bed. "Don't talk," she said. "You're still not well."

"Ginnevra, the lamia...you have to kill her..." Caterrina stopped for a long time between sentences. She licked dry, cracked lips and continued, "She passes for human...Lady Jiulliana..."

"I know, Aunt. The lamia is dead. Eodan and I killed her. It's all right." Ginnevra helped her sit and gave her a drink of water. Caterrina swallowed a mouthful or two and relaxed.

"Bad luck...full moon," she said, her voice sounding a little stronger. "Bright One's creatures...strongest."

"She couldn't have overwhelmed you together otherwise," Ginnevra agreed. She looked at the Revered and said, "You've seen true evil now, Revered, in confronting the monster Lady Jiulliana was. Look at Eodan. He's nothing like the lamia. He and many of the werewolves have turned their backs on their creator, and they only want to live in peace with us. Eodan fought that lamia by my side—do you really think he would have done that if he was its ally?"

The Revered stared at her, her mouth slack with astonishment. Then she ran for the door, pushing past Pellarius so he nearly fell over. "No!" Ginnevra shouted, and stood to follow her. Caterrina's hand on her arm stopped her. Ginnevra looked at her aunt, whose eyes were closed but whose grip was firm.

"You can't force people to see the truth, Ginna," Caterrina said. "She's been through a lot. Give her time."

Ginnevra sank back down to kneel beside the bed. "I know," she said. "But I hoped..."

Caterrina didn't respond. Her breathing had slowed, and she appeared to be falling asleep again. Ginnevra rose and crossed to Eodan's side. He looked up at her and smiled.

"It's over," he said. "Ginnevra, rest."

"The paladins will be here tomorrow," she told him. "It's not over."

Eodan took her hand. "Then we'll deal with them tomorrow. For now...lay down that burden, please?"

Ginnevra nodded. Eodan closed his eyes. In a minute, he too had fallen asleep.

Ginnevra glanced at Pellarius, who'd taken a seat with his crutch splayed out beside him. "What paladins?" he asked.

She shook her head. "Eodan's right, that's a problem for tomorrow. But, if you're at all a praying man, you might pray for them to have open minds and a reluctance to kill monsters on sight."

Pellarius smiled slightly. "You're persuasive," he said. "Eodan's fate is in good hands."

Ginnevra brushed the hair out of Eodan's face and rested her hand lightly on his cheek. She hoped Pellarius was right, for both their sakes.

She ended up making herself a pallet on the floor so she could watch both Caterrina and Eodan, having paid Drommio a larger sum than she thought was strictly fair to look the other way. She wasn't sure which of her patients to worry about more. Caterrina continued to sleep, waking for a few minutes around sunset to ask for more water, and while Eodan woke an hour or so after that, he was so quiet and submitted to having his wound checked again so meekly it scared Ginnevra, who was used to him refusing to admit his wounds were serious. She ate a light meal just before Eodan woke and worried further that he refused food when she offered it.

She sat on the pallet with her back against the wall and let herself give in to despair, just for a moment or two. Eodan was too injured to be moved. He certainly couldn't defend himself against a company of paladins. And while their current location was out of the way, the Revered knew where they were and would have no trouble directing the paladins here. Which meant all that stood between Eodan and death was Ginnevra. The thought couldn't help but deepen her despair.

She mulled over other possibilities. She might hire a wagon and get Eodan out of town that way—but that meant abandoning Caterrina, and Ginnevra refused to do that. She might move them all to a different inn, one the Revered didn't know about—but moving the injured could hurt them further, and they both looked bad enough off she was reluctant to do that. She might threaten the Revered, get her to tell the paladins it was a mistake and the werewolf was gone—but that was an even stupider idea, since no Revered was going to lie to a paladin, especially not about a dangerous monster loose in the city.

No, the only solution was the one she'd started with: confront the paladin company and its captain and try to convince them of Eodan's harmlessness and goodness. That seemed an impossible task even if the captain did know Ginnevra. She thought back to the time, two months ago, when

Eodan had saved her life. Even that hadn't been enough to convince her immediately he wasn't evil. Convincing strangers of the truth...

Ginnevra tilted her head back, closed her eyes, and sighed. She brushed her fingers over the grace at her throat and whispered, "Dark Lady, You know the truth. You put me in a position to learn the truth for myself. I want so much for the werewolves to receive justice, and this is my chance to convince a few of Your servants that they're not all evil. Please, Goddess, guide my actions and my words that my sister paladins will hear I speak truth. The rest is up to them."

The room was still and silent except for Eodan and Caterrina's breathing. Ginnevra let her thoughts drift, hoping to hear something, some message from the Goddess, but nothing came, not even a sense of rightness or peace in her heart that might be the Goddess touching her. She sighed again and opened her eyes. The lamps burned low, and no light came from beneath the door.

"Ginna..."

Ginnevra rose immediately and crossed to Caterrina's side. "Yes, Aunt? Can I get you water, or...are you hungry?"

Caterrina shook her head, a more decisive movement than she'd managed before. "I feel stronger," she said, and her voice did sound less weak. "I didn't know how much this meant to you."

"What do you mean?"

"The werewolves. Or is it Eodan you care about?"

Ginnevra blushed at the realization that someone had heard her pray. "Of course I care about Eodan, but it's all the werewolves, really. All the ones who choose not to worship the Bright One. It's just so unfair that we should treat them like enemies when we have so much else in common."

"I agree." Caterrina let out a low chuckle. "I killed so many werewolves in my day, I hate to think that some of them might have been allies if circumstances had been different. We killed them, they killed us...how much of that was misunderstanding?"

"Aunt, why did you believe me about Eodan? You must hate werewolves more than I do. Did. Why did you listen?"

Caterrina's gaze fixed on the ceiling, past Ginnevra. "You have always lived by your sense of right and wrong, Ginnevra. I've never known you to flinch from doing the right thing once you knew what it was. You are the last person I expect to be swayed by evil, no matter how handsome its face. And...Ginger trusted Eodan enough to let him ride. Horses are hard to fool when it comes to monsters."

Ginnevra laughed and covered her mouth to hold back the sound. "The witness of a horse. I might have known it's something you'd consider valid."

Caterrina chuckled again. "That combined with your word was enough."

"But these paladins arriving tomorrow—they probably don't know me. Why should they believe my word?"

Caterrina put her hand over Ginnevra's. "You have truth on your side. Have faith, Ginna. You can't compel the future—you can only prepare to meet it, however it comes."

Ginnevra nodded. She turned her hand to clasp her aunt's. "Thank you. I needed that reminder."

She helped Caterrina sit up to have a drink, then settled her more comfortably and turned to check on Eodan. He lay on his back, snoring lightly. It was such a reassuring sound, a familiar sound she'd so often fallen asleep listening to, that her heart eased. Caterrina was right; she couldn't guarantee the future, couldn't make those paladins bend to her will, but she could speak the truth as clearly as possible. What paths opened up beyond that, only the Goddess knew.

TWENTY-THREE

S he divided her time the next day between tending Eodan and Caterrina and running last-minute errands and preparing to meet the paladins. They couldn't arrive much before sunset, and there was no point fretting about what would happen when they reached Uparde. So she groomed Dauntless and Ginger, who didn't really need the attention, given the kind of care they got from the Golden Sickle's stable master, but who seemed to appreciate her presence anyway. She brought her armor from Caterrina's house and went over it, polishing the plate until it gleamed.

Caterrina woke that morning much more energetic, as if she'd turned a corner in her recovery. She was able to sit up and eat a bowl of broth and even complain about wanting something more solid. Her bruises were faded to smudges of yellow, the swelling in her broken foot had gone down, and the cuts on her face and broken arm had nearly closed over. How much scarring they would leave, Ginnevra didn't know, but her aunt seemed not to worry about it, so she decided she wouldn't either.

Eodan, on the other hand, did have her worried. He rarely woke all that day, even when Caterrina and Ginnevra talked, and his color hadn't returned. When Ginnevra checked his wound, she was dismayed to find it was still bleeding a little and the edges were so dark a red as to be nearly black. The knowledge that she'd been the one to hurt him made her anguished and furious by turns, anguished with the memory of her sword driving into his body, furious that the lamia had made her do it.

Around sunset, Ginnevra donned her armor and left Pellarius to watch over the injured pair. She saddled Dauntless and guided the blue roan through the streets. She knew without being told where the paladin company would arrive.

She arrived in the great plaza outside the chapel as the sun kissed the distant mountaintops. Throngs pressed her on all sides, some citizens going home to their suppers, others arriving at the chapel for evening services. She stopped beside the ruined black fountain and waited.

Time passed. The crowds thinned, though many people still stared at her as they passed. She thought about going in for services and decided she wouldn't be able to sit still or pay proper attention, not to mention she wasn't sure she was ready to face the Revered. No, better not to disrupt everyone else's worship.

Dauntless stood still in the patient way of a good warhorse. She stroked his mane with her gloved hand. The plaza was almost empty now except for something large that moved at the street entering it on the south. Something that gleamed in the last light of the setting sun, distant ruddy rays reflecting off metal.

Ginnevra waited, controlling her impatience. They would come to her soon enough. Her enhanced vision made out two columns of riders, with one paladin riding ahead. They approached the chapel slowly, without deviating in their path. The few remaining pedestrians got out of their way and stayed where they were, watching the paladins pass. Ginnevra discovered her fears and worries had vanished. There was only the moment, and it was what you made it.

As the company neared the chapel, Ginnevra guided Dauntless away from the fountain and rode to meet them. The lead rider slowed and signaled to the others to halt. Ginnevra came to a stop about five feet away. She'd strapped her sword to her back in a position she couldn't draw it from, signaling that she had no intention of drawing a blade against her sister paladins while reminding them that she was entitled to carry the sword. The lead rider, the captain, eyed its position but said nothing. Ginnevra, too, remained silent. It was down to the captain to speak first.

Finally, the captain, whose lined face proclaimed her to be much older than any captain Ginnevra had seen before, said, "You are Ginnevra Cassaline, the heretic?"

That wasn't a good sign. "I am Ginnevra Cassaline. I am no heretic. The Blessed—"

"We have a report of a werewolf in Uparde," the captain said. "Revered Massina Parenogne claims you defended that monster and refused to do your duty in killing it."

"Revered Parenogne lacks all the facts," Ginnevra said. "The werewolf is not evil. He is not a monster to be killed, but an intelligent creature who has turned his back on the Bright One who created him."

A murmur of speech washed over the paladins in column behind their captain. The captain raised a gloved hand for silence, and sunlight glinted off her vambrace. "You speak nonsense," she said. "Werewolves are evil. You are corrupted if you believe otherwise."

"I told the Blessed what I learned, and she gave me her blessing," Ginnevra said, as calmly as if her heart weren't pounding like a frightened rabbit. "She knows the truth."

"And yet she didn't tell us," the captain said. "Convenient, that she's not here to attest to your claim." She maneuvered her horse closer to Ginnevra. "Why do you defend this monster? Did it enthrall you?"

"Werewolves can't enthrall, and even if they could, I wouldn't realize it if he had," Ginnevra pointed out. "I love him, and I want him to receive justice."

The captain recoiled, a look of disgust on her wrinkled face. "You confess to such deviant behavior and expect me to honor you for it?"

The chapel door opened, and men and women began streaming out, slowing when they saw the paladins. Ginnevra didn't dare look away from the captain to see what the worshippers thought of this confrontation. "Think what you like of me," she said, "but I know the truth. He is no monster, and I am not ashamed of loving him. Please believe me. If you kill him, you will be murdering an innocent man."

The captain, too, ignored the press of worshippers surrounding them. "You will tell us where the monster is, and we will do our duty and then escort you to Abraciabene for trial. Resist, and we will cut you down where you stand."

"Captain," someone said.

Ginnevra, startled, looked away and discovered the Revered standing near her stirrup. The Revered looked perfectly composed, her robes and her hair tidy as they had not been the last time Ginnevra had seen her, and she had her gaze fixed on the captain.

"Captain, I am Revered Massina Parenogne," she said, "and I am the one who summoned you here."

"Revered," the captain said, saluting her with left fist over heart. "We intend to rid Uparde of this evil."

"I see," the Revered said. "I know where the werewolf is, and I will take you there."

Ginnevra sucked in a sharp breath. "No—"

"You will not interfere in my duty," the Revered said. Her jet grace in its hematite bezel lay openly on her chest, and she laid the first two fingers of her right hand against it and said, *"By Your grace I bind my foe."*

Ginnevra's arms felt suddenly heavy and stiff, as if they were strapped to her sides. She struggled to get free and nearly fell off the horse. "No," she said, feeling afraid. "No, don't do this. You know—"

The Revered took Dauntless's fallen reins and handed them to the captain. "I know the truth," she said. "Follow me, captain."

The captain led Dauntless along beside her and fell in behind the Revered, who walked confidently in front of their procession. Ginnevra blinked away tears she couldn't raise her hands to wipe away. So, this was how it ended. She would watch the paladins kill Eodan, who was helpless to stop them, and then she would go to the holy city and watch the Blessed tell this captain she'd killed an innocent man who was no monster. And she would be vindicated, but it wouldn't matter, because Eodan would be dead.

They must have made a strange-looking procession, eighteen mounted paladins following one small, plump woman in an anointed's robes through the streets of Uparde. Everyone stood aside to let them pass. Some people held their children up to watch the paladins go by, which broke Ginnevra's heart more, though she didn't know why. Maybe because those people had no idea that the paladins they revered were about to commit murder.

They came within sight of the Golden Sickle, and Ginnevra, desperate, said, "Please, captain. The Blessed will tell you—this is wrong, you're making a mistake!"

The Revered stopped by the inn's front door. "On the left, the fourth door on the right," she said. "Bring him here so all may witness."

"*No!*" Ginnevra screamed, and this time she did fall off the horse, cracking her shoulder hard against the cobblestones. "You can't! Please, he's helpless, please don't do it!"

Two paladins near the head of the column dismounted and entered the inn. Ginnevra could barely see for the tears in her eyes. The smell of mint and pine choked her, made her feel like vomiting. This was all her fault—she should have made Eodan leave no matter what he'd promised her. She loved him, and now she was going to watch him die.

She heard shouting from within the inn that cut off abruptly, making her heart ache worse at the thought of Pellarius trying to stop a couple of paladins who would think nothing of tossing him aside like so much worthless garbage. Even Caterrina couldn't do anything to stop them. Why they wouldn't question their orders, why they wouldn't wonder why a werewolf and a paladin shared quarters peacefully, she didn't know, but she was convinced now that the conclusion of this path was very near, and regardless of her beliefs in the Goddess's gift of free will, she knew how it would end.

Footsteps, and the sound of something heavy being dragged, drew near, and soon the paladins appeared in the doorway with Eodan between them. He wasn't fighting them, didn't even appear fully conscious, and Ginnevra screamed his name from where she lay on the ground. The captain dismounted and lifted Ginnevra to her feet. "You will watch, and you will confess your heresy," she said.

Ginnevra struggled against the woman's grip, but succeeded only in wrenching away to fall again. The paladins dragged Eodan to collapse on the ground in front of the Revered, where he lay unmoving.

The Revered looked over her shoulder at Ginnevra, then at the captain. She removed her grace from around her neck and closed her left hand around it, letting the chain dangle. "Let all witness the Goddess's will being done here today," she said in a loud, carrying voice.

The captain stepped forward, drawing her sword, but the Revered stepped in front of her, blocking her way to Eodan. Then, to Ginnevra's shock, she gripped Eodan's injured shoulder. Eodan cried out in pain, but weakly, and Ginnevra's voice echoed his. With her other hand, the Revered raised her grace high and shouted, "*By Your grace I make all things whole!*"

Brilliant light like a million fractured rainbows surrounded the Revered and Eodan. Ginnevra threw up her arms to protect her eyes, only afterward remembering she was bound and that should have been impossible. The air sang like a fingernail on crystal, and then a gust of wind buffeted Ginnevra and the captain, rocking them both. Behind her, Ginnevra heard exclamations of surprise as the wind swept past the columns of paladins. She wiped tears from her eyes and slowly got to her feet.

The light was fading, but the colors remained, as if filmy colored gauzes hung like curtains surrounding Eodan and the Revered. The Revered had lowered her hand to hang her grace around her neck again. Her other hand still rested on Eodan's shoulder, though not tightly. Eodan knelt before her, his head bowed. Ginnevra took a step toward them, and Eodan raised his head. His eyes were clear, brilliant blue, with no shadow of pain over them. Slowly, he got to his feet and removed the bandage to reveal whole, unwounded skin without even the scar Ginnevra expected from a silver-tainted wound.

The captain's sword still hovered nearly at the ready. "What madness is this?" she exclaimed, her voice hoarse as if she'd been the one screaming.

The Revered turned, her face serene. "Yesterday, the impossible happened. A werewolf fought beside a paladin to kill a monstrous evil. I didn't want to believe it. Werewolves are evil—we all know this. But I have spent the day in prayer to learn whether what we all know is a lie."

Now the captain lowered her sword. "What are you saying, Revered?"

"I am saying I was mistaken." The Revered walked toward them, her attention fixed on Ginnevra. "I don't understand it, and I think I have more praying and thinking to do. But it's true, captain. Some werewolves—this werewolf, certainly—are no monsters."

"That's impossible," the captain said, but she didn't sound certain.

"Which is why I wanted a witness," the Revered said. "The Goddess will never grant Her grace to bless evil. You have seen Her power heal this man as a sign to everyone here. You cannot deny the truth of what Ginnevra Cassaline has sworn to—what I swear to as well."

Ginnevra looked at the captain. The elderly woman still looked stunned. "It's true," Ginnevra said. "It's all true. Not all werewolves are good—there are still many who worship the Bright One—but the ones who turn their backs on Her don't deserve to be treated as monsters. Please, captain. You have faith —show us how far it goes."

The captain turned her head to look at Ginnevra. Then she sheathed her sword and removed her helmet and coif, revealing short, curly gray hair matted with sweat. "I will never deny the evidence of my eyes," she said. "You have my word. This werewolf is no monster."

Ginnevra let out a deep breath. Eodan approached, moving as

easily as if he'd never been wounded. He bowed to the captain. "Thank you," he said. "I know it's hard to believe."

"I've seen much stranger things in the Goddess's service," the captain said, and smiled, deepening the wrinkles around her eyes. "A good werewolf, though..." She shook her head ruefully. "What the hell am I supposed to do with that information?"

"I don't know," Ginnevra said. "Keep an open mind, I suppose? It's not as if you can approach every aggressive werewolf and question him about his religious affiliation. But...not killing Eodan is pretty much the extent of what I hoped for."

The captain eyed Eodan speculatively. "Do you suppose this inn has room for seventeen paladins?" she asked. "I'd like to hear the story of how this all happened once we're settled."

"Drommio will be thrilled," Eodan said. "And the story is one we never tire of telling."

THE CAPTAIN TURNED out to be ruthless in more than one way: she casually evicted all the patrons from Drommio's private parlor and commandeered it for the paladins. Seventeen women, plus Ginnevra, Eodan, Pellarius, and the Revered, made for a noisy, cheerful party. Even Caterrina, still not fully recovered, joined in the exuberant fun, though she was quieter than Ginnevra remembered her being. When she pressed her aunt, Caterrina only said, "It's going to take time for me to forget everything that happened in that monster's house," and Ginnevra knew better than to say anything else.

She told the story of meeting Eodan and falling in love with only a few interruptions by her werewolf lover, most of them the kind of interruption that left their listeners howling with laughter. Ginnevra's own laughter felt like it had a slightly manic edge, but she was so relieved at how everything had turned out she felt that was reasonable.

The laughter died away when Ginnevra described the Goddess's intervention on behalf of an injured dragon, until at the end, the room was silent. Finally, the captain said, "I would never have thought to do that. You seem to have a remarkable compassion for the misunderstood. Aren't you afraid that will work against you someday? That you'll take pity on a creature that will tear your throat out?"

"I felt no pity for the lamia," Ginnevra replied, "and most monsters really are monstrous and dangerous. I simply try to keep in mind the possibilities."

"You're on a path I don't envy," the captain said, and topped off Ginnevra's wine glass with a rueful smile. "But it's one I honor you for. And maybe, as a prime, you're better suited for that path than I imagine."

Ginnevra, embarrassed, merely smiled, and let Eodan start in on another story, one less fraught with emotion, and gradually the mood lightened. But she couldn't stop thinking about the captain's words. Until that moment, she hadn't thought of her choices as relating to any particular path—but that was what the Goddess taught, wasn't it? That the choices one made shaped the path one followed? It wasn't destiny that had brought her to Uparde and the lamia, but it wasn't unreasonable or blasphemous to see that her choices had prepared her for that conflict.

Eventually, the paladins, who'd ridden hard to reach Uparde in less than a day, drifted off to their rooms, until finally the captain said good night and it was only the five of them alone in the parlor. Ginnevra leaned against Eodan and closed her eyes, breathing in the werewolf musk and feeling deeply grateful for how everything had turned out.

"So," the Revered said, pouring herself another glass of wine, "where will you go now?"

"I still haven't ever seen the sea," Eodan said. "Devoyenne, next."

"And I'll have to report in to the sanctuary there and see if they have messages for me," Ginnevra added. "If the Blessed has an assignment, we'll do that."

The Revered nodded and sipped her wine. Ginnevra wasn't used to how relaxed the woman was now that she wasn't enthralled by the lamia. She was nothing like she had behaved after her reappearance, and Ginnevra couldn't stop herself staring every time the Revered came out with a joke.

"But you'll stay a few days, won't you?" Caterrina said. "We never had a proper visit."

"We'll stay," Ginnevra said. "At least long enough to see Pellarius off."

"End of the week," Pellarius said. "Then it's back to Guinio, and back to my old life."

"Not hunting anymore?" Eodan said with a grin.

Pellarius saluted him with his wine glass. "Hunting is a valuable profession, but I don't think it's for me. But I'm not sure I want to go back to being a tax inspector."

"I thought that was a lie you told to get into Lady Jiulliana's house," Ginnevra said.

Pellarius reddened slightly. "Only in the sense that I have no authority in Uparde. I was a tax inspector in Guinio for years before giving it up to hunt. And now...you know, I think I'd like to stand for a justicer? Now that I've seen what good someone who cares about the law can do."

"That's an excellent and thankless profession," Caterrina said. "I wish you luck."

"It's worth doing," Ginnevra said. "Besides, you can't be worse at it than Ciutto Baroccius."

"Whatever happened to him?" Eodan asked.

Ginnevra shrugged. "I checked in at the justiciary this morning, in case they needed my testimony or something, and the clerks told me he'd been dismissed for not taking his duties seriously and by extension letting all those people get killed. I can't imagine he didn't deserve it. I'm just disappointed it wasn't for taking bribes."

"Bribery is the grease that oils the wheels of justice," Caterrina said. "Paladins may not take that path, but you need to be aware of what motivates mundane officials. You'll meet any number of corrupt Lords Mayor or councilmen or dukes or princes—don't let your principles interfere with seeing the truth."

"That's very wise," Ginnevra said. "I hate it, but it's wise."

Caterrina yawned. "I need sleep," she said, "and tomorrow I'd like to return home, if you think I'm healed enough."

"I think you're recovering well, and you'll recover even better in your own home," Eodan said. "Ginnevra?"

Ginnevra lifted Caterrina in her arms. The Revered stood as well. "It's been an extraordinary day, hasn't it?" she said. "And what a story I'll have to tell the other anointed. Good night, all."

Ginnevra and Caterrina bade the others good night, and Ginnevra carried her aunt back to her room and settled her in her bed. Caterrina gripped Ginnevra's hand when she would have withdrawn. "I'll be fine on my own," she said, "if you'll put the pitcher where I can reach it."

Mystified, Ginnevra did as she asked, then realized Eodan hadn't followed them in. "Good night, then," she said, and left to find Eodan.

She found him at the end of the hall near the stairs. "What are you—"

Eodan took her hand and pulled her close. "Upstairs," he said.

She followed him to the second floor, then down another hallway to a room near its end. "I talked to Drommio," Eodan said, "and he agreed you deserve something special, what with killing a dangerous monster and freeing its captives." He pushed open the door and bowed.

Ginnevra entered and was struck mute. The large room, bigger than she had thought the Golden Sickle offered, was furnished as elegantly as a rich man's manor, with a bed sumptuously draped in velvet, a bearskin rug thick enough to bury her feet in, and lanterns on every wall shedding a brilliant, warm light over the furnishings. A couple of padded chairs next to a small table suggested leisurely private meals, catered to by servants. Paintings, not terribly expensive ones but nice nonetheless, hung at intervals on the walls. "This is nice enough I'd want to live here," she breathed.

Eodan took her hand and led her to the large window paned with thin sheets of perfectly clear glass. It looked out over a garden Ginnevra hadn't known the inn even had, and when Eodan opened the casement, the scents of cool green growing things filled the room as if the garden had come indoors.

Ginnevra leaned out of the window, breathing in the delicious smells, until Eodan put his hands on her waist and drew her back to lean against him. "It's been a day of miracles," he whispered in her ear. "What do you say we see what kind of miracles the night will bring?"

Ginnevra turned in his arms to face him. "Miracles beyond belief," she said, and pulled him close for a kiss.

About the Author

In addition to the Books of the Dark Goddess, Melissa McShane is the author of many other fantasy novels, including the novels of Tremontane, the first of which is *Servant of the Crown; Burning Bright*, first in The Extraordinaries series; and *The Book of Secrets*, first book in The Last Oracle series.

She lives in the shelter of the mountains out West with her family, including two very needy cats. She wrote reviews and critical essays for many years before turning to fiction, which is much more fun than anyone ought to be allowed to have. You can visit her at her website **www.melissamcshanewrites.com** for more information on other books and upcoming releases.

For news on upcoming releases, bonus material, and other fun stuff, sign up for Melissa's newsletter **here**.

If you enjoyed this book, please consider leaving a review at your favorite online bookseller!

ALSO BY MELISSA MCSHANE

The Book of War

The Book of Destiny

THE LIVING ORACLE

Hidden Realm (forthcoming)

THE NOVELS OF TREMONTANE

Pretender to the Crown

Guardian of the Crown

Champion of the Crown

Ally of the Crown

Stranger to the Crown

Scholar of the Crown

Servant of the Crown

Exile of the Crown

Rider of the Crown

Agent of the Crown

Voyager of the Crown

Tales of the Crown

COMPANY OF STRANGERS

Company of Strangers

Stone of Inheritance

Mortal Rites

Shifting Loyalties

Sands of Memory

Call of Wizardry

THE DRAGONS OF MOTHER STONE

Spark the Fire

Faith in Flames

Ember in Shadow

Skies Will Burn

THE CONVERGENCE TRILOGY

The Summoned Mage

The Wandering Mage

The Unconquered Mage

THE BOOKS OF DALANINE

The Smoke-Scented Girl

The God-Touched Man

Emissary

Warts and All: A Fairy Tale Collection

The View from Castle Always

www.ingramcontent.com/pod-product-compliance
Lightning Source LLC
Chambersburg PA
CBHW060625260626
47161CB00008B/2802